Allen,
Mur

MURDER
ON THE
CARONIA

Also by Conrad Allen

MURDER
ON THE
CARONIA

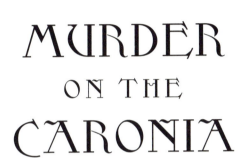

Conrad Allen

ST. MARTIN'S MINOTAUR ⚬ NEW YORK

www.minotaurbooks.com

ISBN 0-312-28091-2

First Edition: January 2003

10 9 8 7 6 5 4 3 2 1

To Benjamin Sevier,
with many thanks for
his expert assistance
in bringing the *Caronia*
safely into port

MURDER
ON THE
CARONIA

ONE

It was never the same. That was what was so remarkable. Though he had crossed the Atlantic over a dozen times in each direction, George Porter Dillman had never become bored or blasé. He remembered each voyage as a separate experience, filled to the brim with its own excitements and charged with individual drama. There were so many variables. Weather conditions could swing between the benign and the tempestuous. A ship's company might be anything from superb to merely competent. Each vessel had her own distinctive character. Cunard's two greyhounds of the seas, the *Lusitania* and the *Mauretania*, were sister ships, built to the same specifications and embodying the same bold patriotism, yet they differed considerably. Dillman had been fortunate enough to sail on the maiden voyages of both and he had found them anything but interchangeable. Their interiors were markedly different and their performance in the water dissimilar. Their personalities set them even further apart. The same could be said of the *Lucania*, the *Ivernia*, the *Saxonia*, the *Carpathia*, the *Aurania*, and all the other Cunard ships on which Dillman had traveled. Each was unique.

It was the passenger list that made every voyage such a special event. When large numbers of people crossed the Atlantic, the vessel that carried them was a microcosm of American and European society. Every class was represented, from the titled to the underprivileged, from wealthy families enjoying the luxury of first-class travel to poverty-stricken emigrants suffering the multiple indignities of steerage. New people brought new problems each time. Dillman had been a detective for long enough to know that the law of averages worked aboard ship just as inexorably as on shore. The vast majority of passengers would be decent, God-fearing, law-abiding souls who would create no trouble at all but there would always be a smattering of those with more criminal tendencies, using the voyage to further their ends. Identifying and arresting them was Dillman's job.

As he stood that Saturday morning on a lower Manhattan pier, he watched the passengers converging on the *Caronia* and wondered which of them would need his particular attention. Over two thousand people would be making the crossing. Among so many it would not be easy to spot the dangerous few, but his instincts had been sharpened by experience. Dillman would rely heavily on those instincts. Observing the passengers at such close quarters, he could feel their collective exhilaration. Even those who had made the journey to Liverpool before stepped onto the gangway with renewed eagerness. First-time travelers were more openly enthusiastic, agog at the size of the ship and excited by the thought that they would be sailing three thousand miles across an ocean. Children were especially animated. Dillman could see the joy in their faces and hear the wonder in their voices. Doubts and fears vanished in the general elation. Everyone hurried aboard. For the best part of a week, the *Caronia* would be their home.

Dillman looked up at the vessel with admiration. He had sailed on her sister ship, the *Carmania*, but this would be his first trip on the *Caronia*. He was looking forward to it. The two ships were known as "the pretty sisters." Externally, they looked identical, elegant vessels of almost twenty thousand tons apiece that stretched to 676 feet in length. Both were surmounted by massive twin funnels, painted in the standard Cunard colors of red and black. The major difference between them lay in the engine room. By way of an experiment, the *Carmania* had been fitted with turbines while the *Caronia* was powered by conventional steam engines. The fact that the *Carmania* averaged a full knot faster in speed with the same consumption of coal justified the experiment. Dillman was curious to find out what else separated the two sisters.

His gaze shifted back to the stream of passengers. In the course of the voyage he would get to know several, mingling freely with them in order to pass as just another traveler. Dillman worked far more effectively as an insider. The easy friendships of shipboard life were an invaluable way to gather intelligence across a wide field. He was tall, cultured, and presentable. Most people found him charming and debonair, pleasant company at all times. Ladies—old, young, and middle-aged—were drawn by his handsome appearance and by his impeccable manners. Only the villains on board ever learned that the courteous American was actually employed by the Cunard Line as a private detective. By then, it was usually too late.

Dillman was about to join the queue at the gangway when he caught sight of some late arrivals. Walking briskly toward the ship was a group of people who commanded immediate attention. Two uniformed policemen set the pace. They seemed to have been chosen for their height and bulk because they towered over the quartet behind them. At their heels was a slim, upright man in his forties, wearing a long coat, a bowler hat, and an expression of quiet determination. Behind him were two figures, a man and a woman, who looked so sad and humiliated that Dillman felt sorry for them. Well into his fifties, the man was short and plump with a beard liberally flecked with gray. His companion, some twenty years younger, was thin and anguished. Heads held down with shame, the couple shuffled along behind their captors. Dillman could see no handcuffs but it was obvious the pair were under arrest.

It was the last man in the party who really sparked his interest. A brawny character of medium height, the man wore an ill-fitting suit and a large cap. The lower half of his face was dominated by a walrus mustache. Clearly proud of it, he stroked the mustache repeatedly with his free hand. Under his other arm, he carried a shotgun and moved along with the arrogant strut of a big-game hunter who has just killed a lion. Dillman wondered what unspeakable crime the couple had committed to justify such close supervision. He also wondered why the man with the shotgun was enjoying himself so much, grinning broadly with a mixture of pleasure and self-importance. A weapon of any kind was surely unnecessary. The captives were too overcome with remorse even to consider an attempt at escape. And what hope would they have against four strong men? The scene worried Dillman. It was contrived to gain maximum effect.

Other passengers parted obligingly to let them through. As the prisoners were escorted aboard, a cluster of waiting cameramen took photographs of them for their respective newspapers. The two New York policemen waved a farewell then took up a position near the bottom of the gangway. Dillman strolled across to them.

"Good morning," he said politely.

One of them grunted a reply but the other merely nodded without taking his eyes off the ship. The passengers who had caused such a commotion had now disappeared, leaving those in their wake to indulge in wild speculation.

"What sort of people need a police escort?" asked Dillman.

"The wrong sort," said the older man.

"They looked English to me."

"They were, sir."

"So those detectives were from Scotland Yard?"

"Yes, sir."

"They came a long way to make the arrests."

"Inspector Redfern wouldn't let them get away with it."

"With what?"

"Murder, sir," the policeman said grimly. "That's who you're traveling with on the *Caronia*. A pair of ruthless, cold-blooded killers."

Genevieve Masefield had boarded the ship long before her colleague. Though she and Dillman worked as a team, they always traveled independently so that they could develop their own circles of friends. As a couple their movements would have been restricted and their acquaintances more limited in scope. Operating singly, each could reach places inaccessible to the other, and gain confidences more easily. During a voyage they took care to remain apart in public. Meetings between them were essentially private matters, and that very privacy added a frisson of pleasure for Genevieve. She relished the fact that, while Dillman invariably attracted a lot of female interest aboard, hers was the only cabin he would visit. Genevieve always collected her own share of suitors. Her blend of beauty and intelligence turned the heads of married men just as frequently as those of bachelors and she had endured more than one unwelcome declaration of love in the course of her work. She took care to describe such embarrassing moments to Dillman in the hope of gaining his sympathy and, by the same token, provoking mild jealousy.

As she finished unpacking the trunk in her cabin, Genevieve wondered how much of her partner she would see on the voyage. Both were traveling first-class but they were merely two among three hundred passengers. They would also be keeping an eye on the second-class areas of the ship, more than doubling the number of people they had to watch. It would leave little time for them to be together. Work took priority. Technically, they were never off-duty. Genevieve's cabin was comfortable rather than luxurious, a large rectangle in which everything had its appointed place. The bed, she discovered, was invitingly soft. The one defect was the absence of a bathroom. Only the most expensive suites had private bathroom facilities. When she wanted a bath, she would have to make a reservation with her steward. It was a minor inconvenience when she had all the other advantages of first class at her disposal.

After taking a final, satisfied look around, she decided to go up on deck to watch the ship leave. Departures had their own mystique. She reveled in them. They induced such a strange feeling of delight and regret, the euphoria of embarking on an adventure, tinged with an odd sensation of loss. Genevieve was perpetually moving between two worlds, the land of her birth and the country to which she had once tried to flee. In between the two was the most dangerous ocean in the world but it held no fears for her. Time had turned her into a seasoned voyager yet the magic of departure remained.

When she stepped out into the corridor, she saw she was not the only person anxious to be on deck at the critical moment. An attractive young woman was walking toward her. Seeing Genevieve, her face lit up.

"Miss Masefield!" she said.

"Hello."

"Are you going where I'm going?"

"I think so, Miss Singleton," replied Genevieve.

"Do you have anyone to wave you off?"

"Not really, but the moment of departure is always rather special."

"This is my first trip," confided the other. "I feel so *excited*."

"So do I. It's a feeling that never quite leaves you." Genevieve pointed toward the exit. "Shall we go on deck together?"

"Yes, please!"

Isadora Singleton had a girlish quality about her that was very appealing. Genevieve had liked her from the moment they met. Genevieve had been standing in line in the customs shed when she fell into conversation with Isadora and her parents. As soon as they heard her English accent, all three of them warmed to her instantly. Introductions were made and, responding to a sharp nudge from his wife, Waldo Singleton had expressed the hope that Genevieve would dine with them on board at some stage. Isadora was thrilled with her new acquaintance. Trembling on the verge of adulthood, she was being taken to England by way of celebration and she clearly had many romantic illusions about the country. In Genevieve, she saw a potential friend, guide, and confidante.

For her part, Genevieve was struck by Isadora's porcelain loveliness and by the fact that the girl seemed totally unaware of it. There was an unexpected bonus. The Singletons were from Boston. Since Dillman also hailed from the city, Genevieve had picked up a great deal of information about it and was ready to learn more. She hoped Isadora Singleton and her parents would be able to fill some of the gaps left by Dillman's accounts of his birthplace. Following her young friend along the corridor, Genevieve was conscious of a paradox. While she came from a rich family, Isadora was wearing the plainest of clothing and exuded no sense of prosperity. Genevieve, by contrast, was stylish enough to suggest a person of wealth yet she had little beyond her income from the Cunard Line. Appearance was everything. Anyone seeing them together would have taken Genevieve as a moneyed lady with her poor relation.

"Isn't this wonderful?" said Isadora.

"Wait until we actually set off."

"Have you sailed on the *Caronia* before?"

"No," said Genevieve, "this is my maiden voyage."

"Then we'll have something in common."

Isadora led the way out on deck. The imminence of departure had brought large numbers of people out of their cabins and it took the newcomers a moment to find space at the rail. They looked down on the crowd of well-wishers below. Isadora gave them a friendly wave before turning to her companion.

"I'm so glad we met, Miss Masefield," she announced.

"So am I," said Genevieve with a smile, "but I don't intend to spend the next three thousand miles being addressed by my surname. Please call me 'Genevieve.' "

Isadora was overjoyed. "May I?"

"As long as you return the compliment."

"Oh, yes. Of course I will. I hate to stand on ceremony.

7

Mother criticizes me for being so forward at times but I don't see the point of playing those silly social games. If you make friends with someone, you don't want to spend an eternity before you can even whisper their Christian name. Do you, Genevieve?"

"No, Isadora."

They exchanged a laugh, glad that one barrier between them had been cleared.

"What's your cabin like?"

"Very nice," replied Genevieve. "You must come and see it sometime."

"I'd like that," said Isadora. "We have staterooms with an interconnecting door. Father always insists on the best. I never expected to find anything so palatial aboard a ship. Even the bathroom is ornate."

"I envy you, Isadora. Most of us don't have that amenity in our cabins."

"You mean that you have to share a public bathroom?"

"They've been designed to a very high standard."

"Perhaps they have," said Isadora, showing a first hint of snobbery, "but it's demeaning to queue whenever you want to take a bath. You must feel free to use ours," she decided graciously. "I'm sure Mother and Father will agree."

"I wouldn't dream of intruding."

"We'll insist."

Genevieve glanced over her shoulder. "Where are your parents, by the way? I thought they'd be as keen as you to be on deck when we set sail."

"Oh, they will be," said the other with a sigh. "They never let me out of their sight for long, I'm afraid. Especially Mother. That's why it's such a treat to meet someone like you. If they see that I have a chaperone, they may give me more license to roam."

"I'm not sure that I like the idea of being a chaperone."

"You're not, Genevieve. You're a friend, and I know you'll be a good one. It's just that my parents will see you as a . . .

well . . ." She searched for the right word. ". . . as a kind of safeguard."

Genevieve grinned. " 'Chaperone'? 'Safeguard'? I can't decide which is the less flattering. Besides," she went on, "you'll make lots of other friends on this voyage. You won't need me to hold your hand all the time."

Her tone was lighthearted but Genevieve was making a serious point. Much as she liked Isadora Singleton, she did not want to be monopolized by her. It would hamper her work. The young Bostonian had great natural charm and an engaging innocence. What she lacked was any flair for independent action. Evidently it had been stifled by her parents. Given the opportunity, Genevieve feared, her companion might turn a casual relationship into a binding commitment. That was to be avoided at all costs.

"Do you know anyone else on board?" asked Isadora.

"Not yet."

"Neither do we. It's such a blessing that we met when we did. I could see from the start that we'd get on famously. Did you have that feeling as well?"

Genevieve was guarded. "Up to a point," she said.

"Mother and Father liked you as much as I did. That's very unusual."

"Is it?"

"Yes, Genevieve. They don't often approve of friends that I choose for myself. Mother says I'm too open; I need to take more care where I place my affections. That's why she interferes so much."

"Do you resent that interference?"

"Yes and no," said Isadora with a shrug. "I resent it at the time because it makes me feel like a child but then I tell myself that Mother is only acting in my best interests."

"I see."

"And she does so in the kindest way."

"It must still be rather irritating."

"Nobody can be irritated by Mother for long. She has such

a sweet disposition. She's not cold and tyrannical, like some mothers."

"But she does overprotect you, is that what you're saying?"

"Mother is only doing what Grandmother did to her. It's a family tradition."

"You seem to have survived it pretty well so far," said Genevieve, wanting to encourage her. "And you won't have to put up with your parents' control for much longer. You'll be twenty-one soon, Isadora. You'll be able to spread your wings."

"Oh, I don't think I'm ready for that yet," said Isadora with a touch of anxiety. "I've so much still to learn. I'm hoping you'll be my teacher for the next week."

"Me?"

"You're so poised, Genevieve, so sophisticated." She gave a wan smile. "Beside you, I feel so ridiculously juvenile. How do I achieve the same assurance?"

"It comes with time."

"There must be more to it than that."

"Perhaps," conceded Genevieve, "but you have no reason to be self-critical. You have all the qualities a young lady ought to have. And I'd better warn you now, I won't be the only one to notice that. Before too long, you'll have a swarm of male admirers buzzing around you. Even a chaperone won't be able to keep them at bay."

Isadora giggled. "That would be tremendous fun," she said.

"Enjoy it while you can."

Another sigh. "If only I could, Genevieve."

"What do you mean?"

"Mother and Father have very firm ideas about what would be a suitable match for me. It's one of the reasons they're taking me to England." She lowered her voice. "I wouldn't tell this to anyone else but I know I can trust you. The truth is that my parents have set their hearts on a son-in-law with a title."

"A title?"

"Yes," Isadora said with foreboding. "In their eyes, it's the best possible birthday present. They want me to marry into the British aristocracy."

TWO

During the first couple of hours at sea, the busiest person on the ship was the purser. The navigational crew was sailing the ship, the stokers and trimmers were slaving away in the engine room, and the cooks were preparing the first meal of the voyage. All were going through a well-established routine. The purser had a more difficult job. Faced with a battery of requests, suggestions, and demands from a host of passengers, he had to make instant decisions on the hoof. Some of the calls made upon his time were habitual but most were specific to that particular crossing. The purser had to work flat-out to oblige, reassure, or appease those who came knocking at his door in an endless line.

Aware of the pressures put upon him, George Porter Dillman delayed his own visit to the purser until well into the afternoon. By that time, the detective had settled into his cabin, enjoyed his lunch, and explored the *Caronia* from stem to stern.

Paul Taggart gave him a cordial welcome, pumping Dillman's hand vigorously. A tall, angular man in his early forties, the purser was a New Yorker who had been born and brought up within sight of the Hudson River. A childhood spent haunting the harbor had prepared him well for a life at sea. Nothing else would have satisfied his primal urges. Taggart had a long, lean, pleasant face that was remarkably unlined. His smile was warm and his voice deep.

"Good to have you aboard, Mr. Dillman," he said.

"Thank you, Mr. Taggart."

"Your reputation goes before you."

Dillman was modest. "I've been lucky, that's all."

"Luck is a decisive factor in your trade."

Taggart perched on the edge of a desk piled high with paperwork. Maps and charts covered the walls. Wooden filing cabinets took up much of the remaining space. On top of one of the cabinets was a framed photograph of Taggart, in uniform, with his wife and two young sons. All four of them were beaming happily at the camera. Dillman glanced at it.

"That was taken a few years ago," explained Taggart. "The boys are twice that size now. I don't know what my wife feeds them on, but it certainly does the trick."

"Are they going to follow in their father's footsteps?"

Taggart gave a hollow laugh. "Not if I can help it!"

"The call of the sea tends to run in families."

"I sometimes wish that *I'd* never heard of it, I know that."

"Busy?"

"I've been swamped, Mr. Dillman."

"The purser always gets the real headaches."

"I know," Taggart said tolerantly, "and I complain like mad about it. But the simple fact is that I love this job more than anything else in the world. If you're a student of human nature, there's nothing to beat it. Something happens to people when they're at sea. They behave in ways they'd never even think of on land."

"I've noticed."

"What about you, Mr. Dillman? I guess you like your job as well."

"Very much."

"Any red-blooded man would enjoy working alongside Miss Masefield."

Dillman was surprised. "You've met Genevieve?"

"Yes," said Taggart. "She reported to me half an hour ago. Her timing was perfect. I'd just got the last of the passengers off my back." He smiled admiringly. "Miss Masefield is a delightful lady. I'd never have taken her for a detective."

"That's her main advantage."

"Is she efficient?"

"Extremely efficient."

"Then she's got everything. Looks and brains."

"Not to mention courage," said Dillman. "Genevieve is the ideal partner."

"I can see what you mean about being lucky." Taggart became businesslike. "Okay, let's get down to brass tacks. I'll tell you what I told Miss Masefield. Most of your work will be pure routine, looking out for the thieves, pickpockets, and cardsharps we always seem to attract. But our main problem concerns narcotics. We've had a tip-off that the *Caronia* is being used to carry drugs on the eastward crossing. What kind—and in what quantities—I've no idea, but I take the warning seriously. I don't want this ship to act as a mule for some lousy drug-runners. We're proud of this vessel. She has to be kept clean of that kind of thing."

"Do you have any information to go on?"

"Precious little."

"How reliable is the tip-off?"

"That's for you to find out, Mr. Dillman."

"Drugs are big business," said Dillman, stroking his chin. "The people involved go to any lengths to protect themselves. They're likely to be armed."

"That's what I told your partner."

"They're also inclined to travel in comfort. If they make huge profits out of crime, they don't cross the Atlantic in steerage. They expect luxury."

"Not on my ship," Taggart said sharply. "Run them down for me, Mr. Dillman, and the master-at-arms will arrange more basic accommodations for the skunks."

"Does he have those other prisoners locked up?"

"Prisoners?"

"The two people I saw being escorted onto the ship by detectives."

"Oh, that pair. No, they're not in one of our cells but they are confined to their cabins. Inspector Redfern will give you the details," he went on, picking up some sheets of paper from the desk. "I promised to send you along to him when we'd finished here. Take your partner with you. It will save repetition."

"Where will I find Inspector Redfern?"

Taggart handed over the papers. "Here's a copy of the passenger list for the entire ship. As you'll see, Inspector Redfern and Sergeant Mulcaster are sharing a cabin."

"What about their prisoners?"

"Right next door."

"Together?"

"No, Mr. Dillman. On either side of them."

"Why was Sergeant Mulcaster carrying a shotgun when he came aboard?"

"He likes to let people know who he is."

"You've met him?"

"Oh, sure," said Taggart, rolling his eyes, "but I won't claim I enjoyed the experience. Inspector Redfern is a good, honest, straightforward cop but the other guy is a pain in the neck. If I were you, I'd keep clear of Ronald Mulcaster."

"Why?"

"He's just like that shotgun of his—liable to go off with a bang."

After lunch in the first-class restaurant, Genevieve Masefield had disentangled herself from Isadora Singleton and made her way to the purser to introduce herself. When he had briefed her, she went up on deck to enjoy the sea air in solitude, striding purposefully along to discourage people from trying to speak to her. She was approaching the stern of the vessel when she heard the patter of feet behind her. Genevieve walked briskly on but she was soon overtaken. A tousle-haired young man in a white running vest and knee-length shorts jogged past her and weaved his way expertly between the people ahead of her. Only when he reached the stern did he pause to catch his breath. He was tall, slim, and wiry. After supporting himself on the rail for a few moments, he turned to see Genevieve coming toward him and his face was split by an amiable grin.

"Hi," he said, waving a hand. "How are you?"

"Very well, thank you," she replied, pausing beside him. "Though I could never run like that after such a large meal."

"I didn't have a large meal. Wes keeps me on a diet."

"Wes?"

"My coach and manager. At least that's what he calls himself. I think he's a professional torturer, but then, I'm the guy stretched out on the rack." He extended a friendly hand. "I'm Theodore Wright, by the way. 'Theo' to friends. If you like to promenade on deck, you'll see a lot of me."

She shook his hand. "I'm Genevieve Masefield," she said, "and I'm hoping to have a less arduous crossing. You're obviously in training for something."

" 'The Big Event.' "

"Are you a boxer?"

"Hell no," he replied with a chuckle. "I'm ugly enough as it is. I don't want some two-fisted gorilla to make me look even worse. Anyway, boxing is for suckers. It's a short life and a painful one. No, lady, I chose a real sport."

"And what's that?"

"Cycling."

"Are you a professional, Mr. Wright?"

He chuckled again. "I can see that you didn't read the sports pages while you were in the States," he said. "The name of Theo Wright pops up in them all the time. I'm the American champion. That means I have to keep myself really fit."

"Will you be racing in England?"

"Yes, Miss Masefield."

"How did you know I wasn't married?"

"Because no husband in his right mind would let you wander around the deck of a ship on his own," he said cheerfully. "But, to answer your question, I do have a few races lined up in England but the real point of this trip is to get to France."

"Why?"

"Even you must have heard of the Bordeaux-to-Paris race."

"I'm afraid not, Mr. Wright."

"It's the Holy Grail of cycling. Whoever wins that really is the champ, and I aim to be first across the line this year. If I'm not, Wes will murder me."

Genevieve was impressed. "Bordeaux to Paris? That's a very long race."

"Now you can see why I have to build up my stamina. The best place to do that, of course, is in the saddle but I can hardly cycle along here with so many people around. Wes is going to work out a timetable for me so that I can pedal up and down the deck when it's deserted."

"You must be dedicated."

"I like to win."

Theodore Wright was bright, fresh-faced, and personable. Genevieve found him a welcome relief from the polite social rituals she had been going through with others. He was open and unaffected. When he talked about his ambition, he did not resort to empty boasts. Wright had the inner confidence of a true champion.

"I hope to see you around, Miss Masefield," he said.

"Not if you're cycling on deck in the middle of the night."

"Wes is bound to give me some time off."

"Does he control what you eat, as well?"

"I can't even clear my throat without his permission," he added. "Anyway, I've got to go. He'll be waiting for me with his stopwatch. Nice to meet you, Miss Masefield."

"I'm glad we bumped into each other."

He beamed at her. "Yes. You've met your Mr. Wright at last."

With a last chuckle, he ran back in the direction from which he had come. Genevieve looked after him with a mixture of curiosity and amusement. Theodore Wright was an original, quite unlike anyone she'd encountered before on a Cunard liner. His chirpy manner might offend some of the more conservative passengers but it was a breath of fresh air to her. She recalled what he had said about cycling from Bordeaux to Paris.

"That's not a race," she said to herself. "It's an endurance test."

The first thing he noticed when he entered the cabin was the sweet smell. Dillman inhaled the aroma of pipe tobacco and found it oddly soothing. There was a soothing quality about Detective-Inspector Ernest Redfern as well. Alone in the second-class cabin, he had slipped off his jacket and stood there in his shirtsleeves and waistcoat; a watch chain dangled from the pocket. While the two men introduced themselves, they weighed each other up. Redfern was relaxed and quietly spoken.

"I had hoped to speak to your partner as well, Mr. Dillman," he said.

"Genevieve will be here any moment, Inspector. I sent her a note."

"Good. I'd like to put the pair of you in the picture, if only as a matter of courtesy. I know you'll have enough on your plate during the voyage but it's only fair that you should know about our little cargo."

"We'd appreciate that, Inspector. I saw you coming aboard."

"At the last moment, I'm afraid. We're very grateful to the purser for fitting us in at the eleventh hour, so to speak. Cunard has been very cooperative."

Dillman nodded. "They're always ready to help the forces of law and order."

Redfern waved him to a seat then slipped on his jacket before lowering himself into his own chair. He had nondescript features but his eyes glistened with intelligence.

"Mr. Taggart tells me that you once worked for the Pinkerton Agency," he said.

"That's right," replied Dillman. "It was my first introduction to the darker side of humanity. I had no idea criminals could be so devious. It was a real eye-opener. I still remember the sense of pride I felt when I made my first arrest."

"Who was the offender?"

"A pickpocket who operated in the Broadway theaters. The irony was that I'd been working at that same theater myself only a couple of months earlier. I was a penniless actor then. That's why I had such satisfaction in catching the guy," he confided. "I mean, there were we, toiling away onstage for modest wages while this fellow had rich pickings among the spectators. It seemed indecent."

"How did you come to work for Cunard?"

"That's a long story."

"I'd like to hear it sometime," said Redfern, with genuine interest. "And I certainly want to hear more about the Pinkerton Agency. We must compare notes. I suspect that its methods are rather different from ours at Scotland Yard."

"I doubt that, Inspector. Don't forget who founded it. In a sense, the agency was a kind of Scotland Yard as well. Allan Pinkerton came from Glasgow."

There was a tap on the door and Redfern got up to let Genevieve Masefield in. Dillman rose to his feet to perform the introductions then yielded his chair to his partner. When he gave her a wink, she smiled back. Redfern noted the little exchange.

"Well," he said, looking at them in turn, "you're not at all what I would have expected as onboard detectives. The ones I met on the crossing to New York were ex-policemen from Liverpool. I could have picked them out in a football crowd."

"We believe in camouflage, Inspector," said Dillman.

"Yes," agreed Genevieve. "It makes people lower their guard."

"That's something we can never afford to do ourselves," resumed the inspector. "The reason I asked for this meeting was to explain our presence on board the *Caronia*. Briefly, the facts are these. Sergeant Mulcaster and I were dispatched in pursuit of two people we believe to be guilty of the murder of a woman named Winifred May Heritage. The man who is in the next cabin with Sergeant Mulcaster," he continued, jerking a thumb over his shoulder, "is John James Heritage, husband of the victim. And in the cabin on the other side of us is his accomplice, Miss Carrie Peterson."

"The evidence against them must be pretty strong to bring you all this way," observed Dillman. "How did you know they had fled to America?"

"We didn't, Mr. Dillman. Our information was that they'd gone to Ireland. When we tracked them down there, they hopped on the next ship from Queenstown."

"What did you do?"

"Went after them in the *Mauretania*. She's the fastest ship afloat. Even though they had a good start, we overhauled them. We telegraphed the other vessel with details, then made the arrest aboard. It spared us all the hassle of extradition procedures."

"Are you certain they're guilty?" asked Genevieve.

"Innocent people don't make a run for it."

"They do in some circumstances, Inspector."

"Not in this case, Miss Masefield," insisted Redfern. "The victim was poisoned. John Heritage was a pharmacist with access to the poison used. Carrie Peterson was his assistant. On the promise that he would marry her, she became his mistress. But his wife refused to give him a divorce."

"Go on," said Genevieve.

"That's it, in essence. The only way that he could live with Miss Peterson was by killing his wife. Over a period of time, he administered small doses of poison so that she would appear to have died from natural causes. But he gave her too strong a dose one day," said Redfern solemnly, "and she expired that evening. He and his mistress had no choice but to take to their heels."

"Who found the body?"

"The woman who came in to clean the house. It frightened the living daylights out of her. When foul play was suspected, we became involved."

"The evidence so far is only circumstantial," said Dillman.

"Finding the victim's diary was our breakthrough."

"Why was that, Inspector?"

"Because it not only contained details of her husband's relationship with Miss Peterson," said Redfern, "it also had entries that revealed Mrs. Heritage's fears that her husband might be trying to poison her."

"What did she do about it?"

"She made an appointment with the doctor. Unfortunately, she wasn't able to keep it because she died on the evening before the appointment. Do you see what I mean?" he asked. "Posthumously, the victim is our star witness."

They heard a key being inserted into the lock as Sergeant Mulcaster let himself into the cabin. The stocky figure stood in the doorway to appraise them, stroking his mustache while he did so. His cap had been removed to reveal thinning hair that was carefully parted into a herringbone pattern. His face was expressionless. When he was introduced to the visitors, he responded with a gruff politeness. Closing the door behind him, he stayed on his feet.

"How is he?" inquired Redfern.

"As miserable as sin, Inspector," Mulcaster replied. "I'm not looking forward to spending five days in there with John James Heritage, I can tell you. He says nothing."

"We'll take it in turns, Sergeant."

"Why not just leave him alone to stew in his own juice?"

"Will he have any other visitors?" asked Dillman.

"No," snapped Mulcaster.

"Not even a priest? There's a chaplain aboard."

"And what about Miss Peterson?" said Genevieve. "Is she in there alone?"

"Yes," admitted Redfern, "but we make regular visits to go

through her statement with her. It's vital that the two of them be kept apart or they'll have time to concoct a story together."

"And a chance to get up to some hanky-panky," Mulcaster complained. "We're not allowing that. They're criminals. They're not here to *enjoy* themselves."

"How long were they on the run?" asked Dillman.

Mulcaster was blunt. "That's our business." He turned to his superior. "I know you want to let them know why we're here, Inspector, but this is our case. It's not something that should be discussed with outsiders."

"There's no harm in sharing thoughts with fellow detectives," said Redfern.

"I'm sure they've got work of their own to do."

Dillman responded to the cue. Inspector Redfern might be inclined to talk to them about the case but Sergeant Mulcaster obviously had strong objections. Ever since he had come into the cabin, it had seemed crowded and uncomfortable. Nothing would be gained by remaining there any longer.

"We have indeed," said Dillman. "Come along, Genevieve. We're only in the way here." She got up from her seat. "Thank you, Inspector. It was kind of you to tell us what you did. The only thing you didn't explain was why Sergeant Mulcaster thought it necessary to carry his shotgun when you brought the prisoners aboard."

"For God's sake, man!" Mulcaster snarled. "They're dangerous criminals."

"They looked harmless enough to me."

"Tell that to their victim!"

"Calm down, Sergeant," advised Redfern, reaching for his pipe. "Mr. Dillman's question was a perfectly reasonable one. All you needed to tell him is that we were taking no chances. It's the way we do things at Scotland Yard."

"I can see that," said Dillman, opening the door. "Oh, one last thing, Inspector."

"Yes?"

"I assume the prisoners have both confessed to their crimes?"

"Their flight was a confession in itself."

"In other words, they've denied their guilt."

"We'll get the truth out of them sooner or later," boasted Mulcaster.

"How?" wondered Dillman. "By pointing the shotgun at them?"

Before the sergeant could reply, the visitors left the cabin.

THREE

Nobody could accuse Frank Openshaw of hiding his light under a bushel. It blazed before him like a small bonfire. He was a big man in every way. The large body with the wide shoulders and the huge paunch was matched by a loud voice that carried his North Country vowels well beyond the ears of his companions. Nearing sixty, Openshaw had the energy and brio of someone much younger. Since he found himself sitting opposite the ebullient Yorkshireman, Dillman soon heard the story of his life. Sitting back in his chair, Openshaw scratched at one of his muttonchop whiskers and held forth.

"When I were a lad," he said with a wistful smile, "I thought a financier was a fella that kept pigeons. I'd no idea what he really did and I never thought for a moment I'd end up as one myself. Happen I'd be a chimney sweep like my dad, I thought, or go down pit like two of my uncles." He laughed throatily. "There's not much call for financial know-how in jobs like that. Any rate, my elder brother, Bert, helped Dad to sweep chimneys so there was no place for me there, and, when one of my uncles was killed in a pit explosion, I lost all interest in being a miner."

"So what did you do?" asked Dillman.

"Became a bricklayer." He displayed two massive hands. "These have done their share of hard work, I can promise you. Covered in cuts and blisters, they were, for the first three months in the trade. Then they hardened off. So did I."

"Tell them about the house, Frank," prompted his wife.

"I was just about to, Kitty."

"He built our first house all by himself," she announced proudly. "Except that we didn't know we'd live there because we hadn't even met then. Properly, I mean."

"We'd *seen* each other," said her husband. "That was enough for me."

He gave another throaty laugh and pulled his waistcoat down over his paunch. Dillman was interested to see the way the couple behaved toward each other. After almost forty years of marriage, there was still a visible spark of romance between them. Kitty Openshaw was a short, roly-poly woman with a chubby face that gleamed with pleasure. There was a touching humility about her. She had never quite got used to the idea that her husband was a millionaire, and a look of amazement— *Is this really happening to me?*—occasionally came into her eye.

"Tell them about the house," she repeated, nudging Openshaw.

"I built a house not far from Bradford," he said. "Single-handed. Well, that's what I tell everyone but I used both hands, really. Took me ages. I couldn't afford the bricks, you see, so I built it up room by room. It were my hobby at first, then I thought, 'Hey, wait a minute, Frank Openshaw, there's a chance to make some brass here.' So that's what I did. When the place was only half-built, I rented out the bit that had a roof, then used that money to buy more materials. So it went on. By the time I'd finished, I'd rented out two more rooms. Just think on it. I were nowt but a struggling young bricklayer yet I were a landlord as well."

"Then he met me," said Kitty with a coy smile. "Properly, I mean."

"We soon needed the house to ourselves then."

"Frank always had plans. That's what I liked about him."

"Never settle for less," boomed Openshaw. "That's my motto."

Dinner on the first evening afloat was a relatively informal affair but many of the ladies wore full-length gowns and a few of the men opted for white tie and tails. Dillman, like Openshaw, wore a smart three-piece suit. The first-class restaurant was a large room with elaborate decoration and an abiding sense of opulence. As in all public rooms aboard, skylights and a domed ceiling were used to add more light and to create an impression of space. Long tables were set parallel to each other and the upholstered chairs, revolving for convenience, were fixed securely to the floor. Dillman sat directly opposite Kitty Openshaw. To his right, facing Openshaw himself, was a man named Ramsey Leach, a diffident individual who seemed to be overwhelmed by the buoyant Yorkshireman and who had completely withdrawn into his shell. Leach was a thin, nervous, balding man in his late thirties. He was returning to England after his first visit to New York but was reluctant to talk about the trip. Dillman felt sorry for him and tried in vain to draw him into the conversation. Leach preferred to remain silent, concentrating on his food, and throwing a glance over his shoulder from time to time. Dillman had a feeling the man would make sure he never sat in the shadow of Frank Openshaw again.

"And that's how I realized I had a gift," said Openshaw, coming to the end of another chapter of his autobiography. "I had this knack of seeing an opening and going through it. That's all it was. The guts to take a chance." He paused to allow a waiter to remove his plate. "What line are you in, Mr. Leach?"

"I inherited the family business in Tunbridge Wells," Leach mumbled.

"Have you got a factory or something?"

"Not exactly, Mr. Openshaw."

"What do you make, then?"

"Nothing." Leach squirmed in his seat before revealing his profession. "I'm a funeral director," he said. "An undertaker."

"I'd call you a fool," teased Openshaw with a loud guffaw. "Get yourself out of that trade, lad. It's a dead-end job."

Leach gave the weary smile of a man who had heard the gibe a thousand times. He was grateful when Openshaw turned his attention to Dillman. After waiting until the next course was served, Openshaw gave another tug on his waistcoat then raised an eyebrow.

"What about you, Mr. Dillman?" he asked. "How do you earn a crust?"

"Not as a financier, alas," replied Dillman. "I'm like Mr. Leach. I went into the family business in Boston."

"Burying the dead?"

"Quite the reverse, Mr. Openshaw. We try to bring excitement to the living. We design and build oceangoing yachts. They're tiny by comparison with a vessel like the *Caronia*, of course, but they have a definite market."

"I know. Kitty and I have had a cruise or two on private yachts."

"We went all round the Mediterranean," she added. "It were grand."

"Yachts, eh? How d'you start designing a thing like that, Mr. Dillman?"

"It's a question of trial and error," said Dillman.

He talked knowledgeably about his former profession, throwing in enough information to interest them but taking care not to confuse them with technicalities. What he did not tell them was that he had disappointed his father by leaving the firm, then outraged him by trying to make a living on the stage. For the purposes of the voyage, Dillman was content to be identified as someone employed in the nautical world. It was a useful disguise. While he liked to talk, Openshaw could also listen. He and his wife were fascinated by what they learned. Leach, too, took an interest in what Dillman told them. The undertaker was sufficiently engaged to venture a remark.

"So," he noted, "we have a sailor in our midst, do we?"

"A yachtsman," said Dillman. "Someone who sails for pleasure rather than for pay."

"There's money to be made in pleasure," argued Openshaw. "And I don't mean the sordid kind, either. I'll have nowt to do with that. Back in England, I own two theaters and a music hall. Aye, and I've a hotel in Scarborough and another in Blackpool. Holiday resorts, both of them. Invest in pleasure and there's no limit to what you can do."

"Frank proved that," said his adoring wife.

"I did, Kitty, even though I say so myself. 'Frank by name and frank by nature,' that's me. I may blow my own trumpet but you've got to admit that it's a damn good instrument. *Trust*," he declared. "That's been my watchword. My whole career has been built on trust. In all this time, I've never once had a complaint from a business associate or an investor. We trust each other. What about you, Mr. Leach?" he said, switching his gaze to the funeral director. "I bet that none of *your* clients have ever complained, have they? Hardly in a position to do so, six feet under the ground."

Dillman could feel his neighbor wincing with embarrassment.

Genevieve Masefield had a problem. The more she got to know Isadora Singleton, the more she liked her. The girl had a blend of intelligence and naiveté that was endearing. But she was quickly forming a dependency on Genevieve that was worrying, turning to her for advice and using her as a legitimate means to escape the vigilance of her parents. Seated beside her in the restaurant, Genevieve was able to further her acquaintance with the whole family. Opposite her were Waldo and Maria Singleton, a couple who looked so irrevocably married that it was difficult to believe they ever spent an hour apart. Waldo Singleton was a tall, stooping man with wispy red hair curling around the edges of a domed forehead. He had made a fortune out of selling real estate to rich clients but Genevieve caught the whiff of Old Money as well. Only the most expensive tailor could have made his suit. His wife, too, advertised their wealth in subtle ways. Her beauty had faded slightly and her midriff had thickened but she was still a handsome woman. What Genevieve objected to was the woman's blatant snobbery.

"We should have traveled on the *Lusitania*," said Maria Singleton. "That's the finest of the Cunarders."

"The *Mauretania* is supposed to be marginally faster, my dear," said Singleton.

"It's not the speed that concerns me, Waldo, but the food. This meal is pleasant enough in its own way but it lacks character. It needs more individuality. The Ferridays sailed on the *Lusitania* earlier this year and said that the cuisine was beyond compare. They talked about nothing else for weeks. Haddon Ferriday was so impressed that he gave the chef a hundred-dollar tip at the end of both crossings."

"Haddon always was ridiculously extravagant."

"The *Lusitania* has so much more class, Waldo."

"Yes," said Isadora impulsively, "but the *Caronia* has something even better. It has Genevieve on board and she's worth more than a hundred chefs."

"Thank you," said Genevieve, discomfited by the comment. "As long as you don't ask me to cook. My skills in the kitchen are very limited, I'm afraid."

"Mine are nonexistent," Maria proclaimed, as if it were an achievement. "And so they should be. Why toil at the stove when you have servants? Our cook is the best in the neighborhood." She turned to her husband. "Why didn't we sail on the *Lusitania*?"

"I was unable to book passages on her, my dear."

"She's a very popular ship," Genevieve confirmed. "And rightly so. I was fortunate enough to sail on her maiden voyage and it was a wondrous experience."

Isadora was excited. "I bet it was. Tell us about it."

"Yes," encouraged Singleton. "Is she really all she's cracked up to be?"

"According to the Ferridays, she is," said Maria. "They were enchanted. And not only by the meals. Haddon Ferriday said it was like sailing in a luxury hotel."

"Is that how it was, Genevieve?" pressed Isadora. "Do tell us."

"How does it compare with the *Caronia*?" asked her father.

Genevieve took a deep breath and weighed her words carefully before answering. In fact she had sailed on the *Lusitania* a number of times but she did not wish to give the impression of being too familiar with it. As far as the Singletons were concerned, she had been visiting America to stay with friends. They must never be allowed to suspect that she had a professional connection with the Cunard Line. The *Lusitania* would always hold a special place in her affections because it was on the ship's maiden voyage that Genevieve first met Dillman, an encounter that was to alter the whole direction of her life. That fact, too, would be concealed from the Singletons, though it gave her a warm glow simply to remember the event. A smile touched her lips.

"It's difficult to know where to begin," she said.

She described the vessel as best she could and talked about the unique atmosphere of a maiden voyage. Isadora was enthralled, Singleton was intrigued, and Maria kept saying she wished they had been sailing on the *Lusitania*. The trouble was that Genevieve was distracted slightly by a conversation going on to her left. While giving her own brief lecture, she also tried to listen to what was being said elsewhere. Two men and a woman, all American, were involved in a breathless conversation.

"Who told you that, Harvey?" asked one man.

"I saw them being escorted onto the ship," replied the other. "They looked as guilty as anything. And they were obviously dangerous. There were two cops and a detective with a shotgun."

The woman was shocked. "What can they possibly have done?"

"My guess is that they're killers."

"Harvey!"

"What else can they be, Millicent?" Harvey said knowingly. "They wouldn't get that kind of treatment for simply failing to pay a hotel bill. I mean, why are they being taken to England?"

"Because they're wanted by the cops over there," the other man decided.

"Exactly, Douglas. And they wouldn't send two detectives all this way for nothing. There must be a high price on their heads."

"I'd love to know the details," said Douglas.

"Well, I wouldn't," protested Millicent. "I don't want to cross the Atlantic in the company of a pair of murderers. And you say that one of them was a woman?"

"Yes," replied Harvey. "She was about your age, Millicent. But she had the hard-bitten look of a criminal. So did he. I'd believe anything of those two."

Their talk turned to another subject and Genevieve was able to close her ears to them. She concluded her account of her crossing on the *Lusitania* then fielded a number of questions from the Singletons. But her mind kept straying back to what she had just overheard. In common with Dillman, she had been impressed by Inspector Redfern and troubled by Sergeant Mulcaster. Genevieve did not envy anyone who was kept in custody by the man with the walrus mustache. He would be a stern jailer. If the pair were guilty of their alleged crime, she wanted them to pay for it. That did not, however, prevent her from having a lingering sympathy for them, especially for the woman.

"What was the food like on the *Lusitania*?" asked Maria Singleton.

"Almost as delicious as this," said Genevieve, before addressing herself to her rib of beef. "I couldn't fault it, Mrs. Singleton."

Carrie Peterson had a different opinion of the cuisine on board. The meal that had been specially prepared for her stood untouched on the tray. All she consented to do was to drink the glass of water that accompanied it. Inspector Redfern was concerned.

"You have to eat, Miss Peterson," he said gently.

"I'm not hungry," she murmured.

"It's good food. We had exactly the same ourselves."

"Very tasty," said Sergeant Mulcaster, licking his lips. "Try it."

"No, thank you," she whispered.

"It's for your own good," coaxed Redfern. "When did you last eat?"

"It doesn't matter."

"It does, Miss Peterson. We have to look after you."

"There's such a thing as forcible feeding," warned Mulcaster.

Redfern shot him a look of reproof. "It won't come to that, Sergeant."

"We can't have her playing games with us, Inspector."

"This is not a game."

Carrie Peterson's face had been drained so completely of color that it had lost all its prettiness and definition. She looked utterly dejected. She was too frightened even to look at Mulcaster. His manner was threatening. She hoped that she would never be left alone with him in her cabin. When Mulcaster glared at her through his angry brown eyes, she felt as if his rough hands were molesting her. Arms wrapped protectively around her body, she sat on a chair while the men stood on either side of her. Redfern gave an unseen signal and his companion let himself out of the cabin. A wave of relief passed over her. The inspector lowered himself onto the other chair.

"Have you thought over what we told you?" he asked.

"Yes, Inspector."

"Well?"

"I've nothing more to say."

"Then you're being very stubborn. Stubborn and foolish. Help us now and it will stand you in good stead when you go to court."

She gave a shudder. "We didn't do it," she said.

"I'm prepared to believe that you didn't actually administer the poison," he conceded. "How could you, when you were banned from even entering Mr. Heritage's house? And I think it highly unlikely that you helped to mix the concoction since he is the pharmacist and you were merely his assistant."

"Nobody mixed any concoction, Inspector."

"The Home Office pathologist disagrees."

"Our only crime was to want to be together."

"Unfortunately, Mrs. Heritage stood in your way, didn't she?" He leaned in closer. "That's why her husband devised his plan. I'm sure you would never have thought of it, Miss Peterson, and I suspect that you raised a lot of objections at first. But it seemed like the only means by which you and Mr. Heritage could be with each other. Do you understand what I'm saying?"

"Not really."

"At most, you're an unwilling accomplice. The judge will take that into account."

"We don't belong in court at all."

"I'm afraid you do, Miss Peterson."

She looked bewildered. "What will happen to us?"

"That depends on what you tell us."

"We're innocent. I've said that a dozen times."

"Then why did you and Mr. Heritage run away from the scene of the crime? That's what guilty people tend to do. If you had nothing to hide, why did the pair of you take the ferry to Ireland?"

"To start a new life together."

"Leaving the dead body of that poor woman behind you."

"No!" she exclaimed, bursting into tears. "No, no, no!"

Redfern took a handkerchief from his pocket and handed it to her. She dabbed away at her eyes. Carrie Peterson did not look like the kind of woman who might drive a man to kill his wife out of love for his mistress, but that did not matter. The inspector had met criminals before who were practiced in the art of dissembling. They could even summon up real tears, as she was doing now. It was only when they were convicted that the mask was ripped away from them. She looked up at him, her voice trembling as she spoke.

"Will they hang us?"

"That depends on the verdict."

"But they could—if the evidence was against us?"

"Premeditated murder does carry the death sentence," he told her, "but you have an excellent chance to cheat the hangman, Miss Peterson. Help us build our case against Mr. Heritage, and your sentence will be much lighter."

She shook her head. "We did nothing wrong. Nothing wrong at all."

"The jury may take a different view."

"How can they?"

"The facts speak for themselves."

"*Your* facts, Inspector. Not ours."

"Tell me what *really* happened," he counseled.

"No," she retorted with sudden defiance. "I'm not saying a word. And I'm certainly not going to help you to send John to the gallows. You can question me until you're blue in the face but it will be a waste of time." She met his gaze. "You believe we killed her, don't you?"

"I'm convinced of it."

"Very well," she said crisply. "Prove it!"

It was late when Dillman tapped on the door of her cabin but Genevieve was expecting him. She admitted him to the room then checked the corridor to make sure that nobody had seen him enter. Closing the door, she accepted a welcoming kiss on the cheek.

"You're as punctual as ever, George," she said.

"One of my many virtues."

"I've lost count of the others."

"Don't flatter me," he said with a grin. "Interesting day?"

"Very interesting. I've met some people from Boston who

want their daughter to marry into the British aristocracy, and I shook hands with the next winner of the annual Bordeaux-to-Paris race."

"A cyclist?"

"Well done, George! I didn't even know that it was a cycle race."

"And I bet you'd never heard of Theo Wright, either."

"How did you know that is his name?"

"Two reasons, Genevieve," he explained. "Firstly, Theo Wright is the only American cyclist who'd stand a chance of winning that particular race."

"And secondly?"

"I saw his name when I skimmed through the passenger list."

"That's cheating," she said, giving him a playful push.

"What was he like?"

"As fit as a fiddle. He'd jogged the length of the ship a couple of times and he was hardly out of breath. I'd have been on my knees. I liked him. Theo Wright is a lively character. He'll be a change from all the stuffed shirts aboard this ship."

She gave him a more detailed account of her chance meeting with the cyclist, then told him about the way Isadora Singleton was trying to adopt her as an alternative mother. What made his ears prick up was her mention of the conversation she had overheard about the two prisoners.

"That guy, Harvey, may have thought they looked guilty," he remarked, "but so would anyone jammed in between two cops and a loaded shotgun. But they were no brazen villains. To be honest, I thought the woman was about to faint."

"Harvey—whoever he was—made her sound like Lizzie Borden."

Dillman sighed. "Rumors are bound to spread," he said, "and that leads to heated speculation. By the end of the voyage, people will think we have two mass murderers chained up in the cells. I blame Sergeant Mulcaster for that. He didn't need to brandish that shotgun. And they certainly didn't need the police escort."

"Why didn't they just bring the prisoners quietly aboard?"

"Because they wanted to display their trophies, Genevieve."

"Do you think the pair of them are guilty of the crime?"

"Without the full evidence," he said, "I'm in no position to judge. Though I must admit I wasn't entirely convinced by what Inspector Redfern told us. I was just sorry that Sergeant Mulcaster came in when he did. I fancy we'd have learned a lot more about the case if he hadn't butted in."

"I keep thinking about Carrie Peterson," she confessed.

"Why?"

"Well, guilty or not, she must be suffering terribly. They were pursued across the Atlantic, arrested on board ship, marched onto the *Caronia* under armed guard, then kept rigidly apart. Inspector Redfern may be a gentleman when it comes to questioning a suspect but Sergeant Mulcaster looks as if he were trained by the Spanish Inquisition." She shook her head sadly. "He'd make it his business to give her a rough time."

"I was puzzled by the fact that neither had made a confession."

"So was I."

"You expect habitual criminals to deny everything but that's not what we have here. They worked in a pharmacy," he reminded her. "They're intelligent, responsible people. If they did kill the victim, it probably would have been their one and only criminal act. I don't think they'd have been able to lie about it so easily."

"Neither do I."

"We don't know that's what happened, of course."

"True."

"Besides, it's not our case."

"That doesn't stop me from thinking about it, George," she said, "or from wondering if I might be of some assistance."

"In what way?"

"Carrie Peterson may be able to keep two male detectives at bay but she might react differently to a woman. If I could win her confidence, who knows what I could draw out of her?" She

FOUR

George Porter Dillman took the opportunity to familiarize himself with the *Caronia* while most of its passengers were either in bed or lingering in the public rooms over a drink or a game of cards. When he left Genevieve Masefield's cabin, he began his perambulation by stepping onto the boat deck. It was a clear night with stars winking in the sky, but there was a chilly breeze that discouraged any but the most ardent lovers from coming out to stare at the moon as they stood at the rail. As he walked along the deck, Dillman saw only one couple locked in an embrace, braving the cold air, and they hurried into the shadows when they became aware of his approach. He lengthened his stride so that he could pass them swiftly and restore their privacy. At such a time in their relationship, there was no place for a third person.

Since coming aboard, he had liked everything he had seen of the *Caronia*. Apart from an incident three years earlier when she had run aground off Sandy Hook, the ship had an excellent record. Indeed, the *Caronia* and the *Carmania* had been among the most popular vessels in the Cunard fleet from the moment they entered service in 1905. New standards may have been set by the *Lusitania* and the *Mauretania* since then, but "the pretty sisters" were still regarded as favorites by many passengers. Dillman could see why. The *Caronia* was a fine ship, well designed and well run. Captain and crew took a justifiable pride in her. Dillman could understand why the purser was so keen to root out any drugs that might have been smuggled aboard. They defiled the carefully protected image of the *Caronia*.

After completing a circuit, Dillman was about to go down the steps to the promenade deck when he heard a swishing sound behind him. He turned to see a sight that was startling in its novelty. Crouched low over his machine, a young man, wearing a sweater and knee-length shorts, was cycling toward him at speed. So intent was he on maintaining his pace that he did not even spare Dillman a glance. Realizing it must be Theodore Wright in training, Dillman looked after him with curiosity. He admired the cyclist's commitment but he feared the couple enjoying a romantic interlude would be chased off the deck by the whirring wheels. He was still standing there when a short, thickset figure ambled up to him, holding a stopwatch in his hand. The accent seemed to come from somewhere in the Midwest.

"You'd best keep out of the way, mister," he advised.

"I can see that."

"We didn't think anyone else would be out here."

"No," said Dillman. "I'm sure you didn't. And when the other passengers know that a phantom cyclist rules the boat deck at midnight, they won't come near the place." He offered his hand. "George Dillman," he said. "If I'm not mistaken, that was Theo Wright who shot past me just now."

"It was," confirmed the other, shaking his hand. "I'm his coach."

"Then you must be Wes Odell."

The newcomer was astonished. "I didn't take you for a cycling fan, Mr. Dillman."

"I can't claim to be that," Dillman admitted, "but I'm an avid reader of the sports pages in the newspapers. Theo Wright has taken professional cycling to a new level and most articles give you much of the credit."

"So they should."

"What's the secret of good coaching?"

"Being ruthless."

Odell said it with such emphasis that Dillman knew he was not joking. He peered at the coach in the half-light. Odell was a solid character in his forties with the weathered look of a man who had spent most of his time outdoors. He had a broken nose, bushy eyebrows that all but concealed the deeply set eyes, and a bald head that was slightly misshapen. Even though he wore only a shirt, waistcoat, and trousers, Odell was untroubled by the cold wind. He looked down at his stopwatch.

"Wouldn't there have been more room on the main deck?" asked Dillman.

"We tried that. Too many people about."

"This late?"

"Some of them looked as if they were going to sleep there."

"Ah, yes," sighed Dillman. "Steerage accommodations can be pretty spartan. There are usually some people who prefer to sleep under the stars rather than put up with a rock-hard bunk in a tiny cabin that sleeps six."

"They can sleep where they like," said Odell, "but I don't want them getting in Theo's way. When he cycled past, half of them jumped up to complain. That only distracted him. Theo needs a clear run."

"Here he comes again," noted Dillman.

They watched as the cyclist sped past. Odell checked the time again then gave a grunt of approval. Keeping up a steady rhythm, Wright pedaled on as if he were in the middle of an open road.

"There's obviously money in the sport," said Dillman.

"We survive."

"If the pair of you can afford to travel first-class, you're clearly not paupers."

Odell was brusque. "We're not in it for the money, Mr. Dillman."

"You lust after glory, do you?"

"All I want to do is to make Theo the best."

"He *is* the best. In America, at least."

"He has to be tested in France," said Odell. "That's where it really counts. They understand cycling there. The French close whole towns and villages when a big race is on. Can you imagine that happening anywhere else?"

"Probably not."

Dillman was not enjoying the conversation and Odell was making it clear he would rather be on his own to study the progress of his young charge. The coach was an unprepossessing fellow. He might have driven Theodore Wright to the pinnacle of his sport but, Dillman mused, he could never teach him the most basic social skills.

"I'll leave you to it, Mr. Odell," he said.

"Thanks."

"Good night."

But the coach was not even listening. Tapping his foot impatiently on the deck, he was waiting for the cyclist to flash past once more. Dillman took his leave, making his way down through the different levels of the ship. The promenade deck was deserted, as was the shelter deck, but there were a few people walking along the upper deck. Dillman did a circuit there before going down to the main deck. Over a dozen passengers were standing at the rail, delaying the moment when they had to return to their pokey cabins in third class or steerage. Others had elected to spend the whole night in the open air and were huddled together in the stern. Their memories of the crossing would be far less rosy than those of the more privileged passengers on the *Caronia*. Dillman was still gazing at the sleeping figures when someone came up quietly behind him.

"What are you doing down here, Mr. Dillman?" he whispered.

Dillman was taken by surprise. "Oh, I didn't see you there,

Sergeant," he said, turning around to recognize the burly figure.

"I was enjoying a smoke." Mulcaster pulled on his cigarette then exhaled a cloud of smoke. He scrutinized Dillman through narrowed lids. "Are you on patrol?"

"In a way."

"I'd have thought you'd be in bed by now."

"I could say the same of you."

"Like to stretch my legs before I turn in," said Mulcaster. "But I can guess why you're still up," he added with a hint of mockery. "You were a Pinkerton man, weren't you? I remember their motto: 'We Never Sleep.'"

"It served its purpose."

"And what was that?"

"To deter criminals," said Dillman. "To let them know that someone, somewhere, would be on their trail twenty-four hours a day if they stepped out of line."

"I don't rate the Pinkerton Agency all that highly, I'm afraid."

"That's because you don't know enough about it, Sergeant."

"I know all I want to know," returned Mulcaster, dropping his cigarette to the floor before grinding it under his sole. "Allan Pinkerton had a great reputation but he couldn't save President Lincoln from being assassinated."

"That's true," agreed Dillman. "It was a source of profound regret to him that he wasn't at the theater that night to protect his friend. But it's unfair to judge the agency on the strength of one isolated event. You obviously haven't come across Mr. Pinkerton's autobiography."

"I'm not a reading man, Mr. Dillman."

"You should acquire the habit. It might teach you something."

"There's not much I don't know about this game," Mulcaster boasted.

"I think you'd find there is, if you read *Thirty Years a Detective*. It was a revelation to me. I know that Mr. Pinkerton's book deals with the past but most of his observations are still relevant today."

"Such as?"

"Well, he does stress the value of going undercover," Dillman said pointedly. "His operatives were trained to pass themselves off in various guises in order to get inside the criminal fraternity. That's how the Molly Maguires were brought down. If a Pinkerton man hadn't infiltrated them, their reign of terror would have gone on."

"We have our own methods. As you've seen, they work."

"All I saw were two frightened people being herded onto the ship like lambs to the slaughter. I'm surprised you didn't have them in chains as well."

Mulcaster was roused. "If it were left to me, I'd have handcuffed them."

"I'm sure you would."

"Killers deserve no quarter."

"Their guilt has yet to be proved in a court of law."

"What would you do, Mr. Dillman?" sneered Mulcaster. "Put them together in a first-class cabin so they could gloat over the way they murdered that woman?"

"No, Sergeant, but I would treat them as human beings."

Mulcaster snorted. "You'd treat Jack the Ripper as a human being!"

"I would," Dillman said easily. "A very bad example of the breed, but one of us nevertheless. And the next time you pour scorn on Allan Pinkerton for failing to save President Lincoln, you might recall your own record with regard to the gentleman we just mentioned. The assassin and his accomplices were all caught and punished. But with all its resources, Scotland Yard seems quite unable to find any credible evidence as to the identity of Jack the Ripper." Dillman gave him a farewell smile. "As you say, Sergeant Mulcaster, you have your own methods."

He walked away and left his companion fuming in silence. It had not been the happiest of strolls. In the course of his tour, Dillman had spoken to only two people but both had been disagreeable. The bluntness of Wes Odell was complemented by the gruff disdain of Sergeant Mulcaster. Neither man would qualify for a post that entailed tact and diplomacy. Dillman still hoped to spend more time with the amenable Inspector Redfern, but he promised himself that he would dodge Mulcaster whenever he could. After a look around the empty lower deck, he made his way back up through the ship, wondering if Theodore Wright was still cycling away above him. It seemed a strange way to enjoy a trip on a Cunard liner.

It was only when he reached his cabin that Dillman became conscious of how tired he was. Suppressing a yawn, he unlocked the door and stepped inside. Before he could close the door behind him, however, he heard a noise farther down the corridor and paused. It was now well past midnight, an unlikely time for anyone to be about. Applying his eye to the crack between the door and the frame, he saw a man emerging furtively from a cabin with a small case in his hand. After glancing up and down, the man scurried along the corridor. Dillman saw the smile of elation on his face as he passed. Dillman was astounded. Earlier that evening, the same person had sat beside him throughout dinner with the lugubrious expression proper to his trade.

It was Ramsey Leach, the undertaker.

News of the first crime reached Genevieve Masefield as she was finishing her breakfast in the restaurant. A steward delivered a note from Paul Taggart. As soon as she had read it, she got up from the table. She met Isadora Singleton at the door.

"Oh," said Isadora with disappointment, "are you going?"

"I'm afraid so."

"I was hoping to have breakfast with you. Mother and Father are having theirs in the cabin but I was sure that you'd be here. Must you leave?"

"I have an appointment with someone," said Genevieve.

"That means I'll miss you for *two* meals."

"Two?"

"Yes, Genevieve. My parents are having lunch served in their cabin as well. They've invited some friends of theirs, the Van

Wessels from New Haven—such dreary people! I begged them to include you in the party," said Isadora, "but they told me that I wasn't to bother you too much. I'm not bothering you, am I?"

Genevieve gave her a kind smile. "No, Isadora," she said, "of course not. But I'd be out of place in a gathering of friends like that."

"They're not friends of mine," the girl said mutinously. "I hate Nick Van Wessel. He's sixteen years old and thinks that it entitles him to take liberties. He tried to kiss me at a party last month." She pulled a face. "He's disgusting. His breath smells."

"I'm sure you'll meet much nicer younger men aboard."

"But I enjoy being with you."

Grateful that she had escaped lunch with the Singletons, Genevieve assured Isadora they would meet again soon, then detached herself. The purser's note had told her of a theft reported first thing that morning. Few details were given. Genevieve headed for the cabin of the victim. When she knocked on the door, it opened at once to reveal an attractive woman in her early thirties whose face was pitted with anxiety.

"Mrs. Robart?" asked Genevieve.

"Yes."

"The purser asked me to call. My name is Genevieve Masefield and I work for Cunard. I understand that you had something stolen?"

"Yes, I did," said the woman. "Please come in."

When she stepped into the cabin, Genevieve saw that it was almost identical to her own. Cecilia Robart was its only occupant. Evidently she was untidy by nature. A dress lay over the back of one chair, a coat over another. The table was littered with items of all kinds. A case stood open on the floor.

"Excuse the mess," Mrs. Robart apologized, "I haven't settled in properly."

"It takes time."

"I didn't realize there was a female detective aboard."

"Few people do, Mrs. Robart. I'd like to keep it that way, for obvious reasons."

"Oh, don't worry, Miss Masefield. I understand. I won't tell a soul." She moved the dress off the back of one chair. "Do sit down. I'm not usually as chaotic as this."

Lowering herself onto the seat, Genevieve took a pencil and pad from her purse so that she could make notes. Cecilia Robart tossed the coat onto the open case before taking the other seat. She gave a nervous smile. Genevieve noticed she was wearing too much powder on her face and surmised that she had put it on to hide the fact that she had been crying.

"I understand some earrings were taken," said Genevieve.

"Gold earrings, Miss Masefield."

"Could you give me a description of them, please?"

"I can do better than that," said Mrs. Robart, searching among the items on the table. She found a slip of paper and handed it over. "Here's a drawing of them. I'm not much of an artist but this will give you some idea of their size and shape."

Genevieve glanced at the sketch. "Thank you, Mrs. Robart," she said approvingly. "This will be very helpful."

"I simply must have them back."

"Can you tell me how much they cost?"

"It's not the cost," said the other woman, "it's the sentimental value. They were a birthday present from my late husband. Apart from my wedding ring and my engagement ring, there's nothing I treasure more. I was distraught when I saw they were gone," she went on with a sob. "David—my husband—bought the earrings in Bond Street."

"How did you discover that they were missing?"

Cecilia Robart composed herself before speaking. Her account was drawn out by some more needless digressions about the importance of the jewelry to her. Genevieve made sure only the salient facts went into her pad. She was interested in the faint West Country burr in the woman's voice. When she'd taken down all the details, she checked them for accuracy then looked up.

"Do you come from Gloucester, by any chance?" she wondered.

"Not far away," replied the other. "I was brought up in Stroud. Is it that obvious?"

"Not at all, Mrs. Robart. I had relatives in Gloucester, that's all. They had strong local accents. There were moments when I thought I heard the same telltale sounds."

"Oh dear! I've tried so hard to shake off that accent."

"You've succeeded admirably. Nobody else would notice."

"Do you mean that?"

"Yes, Mrs. Robart," said Genevieve, responding to the woman's obvious need for reassurance. She rose to her feet. "Thank you for giving me your time. I'll need to make inquiries elsewhere before I can start the hunt for the earrings. As long as you're quite sure that you haven't mislaid them. . . ."

"I don't think so—though that's not impossible." She looked around the cabin with dismay. "I know I had them last night because I was going to wear them to dinner but I just couldn't find them at all this morning. Someone must have come in here."

"Only a stewardess. I'll start with her."

"Good. Her name is Edith." She got up to usher her visitor to the door then halted as a thought struck her. "Is it true we have two killers aboard?"

"Who told you that?"

"Someone was talking about it over dinner last night. He said that two detectives had boarded the ship at the last moment with a pair of desperate criminals. Apparently they're being taken back to England."

"That's only partially correct, Mrs. Robart."

"Is it?"

"The man and the woman in custody are only suspects. We've no means of knowing at this stage whether or not they're guilty of their alleged crime."

"But it was murder?"

"According to Inspector Redfern."

"Is he from Scotland Yard?"

"Yes, Mrs. Robart. And so is Sergeant Mulcaster."

"I wish they'd chosen another ship."

"Why?"

"Because I don't like the notion of traveling with a pair of murderers."

"Murder *suspects*," corrected Genevieve.

"It amounts to the same thing," said Cecilia Robart, wringing her hands. "I hope they're safely under lock and key. I know they have proper cells aboard. I'd hate the thought that they were being kept in the cabin next to me."

"They're not in the cells, as it happens, but there's no danger. Inspector Redfern has them locked away in separate cabins in second class. He and Sergeant Mulcaster are in the cabin between them." She raised a finger. "I must stress that this is confidential information."

"I won't breathe a word, I promise."

"There are enough rumors flying around as it is. If people get to know where they are, some of the more ghoulish passengers will start hanging around outside their cabins in the hope of catching a glimpse of them." Genevieve opened the door. "That's the last thing we need."

"I appreciate that, Miss Masefield." Her eyebrows rose hopefully. "Is there any chance you'll be able to find my earrings?"

"Most stolen property is usually recovered by the end of the voyage."

"That's a comfort. This experience has shaken me," confided Mrs. Robart. "I've never had anything taken before. It's so unsettling. I mean, it makes you wonder who you're traveling with, doesn't it?"

It was Ernest Redfern's idea to borrow the chess set. During his visit to the scene of the crime, he had noticed that a board was set out with large ivory chess pieces. John Heritage was a man with a hobby. Unable to get any satisfactory answers out of his prisoner by intensive questioning, he opted for another method, believing that a game of chess would help Heritage to relax. The pair of them sat on either side of the table in the cabin where the prisoner was kept. Heritage had slept badly. There were dark circles under his eyes and deeper lines in his brow. As he pored over the chessboard, he knew exactly the game the inspector was playing and he went along with it.

"Did you enjoy your breakfast, Mr. Heritage?" Redfern asked.

"I ate it. I can't say that I enjoyed it."

"If you were on remand, you'd get nothing but bread and water."

"Would I be able to play chess with a warder?"

"Not a chance!"

"Then I'd better make the most of it, hadn't I?"

Heritage looked up with a glint in his eye. He was much more resilient than Carrie Peterson. The shock of their arrest had sent him into a brooding silence but he had now come out of that to reveal a sardonic humor. It was almost as if he was dueling with his captor. After a few moments, he decided on his next move.

"Are you a good Christian, Inspector?"

"I like to think so."

"You believe in defending the faith?"

"Naturally," said Redfern.

"Then you should protect your bishops more carefully," said Heritage, using his queen to sweep a white bishop from the board. "Your move."

Redfern pondered. "How often did you play this game?" he asked at length.

"Every evening."

"With your wife?"

"No," said the other. "Winifred never had the patience for chess. I had friends who came in on certain evenings."

"Miss Peterson was one of them, I presume."

"You presume wrongly."

"Did the two of you never play chess together?"

"A word of warning, Inspector. Don't expose your knight."

"I asked you a question."

"I gave you some free advice," said Heritage, looking up with an enigmatic smile. "The truth is that some evenings, I had no partner. So I challenged myself."

Redfern was skeptical. "You played chess with *yourself?*"

"It's an excellent way to sharpen your wits. I did it properly, you see, moving from one chair to another as I took charge of the destinies of white and black. I set myself some teasing problems," he continued softly. "The beauty of playing against yourself, of course, is that you always win."

"You always lose as well, surely?"

"I learned to cope with defeat a long time ago."

Redfern moved a knight to capture a black pawn. Heritage clicked his tongue.

"I did warn you, Inspector," he said, using his rook to knock the inspector's other knight out of the game. "You have to look over your shoulder all the time. Check."

"You distracted me."

"I thought that's what you were trying to do to me."

"I hoped this would be a slightly more pleasant way of passing the time than simply firing questions at you for the next five days." He shifted his king to safety. "If you'd prefer to play with Sergeant Mulcaster, of course, I can ask him to step in here instead, but it won't be chess. He's essentially a draughts man."

Heritage was waspish. "I'm surprised that he has the intelligence to play that."

"The sergeant is a good policeman," Redfern said defensively.

"Since when has that required intelligence?"

"You're starting to annoy me, Mr. Heritage."

"I wasn't being personal, Inspector," said the other, striking a more conciliatory note. "You've treated us as decently as you can in the circumstances. The same can't be said for that brute of a sergeant you brought along with you. I'll never forgive him for the way he manhandled Miss Peterson."

"He was only doing his duty."

"He grabbed her with excessive force," protested Heritage. "I daresay that she's still got the bruises on her arms. It's not as if either of us resisted arrest."

"We weren't to know that you were unarmed."

Heritage laughed. "I'm a pharmacist, Inspector, not a professional criminal. What did you think I'd do—attack the two of you with a box of laxatives?"

"It's no joking matter."

"You don't need to tell us that." He lifted his head. "How is she?"

"Miss Peterson is as well as can be expected."

"Has she eaten any food?"

"Not as yet."

"The poor woman is still in a state of shock. Let me see her."

"No, Mr. Heritage."

"Let me talk to her for a few minutes, that's all I ask."

"It's out of the question, I'm afraid."

"You can be present throughout."

"The two of you will never meet again until we reach England."

"If anything happens to her . . ."

"Mr. Heritage," Redfern said with growing exasperation, "it may have escaped your notice that you are in custody. It's my job to determine the nature of that custody and I've already been far too lenient. If you make any more futile threats, I'll ask the master-at-arms to lock you up in one of the cells. There'll be no games of chess in there."

"Pity," said Heritage, moving his queen again.

"Why?"

"See for yourself, Inspector. Checkmate."

Redfern looked down and saw that he had lost his third game in a row. Heritage turned the board around and began to set out the pieces for another game. Redfern stood up to signal that the session was at an end. He moved to the door.

"Can I at least write her a little note?" pleaded Heritage.

"Only if it's a signed confession."

Though the pangs of hunger were getting sharper, Carrie Peterson was not tempted by breakfast. The steward who had brought it took it away untouched. She sat alone in her cabin and wondered what was happening to her lover. When she heard a key in the lock, she was lifted to her feet by the distant hope they might be bringing John Heritage to her. Instead, it was the smirking face of Sergeant Mulcaster that came around the door.

"Time to visit the bathroom," he announced. "And don't be long in there, Miss Peterson, will you? Or I'll have to come in and find you. I'd enjoy that."

Gritting her teeth, she offered up a silent prayer then followed him out.

FIVE

In the space of only twenty-four hours, the atmosphere in the first-class restaurant had undergone a radical transformation. Lunch on the day of departure had been served to passengers who were, in the main, excited by the novelty of oceanic travel, yet were also very tentative in their surroundings. Not knowing quite what to expect, they were at first reserved and watchful. By the time they sat down for their second lunch aboard, however, everything had changed. They were relaxed and confident. Friendships had already developed, smiles of acknowledgment were distributed freely on all sides, and there was a pervading familiarity that showed itself most clearly in a greater volume of noise and a substantial increase in laughter. Genevieve Masefield had observed the process on previous voyages but it always amused her. When she came into the restaurant for lunch, she collected nods of welcome from people who would have been too shy even to look at her properly on the previous day.

Liberated from the company of the Singleton family, she sat instead directly opposite Theodore Wright. The cyclist looked rather incongruous in a smart suit. His hair was still unkempt and his face glowed with health. Beside Genevieve was a tall, fleshy man in his thirties with a permanent smile on his face. Stanley Chase had a cultured voice and an engaging manner. She admired the way Chase tried to converse with Wes Odell, who sat opposite him, even though the coach was curt and offhand. When the first course was served, Chase noticed Wright's meal was different from everyone else's, and that his portions were much smaller.

"Do you have a special diet?" he asked.

"I'm afraid so," Wright replied with a mock groan.

"Who chooses what you eat?"

"I do," said Odell.

"Why?"

"I'm his coach."

"Does he have no say in the matter?"'

"None."

"But you're not his mother," said Chase with a chuckle. "Surely Theo is old enough to decide what he wants for lunch."

"I have to get him fit."

"Yes," Wright said jocularly, "by starving me to death."

"Whatever food you're getting," said Genevieve, "you look very well on it."

"I agree," said Chase. "You're obviously in prime condition. And in your game, I suppose it's important to keep your weight down."

Odell was blunt. "Very important."

"It's like training a greyhound, isn't it?"

"No, Mr. Chase."

After delivering his firm rebuff, Odell started to eat his food. There were no special dietary requirements for him, and Genevieve noted the relish with which he consumed each mouthful. Coach and cyclist seemed an ill-matched pair at first sight. While the one was terse and unsociable, the other was effervescent and friendly. Theodore Wright was obviously glad to be sitting with Genevieve and kept up a stream of lighthearted comments. She found both him and Stanley Chase extremely pleasant company. It was Wes Odell who was the specter at the feast. At one point, when she paid Wright a compliment, his coach shot her a glance of stern disapproval. Genevieve could not understand what she had said to deserve it.

When the main course was served, Wright turned his attention to Chase.

"Have you spent much time in the States?" he asked.

"I've made a number of visits," said Chase, "but they've always been in pursuit of business. I never stay long enough to see the place properly."

"You'd need a lifetime to do that."

"Several lifetimes."

"What kind of business are you in, Mr. Chase?"

"Antiques."

Wright grinned. "How much will you offer me for Wes?"

"Oh, I'm afraid he wouldn't qualify," said Chase. "I specialize in antique furniture. Sheraton, Hepplewhite, Chippendale, and people of that ilk. Your coach would need to be at least a hundred years older before I took an interest in him. I ship my merchandise to New York, sell it there, then take special orders from certain clients. It's a good living. I know you've been having severe financial difficulties in America recently but there are still people with plenty of dollars to spread around."

"Where do you get your antiques?" asked Genevieve.

"From all over the country—house sales and auctions, for the most part."

"It must be fascinating."

"It is, Miss Masefield," Chase said affably. "I get to meet the most extraordinary characters along the way."

Wright sat up. "But not as extraordinary as me, surely?"

"No, Theo. You are well and truly unique."

"Who else would cycle all the way across the Atlantic?" noted Genevieve.

By the time they reached dessert, Odell was more forthcoming. He actually initiated a discussion. The coach had only one subject of conversation but there was no denying his expertise.

"Since I took charge of Theo," he asserted, "he hasn't lost a race."

"I wouldn't dare to, Wes," said Wright. "Not with you breathing down my neck."

"Is that how you coach, Mr. Odell?" asked Chase. "With naked fear?"

"No, Mr. Chase. I prepare him thoroughly in body and in mind."

" 'Mind'?"

"Having the right attitude is as vital as being in peak condition. It's not enough to simply to have a desire to win," emphasized Odell. "You must have the conviction that you can't lose. That's what will drive you on through the really grueling phases of a race."

"What about this one in France?"

"It's the blue riband of cycling, Mr. Chase."

"Is that why you're going all this way to take part?"

"Yes. We have to prove that Theo can beat Vannier."

"Vannier?"

"Gaston Vannier," explained Wright. "He's the French champion and he's won the Bordeaux-to-Paris race for the last two years. My job is to stop him making it a hat trick. And to get my revenge."

"Vannier has been making some disgusting remarks about Theo in the French press," Odell said bitterly. "He's been scornful about the times we've recorded in certain races and doesn't think that Theo will even reach the finishing line in Paris. The cuttings were mailed to us and I had them translated. Vannier has been very cruel about Theo."

Wright set his jaw. "Wait till you see what I do to him!"

"He's only trying to put you off, surely?" said Chase.

"Well, it hasn't worked. Vannier can watch out. I'll rub his nose in the dust."

"Deep down," said Odell, "this French guy is scared of Theo. He knows the reputation we've built up. His nasty comments are meant to spook us."

Genevieve was interested. "How long is the race, Theo?"

"Five hundred sixty kilometers, as the crow flies."

"How much is that in miles?" she said.

"Around three hundred fifty, we reckon," said Wright, "though it will be farther than that because of the way the road loop so much. Then there are the hills to climb and there are plenty of those, apparently. They'll make it seem even longer."

"Three hundred and fifty miles?" Chase echoed in wonder. "I'd be exhausted if I drove a car that distance. No wonder you keep yourself in trim, Theo."

"He's won six day-races before now," Odell said proudly.

"How long will the Bordeaux-to-Paris run take?"

"The best part of twenty-four hours."

Genevieve gaped. "You stay continuously in the saddle for *that* long, Theo?"

"Yes," he replied cheerily. "Give or take a few stops to answer to the calls of nature. They're something even Wes can't control."

"What about food and drink?"

"I grab what I can along the way. No time to sit down for a three-course meal in a pavement café, I'm afraid. I guzzle what I can when I have a short break."

"Water's the main thing he needs," added Odell. "It can get very warm at this time of year. Theo must have regular fluid, so I carry plenty of it with me."

"What about Gaston Vannier?" asked Chase. "Does he prefer wine?"

Wright was determined. "Whatever he drinks, he won't catch me."

"I think it's amazing," said Genevieve. "To cycle for twenty-four hours nonstop. What will you be like at the end of it?"

"Holding the winner's check, Genevieve."

"But what sort of state will you be in?"

"Better than you think, Miss Masefield," said Odell. "Wes is fully prepared for it. When he does take a break during the race, I massage his legs to keep them supple."

"You've thought of everything, Mr. Odell," observed Chase. "You're a lucky man, Theo. A good trainer makes all the difference. I saw a boxing match in New York once and one of the fighters was out on his feet at the end of the fifth round. But his trainer really worked on him in the corner. He sponged his face, gave him a drink from a bottle, and talked nonstop into his ear. I don't know what he said but his man came out like a demon for the next round and knocked his opponent all round the ring." He laughed at the memory. "It was only afterwards I discovered that the trainer had given him a drink of brandy from that bottle. *That* was the secret ingredient."

Genevieve was puzzled. "Brandy? Is that legal?"

"Anything is legal in boxing—if you can get away with it."

"Would you like a swig of brandy during a race, Theo?"

"Not me, Genevieve. I'd never be able to cycle in a straight line." Wright held up his glass of water. "I'll stick to this—until we celebrate afterwards, that is. It will be the best champagne then." His eyes twinkled. "A pity you won't be there to share it with me."

Genevieve smiled at him and earned another glare from Wes Odell. When the meal was over, she made a polite excuse then rose to leave. Wright gazed after her with candid admiration. Stanley Chase leaned across to him.

"If Miss Masefield were waiting for me behind the finishing line," he whispered, "I think that *I'd* be prepared to take part in the Bordeaux-to-Paris race as well."

"No chance," said Wright, with feeling. "I saw her first."

George Porter Dillman hoped to catch the purser alone in the lull immediately after lunch but he had to wait until Paul Taggart had finished calming down an irate passenger. When the door finally opened, a large, stone-faced, middle-aged American woman in a tweed suit and a feathered hat came bursting out and waddled off down the corridor. Dillman went into the cabin.

"Who was that?" he asked.

"Mrs. Anstruther," sighed Taggart. "She's only been on board the *Caronia* for a day and she's already notched up five complaints. If she keeps up that rate, I'll need the patience of Job to survive this voyage."

"Were the complaints serious?"

"They were to her, Mr. Dillman, and that's all she's concerned about. First of all, she wanted to be moved to another cabin because she didn't like the color of her carpet. Then she took against her stewardess. Last night, she had a toothache and blamed it on the chef. This morning," he continued in a tone of disbelief, "she ordered me to speak to the captain because the ship was rolling too much. What does she *expect* when we're in the Atlantic?" he wailed. "It has waves. But the latest complaint was the best yet."

"Did she want you to turn the vessel around and take her back to New York?"

"If only I could! No, she'd just come steaming out of the restaurant because, she claims, the man sitting opposite was looking at her."

"He didn't have much choice," said Dillman.

"According to her, he was staring in a meaningful way. As if he had designs on her. Can you believe it?" said Taggart. "Look at the woman. She's a positive Gorgon."

"Is there a *Mr.* Anstruther?"

"There was, it seems. 'If my dear Wilbur were still here . . . ' she kept saying, as if he'd have waved a magic wand and solved all her problems. My guess is that Wilbur took to his heels and ran away years ago."

"What action did you promise to take over this latest complaint?"

"I said that I'd look into it," Taggart said wearily. "Which means, I fear, that I'll have to ask you to have a discreet word with a Mostyn Morris. His cabin number will be on that list I gave you. Mrs. Anstruther described him as having all the attributes of a Welsh mountain goat."

"You won't see many of those traveling first-class on the *Caronia*."

"We won't see any, Mr. Dillman. She's simply having fantasies."

"I'll advise the gentleman to sit elsewhere next time."

Paul Taggart had more work for him. A passenger in second class had had his wallet taken in the lounge and a woman had reported hearing strange noises from inside a locked storeroom. The purser also told him about the case he had assigned to Genevieve Masefield at the start of the day.

"Why didn't the lady put all her jewelry in your safe?" asked Dillman.

"That's exactly what I said to her. Mrs. Robart struck me as being a trifle scatterbrained. I wouldn't be at all surprised if she put those earrings down somewhere and simply can't find them."

"It seems unlikely that anyone got into her cabin to steal them. No thief would make off with a pair of gold earrings when there must have been other valuables he could take as well."

"That thought crossed my mind," admitted Taggart.

There was a sharp knock on the door and Inspector Redfern let himself in. When he saw Dillman, he backed out again.

"I'm sorry," he said. "I didn't realize you were busy."

"Come in, Inspector," urged Dillman. "I was just leaving."

Redfern paused in the doorway. "In that case . . ."

"Any progress?"

"I think so, Mr. Dillman," he said. "I can't claim they've owned up to the crime in so many words, but their manner has convinced me beyond any doubt that they are guilty of the crime."

" 'Their manner'?" repeated Dillman.

"Yes. When we arrested them, they protested their innocence then refused to say a word. It was almost as if they had a pact of silence. But that's gone now," said Redfern. "Heritage came very close to taunting me this morning. And yesterday, Miss Peterson actually challenged me to *prove* their guilt. She'd lost that simpering look completely. Her eyes were blazing."

"That could have been anger at wrongful arrest."

"No, Mr. Dillman. What I saw was a woman, brazenly confident that she and her accomplice had got away with it. Until then, she'd been meek and mild. In a flash her real character suddenly revealed itself."

"Are you sure that they're safe where they are, Inspector?" said Taggart.

"Quite safe."

"A strong man could break out of that cabin."

"Where would he go? Heritage can't escape from this ship. Besides," he said, "the only place he wants to be is with Miss Peterson. Sergeant Mulcaster and I would hear the noise if he tried to break down any doors. We keep a close eye on both of them."

"I wonder if I might make a suggestion," Dillman said gently.

"Go ahead."

"Well, I know that Sergeant Mulcaster doesn't have too high an opinion of the Pinkerton Agency but it has had considerable success. One of the things it taught me was the value of using female operatives, especially when it came to questioning female suspects." He saw Redfern purse his lips in irritation. "We don't want to tread on your toes, Inspector. This is your case and we respect that. I just feel that Genevieve Masefield might be able to talk to Miss Peterson as a woman and draw things out of her that neither you nor Sergeant Mulcaster ever could do."

"Thank you for the offer, Mr. Dillman, but I'll have to decline it."

"Don't you want any help?"

"We don't need it."

"Very well. I won't press it."

"You'd be wasting your time, Mr. Dillman."

"Then let me leave you with this thought, Inspector. You told us, I believe, that both the suspects have repeatedly denied their guilt."

"Most villains do."

"But they're not typical villains, are they?" said Dillman. "Until recently, they were well-behaved British citizens who went about their lawful business without causing a moment's concern. They then commit a heinous crime—allegedly."

"Who else could have murdered Mrs. Heritage?"

"That's beside the point. What I'm asking you to consider is this. The husband may indeed have poisoned his wife—all the signs indicate that—but supposing that Miss Peterson was not directly implicated. . . . Suppose that, until you arrested her, she didn't even know that Mrs. Heritage had been killed?"

"She did seem overwhelmed by the news," Redfern conceded.

"Could that be the reason she was so angry yesterday?"

"What do you mean?"

"Innocent of the crime herself," argued Dillman, "she refuses to believe that her lover could have committed it. That's why her denials are so vehement, Inspector. You can't prove that she has blood on her hands if they're completely clean, can you?"

"That's marvelous!" exclaimed Cecilia Robart. "Where did you find them?"

"I didn't," said Genevieve. "The bath steward did."

"Bath steward?"

"You'd be surprised what people leave in a bathroom. They take off watches, necklaces, earrings, and everything else they're wearing before they get into the water. Then they simply forget to pick them up again. It may seem incredible, but a glass eye was once found in a bathroom on the *Carmania*."

"Who could possibly leave that behind?"

"An old gentleman who was ever so grateful when it was returned to him."

"Well, he couldn't have been more grateful than I am, Miss

Masefield," said Mrs. Robart. "I'd given up all hope of ever seeing the earrings again."

"You're certain they're the right ones?"

"No question of that."

When Genevieve had called at her cabin to return the items, Mrs. Robart was quite overjoyed. Now, taking the earrings across to the mirror, she held them up to the lobes of her ears and beamed happily.

"How on earth did they get into the bathroom?" she wondered.

"Did you have a bath this morning?"

"Yes. I had a reservation, first thing. I don't remember taking the earrings in there with me. Though I did have my necklace for safekeeping," she said, touching the pearls around her neck. "I always wear that when I'm traveling. Even for breakfast." She scratched her head. "I suppose I *could* have had the earrings on. I am a little absentminded at times." She turned to face Genevieve. "Oh, this has cheered me up no end. You must let me give you a reward."

"That won't be necessary, Mrs. Robart."

"But you recovered them within a matter of hours."

"The bath steward must take the credit. He found them when he was putting some fresh towels in there. Why don't you give him a tip when you next see him?"

"I will," agreed the other woman, looking for her purse, "but I'd like to give you something as well. You've soothed my mind wonderfully."

"They *are* beautiful earrings."

"David always knew what to buy for me."

"Take more care of them in future."

"Oh, I will, I promise." She found her purse. "Ah, here we are."

Genevieve held up both hands. "No, Mrs. Robart. Put it away. I'm not allowed to take money. I was only doing my job and I get paid for that. I just hope that every problem I encounter gets sorted out as quickly and painlessly as this one."

"I'm sorry to have bothered you."

"We aim to serve."

"You certainly did that." She opened the door. "Thank you again."

"If I might offer one last piece of advice. . . ."

"Leave any valuables in the purser's safe from now on," said Mrs. Robarts, anticipating the counsel. "I will, Miss Masefield, I guarantee it. I've had my scare. You won't hear another peep out of me for the rest of the voyage, I promise you."

Sergeant Mulcaster was outraged. Bunching up his fist, he brought it down on the table with such a bang that he scattered a pile of papers lying there. They floated lazily to the floor.

"Poke their nose into our investigation?" he roared.

"Calm down, Ronnie."

"I hope you told him to mind his own bloody business."

"It was only a suggestion," said Redfern.

"Well, it's one that we can do without." Mulcaster's pride had been hurt. "When I see Mr. Dillman again, I'll tell him what I think of his offer."

"He was making it on behalf of Miss Masefield."

"That's even worse, Inspector."

"Why?"

"Because the lady is an amateur!" snarled Mulcaster. "She's nice to look at, I grant you, but she's had no experience of real police work. At least Dillman has had some professional train-ing—if you can call it that. But not that well-dressed assistant of his. What on earth did she imagine she could do?"

"Talk to Carrie Peterson as a woman."

"Give me a dress to wear and *I* could do that."

"Ronnie!"

"I'm sorry, Inspector, but this has made my blood boil. We don't need any outsiders butting in on our investigation."

"That's what I said to him."

"How would Dillman like it if we started to do his job for him?" He bent down to pick up the pages on the floor, still seething with righteous indignation. "Blimey! There are five days to go yet. We've got bags of time to squeeze a confession out of Heritage and his fancy woman. By the time we reach Liverpool, we'll have them singing like canaries."

"I'm not so sure about that," said the inspector.

"Oh?"

"They're a tougher proposition than I thought. Especially Miss Peterson."

"Let me frighten the truth out of her."

"No, Ronnie."

"We've been much too soft so far."

"You weren't exactly soft when we arrested them," Redfern reminded him. "You used undue force against her, there's no doubt about it. She's not a strong woman. You had no cause to pounce on her like that."

"I thought she was trying to get away, Inspector."

"Let's be honest, Ronnie. You jumped in too fast and too hard. And it's not the first time it's happened, is it? You've been disciplined twice for handling suspects too roughly."

"They deserved it."

"Only if there's provocation."

"Well, I was provoked."

"That's not the view the superintendent took. If I hadn't spoken up for you, he might well have suspended you. And you'd never have been given this assignment," stressed Redfern. "I had to defend you all the way."

"Yes, I know," said Mulcaster, restoring the papers to the table. "Thank you."

"I don't want thanks, Ronnie. I just want recognition that I'm the senior officer here, which means I make the decisions. There'll be no strong-arm methods with Carrie Peterson. That could get us both into trouble."

"It would also get us the confession we need."

"The evidence is strong enough as it is."

"It's not enough for me, Inspector," said Mulcaster, rubbing his hands together. "When I've got someone in custody, I like

to break them down bit by bit. It saves so much time in court."
He nodded toward one wall. "What do you think she's doing
in there now?"

"Thinking about Heritage, probably."

"And him?"

"I daresay he's playing chess with himself."

"Eh?"

"That was my reaction at first, Ronnie, but it is possible." He
heaved a sigh. "John Heritage can certainly give himself a better
game than I can. He trounced me good and proper at chess.
It's a pity there's no dartboard in that cabin." A reflective smile
spread over his face. "Now, there's a game where I'd take on
anybody. I've won cups at it."

"I could win cups at interrogation—if I was given free rein."

"Well, you're not."

"What are we going to do, Inspector?"

"Bide our time."

"Let me have an hour alone with Heritage."

"No, Ronnie."

"I won't lay a finger on him," said Mulcaster. "I'll just talk to
him. Face-to-face."

"That's what you said last time, and the suspect finished up
with a split lip and three missing teeth."

"He threw a punch at me. I had to restrain him."

"Well, I'm restraining you now," said Redfern, fixing him with
a stare. "I want to get those two back in one piece. This case
could be the making of us, Ronnie. Think of the headlines in
the papers. 'Detectives Cross Atlantic to Capture Murder Suspects.' There'll be photographs of us, probably. And of them, of
course," he added, taking his pipe out of his pocket and slipping the stem into his mouth. "We have to keep Heritage and
his mistress looking pretty for the camera."

Mulcaster gave a low cackle. "And for the hangman," he said.

Frank Openshaw was a gregarious man. In the course of a single
day afloat, he had befriended a large number of people. As he

strolled along the boat deck, he was able to greet several passengers by name. George Porter Dillman was one of them.

"Good afternoon, Mr. Dillman."

"Hello, Mr. Openshaw."

"I'm just taking my constitutional," said the Yorkshireman, patting his stomach. "It's the only way to keep this from getting even larger."

"How is Mrs. Openshaw?"

"Not too well, I fear. A touch of seasickness. Kitty is having a lie-down in the cabin. For some reason, it always happens like this. She's fine on the first day out, then has an upset tummy on the second. You're a sailor, Mr. Dillman," he recalled. "Do you know a cure for seasickness?"

"Yes," replied Dillman. "Stay on land."

Openshaw chortled. "That's a fair comment."

"I was being facetious. Seasickness is not amusing to those who suffer from it."

"Kitty could confirm that."

Dillman had just returned from interviewing the man in second class whose wallet had been stolen. A pickpocket was evidently at work in the public rooms and the detective would need to stalk him. He had also dealt with the other problem reported to the purser. When Dillman unlocked the storeroom from which noises had been heard, the ship's mascot, a large cat, came darting out of the prison in which he had inadvertently been locked. During his incarceration, he had managed to knock over a number of small boxes. Dillman had stacked them neatly before locking up the storeroom again with his master key. He was pleased to see Openshaw again. They had lunched at separate tables so had not spoken since the previous day.

"I was interested to hear that you owned two theaters," said Dillman.

"Both in London's West End. The music hall is in Manchester."

"What sort of plays do you present?"

66

"Ones that make money, Mr. Dillman."

"Pinero? Shaw? Henry Arthur Jones?"

"Don't ask me the names," the other said dismissively. "I hardly ever go to the theater, myself. I usually fall asleep. Music hall is my passion. I do love that. But I cater to all tastes," he went on. "One of my theaters put on a Shakespeare play last year."

"There's a certain amount of vaudeville in some of those," opined Dillman.

It was not a point he had any chance to develop. At that moment, a figure tried to sidle past them without attracting attention. Openshaw spotted him at once.

"Mr. Leach!" he called out, moving to intercept him.

Leach came to a halt and exchanged reluctant greetings with the two men. Wearing a long black coat and a black hat, he looked as if he were about to attend another funeral. Dillman recalled the way Leach had left his cabin the previous night.

"Where have you been hiding?" asked Openshaw.

"Nowhere," said Leach.

"We didn't see you at dinner last night or at lunch today."

"I was there, Mr. Openshaw."

"Well, I hope you'll be able to join us for drinks before dinner," said Openshaw, with a benevolent wave of his arm. "You, too, Mr. Dillman. Kitty so enjoyed your company, and I'm sure that she'll have recovered completely by this evening. We're in cabin number six. Can I count on seeing you there, Mr. Leach?"

"No, I'm afraid not."

"You can tell us about the tricks of your trade."

"They don't make for polite conversation."

"There must be some yarns you can tell us. And you'll be able to meet some of our other friends as well. They include a couple of attractive single ladies," he said with a roguish smile. "They're the best decoration of all at a drinks party, I always think. Come along and say hello to them, Mr. Leach."

The undertaker looked alarmed. The invitation was unwelcome but he seemed unable to find the words to refuse it. Eyes darting, he shifted his feet uneasily. Dillman could see how uncomfortable the man was. Frank Openshaw waited for a reply that never came. Unable to find an excuse, Ramsey Leach simply turned on his heel and scuttled away as fast as he could. Openshaw turned in surprise to Dillman.

"By heck!" he said. "What did you make of that?"

SIX

John Heritage had grown increasingly worried about the condition of Carrie Peterson. Not having seen or communicated with her for over twenty-four hours, he began to fear the worst. She was not the most robust person, and the predicament in which she found herself would be almost unbearable. He blamed himself for landing the two of them in the dire situation they faced, and longed for an opportunity to relieve her suffering in some way. Locked in his cabin, he could do little but anxiously pace up and down. However, when he was accompanied to the bathroom by Inspector Redfern, he saw his opportunity. They had to walk right past Carrie Peterson's cabin. He was under no restraint. On the way back from the bathroom, therefore, he waited until he reached her cabin, then broke away to bang hard on the door.

"Carrie, it's me!" he yelled. "Are you all right?"

"I'm fine, John!" she called. "What about you?"

"Come away from there," said Redfern, grabbing him by the arm.

"You must eat, Carrie," urged Heritage. "Keep up your strength."

The inspector dragged him away. "This way, sir."

"I love you, John," she declared from the other side of the door, waiting for a reply that never came. "John!" she said. "John, are you still there?"

But Heritage was already being hustled into his own cabin by Redfern. Hearing the commotion, Sergeant Mulcaster came in from next door to see if he was needed.

"What was all that about?" he asked.

"Mr. Heritage broke the rules," Redfern said irritably.

The prisoner gave a shrug. "I simply wanted to speak to her."

"That comes under the heading of 'privilege,'" said Mulcaster, "and you don't have any. That was a very silly thing to do."

"I just wanted to know how she was."

"Safe and sound."

"Has she had any food yet? You told me she wouldn't touch anything."

"She ate some lunch," said Redfern. "Not very much, it's true. But we did coax her into eating a sandwich. At least, Sergeant Mulcaster did."

Mulcaster grinned. "I want to keep her alive for the trial."

"Do you need to take quite so much pleasure out of it, Sergeant?" complained Heritage. "Miss Peterson and I are completely innocent. It's demeaning to be treated like a pair of convicts."

"In my book, that's what you are."

"They're suspects in a murder investigation, Sergeant," corrected Redfern. "The burden of proof lies with the prosecution. Not that I have any qualms on that score," he said, flicking his eyes to Heritage. "As for you, sir, we'll have no more of the stupidity I just witnessed. If you try to make contact with Miss Peterson again—even by calling out to her—I'll have to take you to the bathroom with a gag in your mouth."

"Let me do that," Mulcaster suggested, eager to take on the role.

"I'm hoping it won't be necessary. Will it, Mr. Heritage?"

"Perhaps not," mumbled the prisoner.

"I want your word on that," said Redfern.

"You have it, Inspector—as long as you treat Miss Peterson with respect."

"We do, sir."

"Yes," added Mulcaster. "I always bow three times when I enter her cabin."

"That's enough, Sergeant," warned Redfern. "There's no call to gloat."

"She needs the company of another woman," Heritage argued. "Not someone like Sergeant Mulcaster. He doesn't know how to behave with a lady."

"I don't see her as a lady," Mulcaster retorted. "Only as your accomplice."

"That's absurd."

"So you keep telling us."

"She's the last person in the world to lend herself to any type of crime."

"Unless she was driven to it by desperation," said Redfern.

"We wanted to be together, Inspector. Can't you understand that?"

"Only too well. But there was the small matter of your wife."

"That's why we ran away to Ireland."

"Having killed her beforehand."

"No, Inspector."

"Then why bother to flee like that?" asked Redfern. "If your wife died by natural causes, then you had everything you wanted. Freedom to marry Miss Peterson and to spend the rest of your life together."

"It was not as simple as that."

"It never is, Mr. Heritage. We talked to the family doctor. He told us your wife was in the rudest of health. Not surprising, when she was married to a trained pharmacist. You could cure any minor ailments she had, couldn't you?"

"That's beside the point."

"I don't think so."

"Mrs. Heritage came to trust you," said Mulcaster. "When you brought pills and potions back from the shop, she took them without questioning your judgment."

"You know nothing about my marriage, Sergeant," said Heritage testily.

"We know that it came to a sudden end."

"Death by unnatural means," said Redfern. "And you did not even stay around to mourn your wife's passing. You planned it very well, didn't you? When you shut up the shop on Saturday evening, you told your business partner you'd be taking a few days off at the start of the following week. That gave you ample time to make your escape. You also sent a note to the cleaning lady, telling her not to come on her usual day. That delayed the discovery of the body."

"It may look like that, Inspector," said Heritage, "but you're quite wrong."

"Am I?"

"I've told you a dozen times what really happened."

"You've told us what you want us to *believe* happened," Redfern said firmly, "but we're not that easily fooled. I'd bet a month's wages that you were responsible for the death of Winifred Heritage. The only point on which I have the slightest doubt concerns Miss Peterson. Was she a party to the murder or not?"

"*Not*, Inspector," pleaded Heritage. "I swear it!"

"You're two of a kind," Mulcaster decided. "Both of you were involved."

"No!"

"She's more or less confessed it by her behavior."

"How can she confess to something that she never did?"

"Guilt expresses itself in a variety of ways," said the inspector. "We know the signs and the pair of you have started to show them in abundance."

Heritage took a deep breath. "For the last time, Inspector, we are innocent."

"Then why has there been no remorse over the death of your wife?" Heritage lowered his head to his chest. "It's because you gloried in it, isn't it? Look at you, Mr. Heritage. You're a middle-aged man who was trapped in an unhappy marriage. You became infatuated with a younger woman. Miss Peterson, in turn, fell in love with you."

"Lord knows why!" said Mulcaster.

"It's a situation that we've seen dozens of times before. Two people have an overpowering urge to be together. Because it's not possible, they're driven to extreme measures. In this case, the murder of a wife."

"That's simply not true, Inspector!" exclaimed Heritage.

"No?" Redfern replied calmly. "Then answer me this. Whenever poison is sold at your pharmacy, you keep a strict record of its sale. Your partner let us examine the record book, and what did we find? A certain John Heritage—the pharmacist himself, no less—is listed as having bought some arsenic and certain other drugs that could be used to induce acute poisoning." He watched his prisoner closely. "Now, sir, perhaps you'd be kind enough to tell us why you did that?"

John Heritage had no answer. Slumping into his chair, he looked desolate.

Genevieve Masefield did not escape her for long. No sooner had she sat down in the first-class lounge than Isadora Singleton came looking for her. The girl was glad to be released at last from the company of her parents and their friends. She talked at length about the extended boredom of her lunch.

"I missed you so much, Genevieve," she said. "Did you miss me?"

"Of course," Genevieve said politely.

"Whom did you sit with?"

"Theo Wright and his coach."

Isadora was mystified. "Theo Wright?"

"You won't have heard of him but he's very famous in his own circles. He's a professional cyclist, on his way to compete in a race in France that takes almost twenty-four hours to complete. Theo is a very engaging young man," said Genevieve, "though I was not so taken with his coach, Mr. Odell."

"I've never met a professional cyclist," said Isadora.

"You can see him in action twice a day."

"On board ship?"

"Yes, Isadora. He trains on deck, last thing at night and first thing in the morning. If you get up at the crack of dawn, you'll see him speeding past."

"What fun!"

"Theo Wright is the American champion."

"Then maybe I should get acquainted with him," said Isadora. "He sounds like livelier company than the Van Wessels. The problem is that Mother and Father would disapprove," she sighed. "Mother, in particular. I can imagine how she would react to a man who made his living on a bicycle."

"There are rich rewards in the sport, apparently."

"It's not a question of money, Genevieve, but of class."

"Your mother will very much be at home in England, then. It's even more class-ridden than Boston."

Isadora grimaced. "I refuse to believe that!"

"Take my word for it. We *invented* class."

Genevieve looked up as a tall figure approached. Stanley Chase stopped beside them to exchange a warm greeting with Genevieve and to be introduced to Isadora.

"It's not fair," he teased.

"What isn't, Mr. Chase?" asked Genevieve.

"The two most beautiful young ladies on the ship are sitting together, on the principle that there's safety in numbers. The *Caronia* is full of amorous young men in search of romance. Why deny them their opportunity?"

"That's not what we're doing."

"I'm sure, Miss Masefield," he said, winking an eye, "and I was only joking. In any case, nothing you could do would prevent admirers from queuing up. I can't speak for Miss Singleton but I know you've already set one heart alight."

"Has she?" said Isadora, agog. "Who is he?"

"A certain cyclist who sat opposite her at lunch."

"Theo Wright?"

"That's the chap."

"Genevieve was just talking about him." She turned to her companion. "Is it true? Have you made a conquest?"

"Of course not," said Genevieve. "Theo was just being friendly."

"I think it may go deeper than that," said Chase. "That's why his coach kept shooting you those dark looks. He could see how fond of you Theo was. Talking of Mr. Odell," he went on, glancing up and down the lounge, "have you seen him around? I wanted a brief chat with him."

"I haven't seen either of them since lunch," said Genevieve.

"Oh, you will, Miss Masefield. I guarantee it. Sooner or later Theo will come in search of you. He can't spend all the time training for his race." He smiled at Isadora. "It was a pleasure to meet you, Miss Singleton. Enjoy the voyage."

"I will, Mr. Chase," said Isadora. She watched him walk off. "What a charming man. He had such a kind smile. But he was wrong about one thing, Genevieve."

"Was he?"

"Yes. He said that you already had an admirer. I think you have two."

"Two."

"Theo Wright and Stanley Chase."

"That's nonsense!" said Genevieve.

"I saw the way his eyes twinkled whenever he looked at you. My guess is that he's carrying a torch for you as well."

"I only met him a couple of hours ago."

"There's such a thing as love at first sight."

"Not in this case."

"He's such an attractive man. I'd be flattered."

"Forget about Mr. Chase," Genevieve ordered. "And about any other imaginary suitors I'm supposed to have. You're the one who's being taken to look for a potential husband. Have you spotted any possibilities on board?"

"I haven't been given the chance."

"There's more than one member of the British aristocracy on the *Caronia*."

"My parents are well aware of that," said Isadora with a sigh. "That's why they're dragging me off for drinks before dinner this evening."

"Dragging you off?"

"To the Openshaws' cabin. Frank Openshaw comes from somewhere called Yorkshire. That's up north, isn't it?"

"Yes, Isadora."

"He's one of those men who went from rags to riches and who insists on describing the journey in detail. He has a voice like a foghorn. Father thought he was frightful and Mother couldn't bear him until he mentioned his close friendships with several aristocrats."

" 'Friendships'?"

"That's what he said," she explained. "Mind you, he did go on to say that he liked to have someone from the nobility on the boards of his companies. It always looked impressive on letter-headings, he claimed. But it was no empty boast. He knows Lord Eddington, who's a passenger on the ship, and there's another friend called Sir Harry Fox-Holroyd, apparently. Both will be there this evening with their wives. That's why Mother insisted we should go as well."

"Even though both these gentlemen are already married?"

"Mr. Openshaw confided that Lord and Lady Eddington have a son who is one of the most eligible bachelors in Sussex. But that isn't the only reason my parents were keen to meet them both. They're hoping it will gain them an introduction to the circles that really matter in England."

"Those aren't all to be found in the aristocracy," said Genevieve.

"Mother believes that they are."

"Then I hope someone enlightens her."

"Will you come with us this evening, please?"

"What?"

"I hate the idea of being on show," said Isadora, "like a china doll in a store window. I don't want Lord and Lady Eddington to look down their noses at me and decide that I'm not good enough for their son. I want you there so I'll have somebody I can enjoy talking to."

"But I haven't been invited."

"I'm inviting you now."

"No, Isadora. It would be quite improper."

"Father can speak to Mr. Openshaw. He seemed very approachable. Oh, by the way," she continued, "I asked my parents if you could use our bath and they agreed without any argument. Do you see, Genevieve? You're one of the family now."

"Not really."

"You're the best friend I have aboard."

"All the more reason for you to meet some new people," said Genevieve.

Isadora was hurt. "I thought you liked me."

"I do, Isadora. I'm very fond of you, but I don't think we should live in each other's pockets. The truth is that I'd feel embarrassed if I went along this evening as part of your family. Don't ask me to explain why. It's one of the penalties of an English education, I'm afraid. We're obsessed with decorum."

"So are we. Boston society thrives on it."

"Then you'll understand how I feel," said Genevieve. "Let's reach a compromise, shall we? You go along to the Openshaws with your parents and I'll promise to sit next to you at dinner. How does that sound?"

"I'd prefer you to be there beforehand."

"I can't be. It's as simple as that."

"Oh."

Isadora was dejected. Genevieve was sorry to have disappointed her but there was no alternative. If it were left to her, Isadora would spend the bulk of each day in her friend's company and that would be a great inconvenience to Genevieve. The girl needed to be weaned off her, to extend her social circle, and to learn the pleasures of being more independent. Before

Genevieve could decide how to achieve those ends, she saw someone come into the lounge and look around with a nervous smile. It was Cecilia Robart. She was wearing the pearl necklace but not the gold earrings. When she recognized Genevieve, she gave a friendly wave before moving off to sit with two elderly female passengers.

Isadora studied the woman. "Who is that?" she asked with faint jealousy.

"Oh," said Genevieve casually, "just somebody I bumped into earlier."

It took only a couple of minutes for George Porter Dillman to deal with the matter. Having found the man in his cabin, he did not even need to reveal his identity as a detective. One look at Mostyn Morris was enough to explain the misunderstanding. Short, shriveled, and gaunt, the Welshman had large eyes that seemed to be on the point of leaving their sockets at any moment. It was as if he were in a continuous state of alarm. He looked up at Dillman.

"Can I help you?" he asked.

"Mr. Morris?"

"That's correct."

"My name is George Dillman. I'm sorry to disturb you but I just wanted to give you a word of warning. I noticed that you were sitting opposite Mrs. Anstruther at lunch."

"Yes," said Morris. "Not the most appetizing experience in any way. She's a handsome woman but Mrs. Anstruther does tend to hog the conversation."

"That's what I wanted to whisper in your ear, Mr. Morris. I had to endure her over a meal yesterday. She means well but, as you found out, she is inclined to talk too much."

"A torrent of meaningless words, Mr. Dillman."

"There is another problem."

"Oh."

"She's a widow, desperate for male company. She never quite got over the death of Mr. Anstruther. She did hint to me that she came on this voyage on the hope of finding a replacement for him."

"Saints preserve us!"

"I just thought you ought to know that."

"Thank you for the warning."

"You seemed so hypnotized by what she was saying."

"The woman just wouldn't take her eyes off me."

"I had the same trouble," confided Dillman. "That's why I've steered clear of the lady ever since. It might be wise if you did the same."

"I will," Morris vowed. "She terrifies me."

"I hope you didn't mind my speaking to you."

"Not at all. You've only said what I secretly feared. Thank you, Mr. Dillman."

Eyes bulging more than ever, Mostyn Morris retreated into his cabin and locked the door behind him. Dillman suspected the man would regret that he had no drawbridge to raise and no portcullis to lower as well. Defenses against Mrs. Anstruther needed to be as formidable as possible. One thing was certain. Those staring eyes would never again get close enough to make her think Morris was having improper thoughts about her. Mrs. Anstruther would have to find another complaint to take to the purser.

Having sorted out a small problem, Dillman made his way down to the second-class deck to address himself to the more serious task of finding a pickpocket. The wallet had been stolen in the lounge. All the victim could remember was that he had been part of a large group of people who had left together. Shoulders had rubbed and there had been some good-natured jostling between the men. It was only when he was back in his cabin that the victim realized someone had deprived him of his wallet. Dillman intended to spend an hour in the lounge, relaxing in a quiet corner from which he could keep the room under surveillance and familiarize himself with the faces of the passengers who were there.

But he got no farther than the shelter deck. Blocking his way, as he descended the stairs, was Sergeant Mulcaster. Instead of giving a warning, it was Dillman's turn to receive one, and it was not issued in the spirit of friendship.

"Keep your nose out of our affairs," growled Mulcaster.

"That's what I've tried to do, Sergeant."

"Then why did you suggest that Miss Masefield should speak to one of the suspects? That's what I'd call unwarranted interference."

"I'd call it an offer of help," said Dillman. "No more, no less."

"We don't need you."

"Inspector Redfern made that point, though in a less hostile way."

Mulcaster squared up to him. "Who do you think you are?" he demanded.

"I'm an employee of the Cunard Line," replied Dillman, meeting his gaze, "which means that I have some jurisdiction aboard this vessel. You have none, Sergeant. You may be traveling in an official capacity but you are, technically, a mere passenger. That means you come within my sphere of influence. I am paid to look after you."

"Clear off!"

"Not until you tell me why you've gotten so riled up."

"I don't like people trespassing on my patch."

"That's not what I was doing."

"Of course it was," Mulcaster said bitterly. "When you ask if Miss Masefield can talk to Carrie Peterson, what you're really saying is that we've failed, so why not let your precious assistant show us how it's done? That's a professional insult."

"It wasn't meant to be. Inspector Redfern understood that."

"I see your offer for what it was."

"Then I withdraw it unconditionally."

"You don't have to, Mr. Dillman. It's been met with total rejection. We didn't come all this way to hand over the interrogation of our prisoners to someone as wet behind the ears as Miss Masefield."

"She's an experienced detective, believe me."

"I'd rather believe the evidence of my own eyes."

"Genevieve would surprise you."

"She won't get the chance," said Mulcaster. "Nor will you. Do you understand? You and Miss Masefield may be able to track down someone's missing collar-stud in first class, but this is a murder investigation. It's way beyond the pair of you. Clear off, Mr. Dillman. You're out of your depth. I won't warn you again."

"I hope that you won't," Dillman replied coolly. "For your sake."

The relaxed and easygoing Theodore Wright came close to losing his temper for once. He and his coach were standing on the boat deck when it happened.

"This is nothing to do with you," he said.

"Oh, yes it is," retorted Odell.

"You're my coach and manager. That's all."

"My job is to get you past that finishing line first."

"And you're doing it, Wes. You devise the training schedule and I stick to it. But that doesn't give you the right to take over my life."

"We can't afford distractions."

"Who's being distracted?"

"You are, Theo—or you soon will be."

"What do you mean?"

"I'm not blind," said Odell. "I saw the way you were mooning over her. I've heard the number of times you manage to bring the name of Genevieve Masefield into the conversation."

"I like her."

"You're hooked on the woman."

"That's my business."

"Not if it affects your training program."

"It doesn't, Wes. You know that. I haven't let up for a moment."

"Keep it that way."

"I'm not going to spend the entire voyage in the saddle."

"Metaphorically, you are."

Wright grinned. " 'Metaphorically,' eh? That's a big word for you. Where did you pick it up from, Wes? More to the point, what the hell does it mean?"

"It means that you keep away from Miss Masefield."

"Who says so?"

"I do, Theo. You're a wonderful athlete but there are two things that can ruin you. Drink and women. I've seen it happen time and again. A guy gets to the top in this game then throws it all away for the sake of booze or, even worse"—he stressed—"because some pretty girl smiles at him."

"Genevieve is not only pretty," Wright said loyally, "she's beautiful."

"Far too beautiful for you."

Wright was stung. "In what way?"

"In every way, Theo. Look at her, will you? She's an English thoroughbred. She's got real class. Miss Masefield is way beyond the reach of someone like you. Can't you see what will happen, Theo?" he urged. "If you start chasing her, you'll only end up being given a polite brush-off and then where will I be? Trying to coach a cyclist with a broken heart."

"It's not like that."

"I don't work with losers."

"I'm a winner," asserted Wright. "On *and* off a bicycle saddle."

Odell stiffened. "I'm ordering you to stay away from that woman."

"And I'm telling you to mind your own business." Pushing his coach aside, he stormed off angrily.

Odell wondered if he should go after him or wait until his ire had subsided. Before he could make up his mind, he became aware of someone standing by his side. Stanley Chase looked apologetic.

"I seem to have come at the wrong moment," he said.

Odell forced a laugh. "Not at all. Theo always blows off steam like that."

"He sounded as if he was really upset."

"It was nothing. Now, then, Mr. Chase. What can I do for you?"

Chase lowered his voice. "I wondered if I might have a word with you."

Dinner that evening provided everyone in first class with an excuse to dress up and show off. The men wore white ties and tails while the women ransacked their wardrobes to find their most striking evening gowns. Jewelry of all kinds was reclaimed from the purser's safe. Expensive perfume was sprayed in discreet amounts and cosmetics used sparingly yet artfully. When the first batch of guests swept into the dining room, it was clear the hairdressers had been busy that afternoon. There was a distinct sense of occasion, heightened by the fact that a small orchestra was playing for the first time. Dinner on the *Caronia* was the special event around which the rest of the day revolved. Everyone entered into the spirit of it.

Genevieve caught only a fleeting glimpse of Dillman but she was struck anew by his elegance. Suave and graceful, he seemed completely at home in his surroundings. She liked to believe that she, too, blended in well. Once again, she sat opposite Waldo and Maria Singleton with their daughter beside her. Whenever her parents were preoccupied, Isadora passed on her comments about the earlier gathering.

"It was a terrible ordeal," she confided. "Far too many people."

"Just as well that I didn't barge in, then," said Genevieve.

"Mother insisted on introducing me to every man under the age of thirty."

"Did you find any of them at all appealing?"

"Not really. They all looked the same."

"What about Lord and Lady Eddington? Did you meet them?"

"I had no choice," said Isadora. "Lord Eddington wore a monocle and his wife looked at me as if I were one of her domestic servants. It was rather unsettling."

"Take that kind of thing in your stride," Genevieve advised.

"The strange thing is that I made a good impression on them. According to Mother, that is. She was triumphant. Lord Eddington owns a string of racehorses, it seems. When he invited us to share his box at Royal Ascot, I thought Mother would faint with joy."

Genevieve was interested to hear all the gossip and offered what support she could. But she also took care to speak to the person on the other side of her, a middle-aged Englishwoman named Pamela Clyne, who was so lacking in confidence that she hardly ventured a word for the first half an hour. She was a plump, round-shouldered woman in a black dress that looked hopelessly old-fashioned. She wore neither jewelry nor cosmetics. Her gray hair was brushed back into a bun that was skewered in place by two bone pins. On her hands were thick black lace gloves. When Isadora spoke to her parents, Genevieve eventually managed to have something approximating a conversation with her other neighbor.

"Was this your first trip to America, Miss Clyne?"

"Yes," whispered the other.

"Did you enjoy it?"

"Very much."

"Where did you stay?"

The question embarrassed her. "With a friend," she admitted.

"And what did you see?"

"New York, principally. It took my breath away, Miss Masefield."

"It is rather splendid, isn't it?"

"I found it a little intimidating."

"So did I, at first."

"They were nice people," said Pamela Clyne. "Very friendly."

"That's what I found. Will you be going back again one day?"

"Oh, no! There's no possibility of that. This visit was very special. People like me don't get to visit America more than once." She looked around uneasily. "Especially in first class. I just don't belong here."

"Yes, you do," said Genevieve, with a smile of encouragement. "Savor every moment of it, Miss Clyne. Think of the stories you'll be able to tell your friends."

"There is that."

Isadora soon reclaimed her but Genevieve did not forget Pamela Clyne. She wondered why such a tense and frightened woman had chosen to cross the Atlantic on her own, among people with whom she had so little in common. A week in the Lake District would have been more suited to her character. What impulse had taken her on a lengthy visit to a foreign country? It was baffling.

Dinner in the second-class restaurant was also a rather grand affair but it was a treat the two detectives had to forgo. Inspector Redfern and Sergeant Mulcaster ate in their own cabin then took a tray of food apiece in to their prisoners. Redfern chose to visit Carrie Peterson and was pleased when she cleaned her plate for the first time. When he got back to his cabin, Redfern passed on the information to Mulcaster.

"Heritage only pecked at his food," said the sergeant. "I think he's finally accepted that there's no way out. We've got him."

"Yes, Ronnie. He gave himself away earlier when I asked about that poison."

"We still haven't got a written confession out of him, though."

Redfern took out his pipe. "It will come."

Now that their charges had been fed and locked away, the two men could relax slightly. All the inspector wanted was to smoke a pipe and think about his wife and children. Mulcaster, a bachelor, had none of the comforts of family awaiting him in England. His mind was filled with visions of the kudos they would earn for their arrest of the two murder suspects. Excusing himself, he went out on deck for a stroll to ease the feeling of restlessness that had plagued him since they had set sail.

Redfern was left alone. After lighting his pipe, he took out his wallet and extracted the sepia photograph of his wife that he always carried with him. She had been alarmed at the thought that he was going three thousand miles in pursuit of two murder suspects, and doubtless would have endured some sleepless nights in his absence. He longed for the moment when he could see her again and reassure her with a warm embrace.

A polite tap on the door interrupted his thoughts. He looked up.

"Yes?"

"The steward, sir."

"What do you want?"

"A message from the purser."

Redfern hauled himself out of his chair and opened the door. But there was no uniformed steward outside it. He found himself staring into the barrel of a revolver held only inches from his face.

"Back inside," ordered a curt voice. "I won't ask twice, Inspector."

Daniel Webb believed he was the unhappiest passenger aboard the *Caronia*. He loathed being at sea, he despised the accommodations in steerage and he detested the country to which he was being forced to return. Old and in failing health, he had tried to start a new life in America with the thousands of other emigrants who flocked there but he had been turned back at Ellis Island. What counted against him were his age, his medical condition, and the fact that he had criminal convictions to his name. He cursed himself for being so honest with the authorities. After being held in custody, he was summarily deported. The only way he could face the return voyage was by drinking as much alcohol as he could beg from other passengers. That night, he had been very successful, telling his tale of misery with such poignancy that he had earned himself a regular supply of beer. Webb had drunk too much too swiftly.

In the hope that the fresh air would clear his head, he went up onto the main deck but his stomach continued to churn even more violently. After being sick over the rail, he stumbled backwards into the shadows and sat down involuntarily on a coil of thick rope. It was dark and late. A gusting wind deterred anyone from trying to spend the night on deck and very few passengers were about. Webb dozed off to sleep for a few moments. When he awoke, he saw something that made him sit up in astonishment. Two men came out of the gloom to approach the rail. The second of them was holding something to the back of his companion's head and pushing him forward. When they reached the rail, the second man suddenly clubbed the other to the floor with a series of vicious blows. He then lifted the heavy body with some difficulty and tipped it over the side of the ship. The noise of the ship's engines muffled the sound of the splash.

Daniel Webb fell back into a drunken sleep.

SEVEN

The alarm was raised on the following morning when the steward assigned to their cabin brought breakfast for the Scotland Yard detectives. Getting no reply to his knock, he used his key to open the door and saw something that almost made him drop his tray. Bound and gagged, Inspector Redfern was lying on the floor in an unnatural position. The back of his head was caked in blood. Flying into a panic, the steward abandoned his tray and rushed off to find the purser. Within a matter of minutes, Paul Taggart had raced to the cabin with Dillman and the ship's doctor in tow. While the detective started to untie Redfern, the doctor examined the victim's head wound. As soon as his gag was removed, the inspector spluttered with relief.

"Thank God!" he gasped. "I thought you'd never come."

"What happened?" asked Taggart.

"I'm not entirely sure."

"You took quite a blow to the head," said the doctor, cleaning the blood away with a piece of lint. "I'll need to put stitches in this."

"Where's Sergeant Mulcaster?" said Taggart.

"I've no idea," replied Redfern.

"Why don't we wait until the doctor has finished?" suggested Dillman, untying the last of the rope and allowing Redfern to flex his legs once more. "What the inspector could do with first, I suspect, is a nice cup of tea." He crossed to the tray. "How do you take it, Inspector?"

"With milk and two spoonfuls of sugar, please."

When Taggart helped him to his feet, Redfern swayed badly. The purser guided him to a chair and sat him down. After giving his patient a more detailed examination, the doctor began to clean the wound again so that he could insert the stitches. A dab of iodine made the inspector wince. Dillman poured the tea and brought it across to him.

"Do you feel able to hold the cup yourself?" he asked.

"I think so, Mr. Dillman."

"How long were you lying there?"

"It seemed like an eternity."

"Two, three hours?"

"All night."

Dillman waited while the doctor took over. Redfern did not flinch as the stitches were inserted, but he was evidently in pain. A night trussed up on the floor had left him with aching muscles and a pounding head.

When he had stitched the head wound and covered it with bandaging, the doctor gave the patient some pills to relieve the pain. He hovered in the background while Taggart and Dillman fired their questions.

"Now," said the purser. "Take it slowly and tell us what happened."

Redfern bit his lip. "All I can remember is that someone knocked last night and claimed to be a steward. When I opened the door, I was staring into the barrel of a gun. A man ordered me back inside and made me turn round. Next moment, I had this bang on the head and fell to the floor unconscious."

"Did you get a good look at the man?" asked Dillman.

"Not really."

"What was his face like?"

"I've no idea, Mr. Dillman. He wore a hood."

"How tall was he? What sort of a build did he have?"

"I didn't have time to take any of that in," Redfern admitted. "When you have a gun pointed at your head, all you can concentrate on is the weapon itself."

"I appreciate that."

"Where was Sergeant Mulcaster?" asked Taggart.

"He went up on deck for a stroll."

"Alone?"

"Yes, Mr. Taggart."

"Why didn't he come back and release you?"

"I've spent most of the night asking myself that question."

"He was intending to come back, then?"

"Of course."

"Forgive me, Inspector," said Taggart, "but I have to ask this. Is there any chance that the sergeant might have . . . slept in another cabin last night?"

"Another cabin?"

"I was just wondering if he might perhaps have had an assignation."

Redfern gave a dry laugh. "Not Ronnie. He has no time for women. Besides, he was on duty. We take it in turns to check on the prisoners every two hours throughout the night." He sat up with concern. "They haven't been released, have they?" he said. "Is that what this is all about? A rescue attempt?"

"I'll check," said Taggart.

Pulling out his master key, he went swiftly out of the cabin. Dillman took over.

"This man who forced his way in here," he resumed. "What was his voice like?"

"Authoritative."

"What sort of an accent did he have? English? American?"

"A mixture of both," said Redfern. "He barked his orders at me, as if he were trying to disguise his voice. Once inside the cabin, he said nothing at all."

"Would you be able to recognize that voice again?"

"I doubt it, Mr. Dillman."

"Can you remember what he was wearing?"

"I'm afraid not. It all happened so quickly."

"The inspector is still groggy," noted the doctor. "He may recall more detail in time. What he really needs to do now is rest."

"How can I rest after something like this?" Redfern said angrily.

"Calm down, sir."

"I want this villain caught."

Taggart came back in.

"Well?"

"They're both still there," confirmed the purser.

Redfern relaxed. "Thank heaven for that!"

"Who would want to release them from custody?"

"I don't know, Mr. Taggart. But I can't think of any other reason why someone would want to disable me like that."

"Not to mention Sergeant Mulcaster," observed Dillman. "Since he didn't return here, we must presume that he was forcibly prevented from doing so."

Redfern was bewildered. "Why?"

"That's what we'll have to find out."

"First of all, we have to track down the sergeant," said Taggart. "I'll organize a search. We'll comb the vessel from top to bottom until we locate him."

"If he's still on board."

"What do you mean, Mr. Dillman?"

"That we have to take every eventuality into account. Sergeant Mulcaster was a strong man, not easily overpowered. He was also devoted to duty," said Dillman, "which is why his failure to return to the cabin is so disturbing. I hope there's a simple explanation for his absence and that he was not attacked like the inspector. But we have to consider the worst possible situation," he warned. "The sergeant may no longer be on the ship."

It was the rain that brought him awake. Carried by a swirling wind, it scoured the ship and kept all but a few passengers away from the unprotected areas of the deck. Daniel Webb opened his eyes to find that his clothes were damp and his face was covered in a wet film. He shook himself like an old dog. It took him a few minutes to get his bearings. When he finally realized that he was at the mercy of the elements, he hauled himself to his feet and sought shelter. The beer he had drunk on the previous night had left his head feeling muzzy and his stomach queasy. What troubled him most, however, was the strange dream he had had. It had been so vivid and frightening. He dreamt he had witnessed a murder that took place only yards away from him. A man had been clubbed to the deck before being tipped over the rail into the sea. Webb could not imagine a more horrible death. As he lurched off towards his steerage quarters, all he could think about was finding some more alcohol. It was the one thing that might block out the dream that was haunting him.

Genevieve Masefield responded swiftly. When Dillman's note was delivered to her cabin, its contents made her abandon her plans for breakfast in the restaurant. She hurried to the cabin occupied by the two Scotland Yard detectives and found Dillman alone in there with Inspector Redfern. The sight of the inspector's head, swathed in a bandage, made her start. Dillman explained what had happened.

"That's dreadful!" she exclaimed.

"I agree, Miss Masefield," said Redfern. "Violence against a police officer is a serious offense. I'll impress that fact on the villain when I catch up with him."

"You're in no state to catch anyone at the moment," Dillman said gently. "You spent the whole night tied up on the floor and you lost a fair amount of blood. Remember what the doctor advised, Inspector. You have to take it easy."

"Not a chance, Mr. Dillman."

"Any sign of Sergeant Mulcaster?" asked Genevieve.

"They're still searching for him."

"Where could he possibly be?"

"We're working on the theory he may have been attacked as well," said Dillman. "It was a case of divide and rule. Someone waited until the inspector was alone in here before seizing his opportunity. That meant the sergeant was also alone." He looked at Redfern. "Would he have been armed, Inspector?"

"No, Mr. Dillman," said Redfern.

"But you did bring weapons aboard."

"Yes. They were issued before we left England."

"Sergeant Mulcaster had a shotgun."

"That's right. And I had a revolver."

"Where are they?"

"Locked away in the wardrobe."

"Are you sure?" asked Dillman. "Do you mind if I take a look?"

"I'll do so myself," said Redfern, struggling out of his chair. He put a hand to his head as the pain surged; Dillman held his arm. "I'm fine," he went on, moving unsteadily across to the wardrobe. "The sooner I get on my feet again, the better."

He opened the door of the wardrobe and started to rummage inside.

"Well?" said Dillman.

Redfern was alarmed. "They're not here. Both weapons are gone."

"Would you like me to see?"

"There's no point, Mr. Dillman. The cupboard is bare."

"Could they be anywhere else in the cabin?"

"Where?" asked Redfern, looking around balefully. "We kept the shotgun and the revolver in there with a supply of ammunition. Is *that* what he was after?" he wondered. "Our weapons? This could be more dangerous than I thought."

"Don't jump to conclusions," said Dillman. "If someone was that keen to acquire weapons, he'd have raided the store kept by the master-at-arms. No, I think your attacker was just trying to disable you even more, Inspector. He was drawing your teeth."

"Why would he do that, George?" said Genevieve.

"I don't know, but he must have had a good reason."

"It doesn't make sense. As you pointed out, the master-at-arms has a supply of weapons. In an emergency, he could always issue replacements to the inspector and the sergeant. Why take such risks to get the weapons from this cabin?" She glanced at the inspector as he sat gingerly back down on his chair. "Besides, the man already has a revolver, doesn't he?"

"No question of that," agreed Redfern.

"We can't be certain it was loaded," Dillman reasoned. "Or that it was a genuine handgun. Some fake weapons can look exactly like the real thing."

Redfern was rueful. "It certainly *felt* like the real thing."

"I just don't understand the motive for the attack," said Genevieve.

"Neither do I, at this stage," Dillman admitted.

"Did someone have a personal grudge against you, Inspector?"

"Yes," replied Redfern. "Two people. John Heritage and Carrie Peterson."

"Perhaps they have friends aboard."

"I think that's unlikely."

"There was no attempt to rescue them, Genevieve. I don't believe the prisoners are implicated in any way here. Though the latest development does raise a question."

"What's that, George?"

"What will happen to Mr. Heritage and Miss Peterson?" said Dillman. "If the sergeant has disappeared or been permanently disabled in some way, who will look after them? It's not something you could easily do on your own, Inspector."

"I realize that," Redfern conceded.

"Then perhaps you'll reconsider our offer of assistance."

"No, Mr. Dillman."

"If you concentrate on Mr. Heritage, then you could leave Miss Peterson to Genevieve. I still feel that a woman's touch is needed there."

Redfern asserted himself. "Thank you for the suggestion but I must ask you not to repeat it. Who knows where Sergeant Mulcaster is? I have every hope that he will be found and be able to resume his duties. If that's not the case," he continued, "then I do have contingency plans. I'll hand Mr. Heritage over to the master-at-arms and keep an eye on Miss Peterson myself."

"As you wish, Inspector."

"I do, Mr. Dillman."

"Then we'll leave you to it."

"I'd be grateful for that," said Redfern, with some asperity. "I know you mean well but your interference is rather annoying."

"We're not interfering."

"What else would you call it? Please stop crowding me. I was knocked unconscious in my cabin, Sergeant Mulcaster has mysteriously disappeared, and our weapons have been stolen. I would have thought those crimes were quite enough to keep you occupied."

Dillman traded a glance with Genevieve. She lifted a meaningful eyebrow.

"That's a fair point, Inspector," said Dillman. "Please excuse us."

Isadora Singleton looked in vain for her friend. She had paid three separate visits to Genevieve's cabin but each journey was futile. Disappointed and bored, she sat alone in the first-class lounge and leafed through a magazine with fitful interest. A shadow fell across her. When she looked up, she saw that it had been cast by a fresh-faced young man with tousled hair. He gave her a disarming grin.

"Good morning," he said politely. "My name is Theo Wright."

"Oh, yes," she replied warmly. "Genevieve mentioned you. You're a cyclist. I'm Isadora Singleton, by the way, and I'm very pleased to make your acquaintance."

"The pleasure's mutual, Miss Singleton."

"Thank you."

"Do you happen to know where Genevieve is?"

"I'm afraid not."

"You seem to be her closest friend on board," he said with a touch of envy. "I've seen the pair of you together a number of times and you were deep in conversation over dinner last night."

"We were. We had a lovely, long talk."

"So where is she now? I haven't seen her all morning."

"Neither have I, Mr. Wright."

"You can call me Theo. Any friend of Genevieve's is a friend of mine."

Isadora beamed. "That's what I think. Call me Isadora, if you like. I hate being known as 'Miss Singleton.' It makes me sound like a maiden aunt."

He laughed. "You're anything but that, Isadora."

"Is it true that you're a champion cyclist?"

"So they tell me."

"According to Genevieve, you ride around the deck twice a day."

"I do," he said. "I was in the saddle at six o'clock this morning."

"Gosh! I was fast asleep then."

"I wish I'd been able to lie in bed as well."

"Where did you cycle, Theo?"

"Well, I usually keep to the boat deck but I couldn't do that today. The rain made it far too slippery for my tires. I went up and down the shelter deck instead. That wasn't quite so bad."

"Isn't the boat deck a little cluttered?"

"That's why Wes chose it."

"Wes?"

"My coach, Wes Odell," he explained. "It's important for me to have to ride around various obstructions, Isadora, since that's what happens in a race, you see."

"But I don't see, I'm afraid."

"You've obviously never watched cyclists in action. Let's just say that they're not the most courteous people on this planet. To start with," he said, using his hands to draw pictures in the air, "there may be a hundred or more other guys in a race. Think of the problems that can give me. I have to dodge and weave all the way."

"I never thought of that."

"If someone comes to grief—and you can bet your bottom dollar that there's always one idiot who comes off his machine—the rest of us have to be careful not to crash into him or we're suddenly out of the reckoning as well. But the real trouble," he confided, "comes from the cheats."

"Cheats?"

"That's what I call them, Isadora, though they'd probably tell you they were acting within the rules. I'm a lone wolf but some guys hunt in packs. They decide which of them is going to win, then impede anyone who's seen as a threat. Namely, me."

"How could they do that?"

"All too easily," he said. "If four guys box you in, it's difficult to break clear. Or they may just fan out across the road and block your way through. At least," he went on with a chuckle, "that's what they *try* to do. But I'm always too fast and too clever for them. Especially on hill climbs. Nobody can keep up with me there."

"I had no idea there was any cheating in the sport."

"You'd be surprised, Isadora. I've even had people trying to push me off my cycle when we were out of sight of the officials. It's war out there, believe me."

"Then you must be very brave," she said with admiration.

He struck a pose. "Bloody but unbowed."

"What about this big race in France?"

"Oh, there'll be all kinds of funny business in that, Isadora."

"How do you know?"

"Because the French are past masters at it," he said blithely. "I've spoken to guys who cycled there. You should hear their horror stories. Barging, blocking, forcing you off the road.

French cyclists will stop at nothing to win. They taunt you as well. They call you so many nasty names that you're grateful you don't understand the language."

"I've always been taught that the French are such a civilized race."

"Not when it comes to cycling."

"Genevieve said the race lasts almost twenty-four hours."

"That's right," he confirmed. "We start on Saturday, cycle all through the night, then reach Paris sometime the following afternoon. Those of us who survive, that is."

"What happens if you get cramp?"

"You hop off your bicycle and let your coach massage your legs. If he's managed to keep up with you, that is. Wes always hires a motorcycle."

"Supposing *that* breaks down?"

"Don't tempt Providence," he said, sitting beside her. "Anyway, if you keep yourself fit, you shouldn't have cramp. After all, you don't have to pedal every inch of the way. There may be some steep hills to climb but you have a breather when you coast down the other side. The secret is being able to pace yourself."

"My parents never let me have a bicycle. They said it was too dangerous."

"It is if you ride it in the Bordeaux-to-Paris race."

"I've always wanted to learn."

"Then why don't you?"

"How can I, Theo?"

"Easily," he said. "I've got two bicycles aboard. You can borrow one of those, if you like. We'll have to lower the saddle for you, of course."

Isadora was excited. "Do you mean it?"

"Why not?"

"Taught by a champion!"

"I'm always ready to introduce someone to the joys of cycling."

"I'll pay you," she said. "I don't expect you to do this for nothing."

He held up a palm. "Keep your money. I wouldn't dream of taking a cent from you." He became thoughtful. "Mind you, there is one reward I'd like."

"Just name it, Theo."

"Put in a good word for me with Genevieve."

Isadora giggled. She felt that she had acquired another friend.

The search was thorough and systematic. Beginning in the second-class areas of the *Caronia*, it went up to first class, then all the way down to the orlop deck. Dillman took an active part in it all, looking into every nook and cranny of the vessel. Stewards were pressed into service. Since the linen had to be changed on every bed in the second- and first-class cabins, they were able to carry out a discreet search at the same time. It was all to no avail. Not the slightest trace of Sergeant Mulcaster was found. Dillman did not give up. He went through some of the cabins in third class and steerage himself, even though it was highly unlikely the missing detective would be found in a place that housed four, six, or even more passengers. Alerted by the purser, the entire crew kept an eye open for any signs of Mulcaster. None came to light.

After the first sweep of the ship, Dillman adjourned to Paul Taggart's office. The purser tried to hide his anxiety. The implications of what had happened were worrying and he feared that there might be unfortunate repercussions.

"Nothing like this has ever occured on the *Caronia* before," he said.

"I'm sure, Mr. Taggart."

"Someone as solid as the sergeant can't just disappear into thin air."

Dillman sighed. "He could have vanished into deep water."

"It doesn't bear thinking about, Mr. Dillman."

"Nevertheless, we may have to confront that possibility."

"Push him overboard?" said Taggart, shaking his head in disbelief. "Who would do such a thing?"

"The same man who knocked Inspector Redfern senseless."

"How did he know the inspector would be alone?"

"Because he watched the cabin, in all probability."

"But how did he know where to find the cabin in the first place?" asked the purser. "Most people on board aren't even aware we have Scotland Yard detectives on our passenger list."

"I suspect that they are, though," said Dillman. "Especially in first and second class. Tongues were wagging over dinner on the first night. I blame Sergeant Mulcaster for that. He insisted on drawing attention to himself with that shotgun. They should have slipped on board quietly, without that police escort."

"It's too late to do anything about that now."

"I know."

"So what do we do?"

"Intensify the search. It may just be that they keep one step ahead of us."

" 'They'?"

"Yes," said Dillman. "My guess is that the man who attacked the inspector may well have an accomplice. If the sergeant is being held hostage somewhere, he could be moved between two cabins before any stewards arrive to change the bedding. Unlikely, I agree, but we can't rule it out."

"You think that he's being held hostage, Mr. Dillman?"

"Frankly, no. There's no apparent motive for that. But it's a more reassuring supposition than the thought that he was dumped overboard during the night."

Taggart nodded. Sitting at his desk, he reached for the passenger list on the desk in front of him. He thumbed through the pages and peered at the endless names. Casting the list aside, he shook his head in dismay.

"It's hopeless. We have almost two and a half thousand suspects."

"A lot more than that," remarked Dillman, "if you count the crew."

"The crew?"

"Sergeant Mulcaster did like to throw his weight around. I can well imagine him getting on the wrong side of someone in the crew. On the other hand, the inspector was attacked as well and he's been much more courteous." He picked up the list. "It's not as daunting as it looks, Mr. Taggart."

"It is, from where I'm sitting."

"We can eliminate female passengers," argued Dillman. "The person who forced his way into that cabin was an able-bodied man. He'd have to be, if he tackled Sergeant Mulcaster as well. Go through this list and I daresay you can exclude the vast majority of names. That would narrow the field considerably."

"What do we do then, Mr. Dillman?"

"Take a closer look at everyone who is left."

"There might still be a sizable number."

"We're not due in Liverpool until the end of the week. That gives us plenty of time." He replaced the passenger list. "The culprit can't go anywhere."

"That's true. Neither can his accomplice—if he has one."

"My suspicion is that he does. I have this hunch."

"Then I'll put my trust in it." Taggart sat back with his hands behind his head. "This is the last thing we wanted," he said. "When I spoke to the captain last night, he told me that we might get some good publicity out of the fact that the *Caronia* was the vessel that helped to bring two murderers back to face justice. What will he say when he hears that one of the detectives was attacked and that the other has vanished completely?"

"Perhaps he'll be philosophical about it."

"You don't know the skipper!"

"Tell him that worse things happen at sea."

Taggart gave a brittle laugh.

"Still, I know you've dozens of other things to get on with," said Dillman, "so I'll get back to continuing with the search."

"Keep me posted at regular intervals."

"I will, Mr. Taggart."

"And remember," said the purser, getting to his feet. "Finding out what happened to Sergeant Mulcaster is very important, of course, but I don't want you to be deflected entirely from the search for those narcotics we believe may be aboard."

"I won't forget," said Dillman.

"Theft, drug smuggling, violence against policemen, a possible murder." Taggart pulled a face. "What is the *Caronia* coming to?"

"You missed one crime out."

"Did I?"

"Mrs. Anstruther. And her stalker."

Taggart groaned. "Keep her away from me today—please!"

After a late breakfast, Daniel Webb cadged a drink off another passenger then went back to his cabin to rest. Ordinarily he shared it with three other people but, since they were traveling together, he was very much the outsider. They had shown little interest in his plight and refused to lend him any money. Since the cabin was now deserted, he took the opportunity to go quickly through their belongings to see if there was anything worth stealing. Finding no cash, and nothing that he could barter with, he lay on a bunk and drifted off into a reverie. The arrival of a steward jerked him out of it. The man had a list in his hand. He bent down to peer at Webb.

"Could I have your name, please, sir?"

"Why?" retorted the old man.

"Just for our records. Are you Tom Carver?"

"No, he's in the bunk above me and his brother is directly opposite. Then there's this noisy Yank from New Jersey who keeps me awake all night. Ben Miller."

The steward checked his list. "Then you must be Daniel Webb."

"I am," agreed the other, "and I have been for all of sixty-five years."

"In that case, I won't trouble you any further, sir."

"No, wait a minute, my friend." Webb struggled to sit up. "There's something behind this, isn't there? Nobody ever bothers about us, here in steerage. They just pack us away in these garden sheds they call cabins and forget all about us. What's going on?"

"Nothing, sir."

"You can tell me."

"I have to get on."

"Come on," coaxed Webb. "It's not a state secret, is it? I can keep my mouth shut. I don't even talk to those three jokers I share a cabin with. Why are you checking up on us, my friend? There has to be a reason."

The steward hesitated. "Maybe there is."

"Go on."

"This is strictly between us, mind."

"Of course."

"Someone is missing off the ship. We're conducting a search."

"You think he's in steerage?"

"Hardly," said the steward, "but orders is orders. Only, we've been told to pretend that we're just checking names so that we don't spread any alarm. Some people would get upset if they thought a passenger had gone overboard."

Webb stood up. "Is that what happened?"

"Possibly, sir. We haven't found the man so far, I know that."

He went out and left Webb to brood on what he had just heard. Sitting on the edge of his bed, the old man scratched his head and began to wonder about the dream that had been causing him so much nagging discomfort.

As she made her way to the restaurant for lunch, Genevieve Masefield caught sight of Pamela Clyne shuffling along with a white-haired lady who used a walking stick. Catching them up, Genevieve fell in beside them.

"Hello, Miss Clyne," she said.

"Oh, hello, Miss Masefield," the other replied shyly. "This is Mrs. Cooney."

"How do you do, Mrs. Cooney? I'm Genevieve Masefield."

"Pleased to meet you."

Mrs. Cooney was an American lady in her seventies with a pale complexion and a pair of deep-blue eyes. There was an almost saintly air about her and Genevieve guessed that she had befriended the other woman out of kindness. The problem was that her proximity made Pamela Clyne seem much older than she really was. So alike were they in size and shape, they might have been taken for sisters, separated by little more than a decade. It worried Genevieve that the younger woman did not seem to mind.

"Are you enjoying the voyage, Miss Masefield?" asked Mrs. Cooney.

"Very much."

"So am I. This is my fifth visit to England."

"That's very impressive, Mrs. Cooney."

"I have a son who lives in London," explained the old lady, "and I see him and my daughter-in-law every two years. I adore sailing. The nice thing about traveling on a Cunard ship is that you always make new friends." She squeezed the arm of her companion. "Pamela and I seem to have known each other for years."

"Yes," said the other woman.

"Companionship is so important on a voyage," said Genevieve.

Mrs. Cooney smiled. "I shouldn't imagine that you'll ever be short of it."

She hobbled into the restaurant with Pamela Clyne at her side like an auxiliary walking stick. After bidding them farewell, Genevieve went off to take her own seat opposite the Singletons. There was the usual flurry of welcomes then Isadora, seated beside her, grabbed her arm.

"Where have you been all morning?" she asked.

"Here and there."

"I looked for you all over the place."

"Isadora, dear," said her mother sweetly, "I've told you not to make a nuisance of yourself to Miss Masefield. I'm sure that she has other friends on the ship."

"She's not being a nuisance at all, Mrs. Singleton," said Genevieve. "The truth is that I was rather busy this morning." She gave Isadora an apologetic smile then turned back to the mother. "I hear you're going to Royal Ascot."

"Yes," said Maria Singleton, clapping her hands together. "Isn't it wonderful? Lord and Lady Eddington have invited us to share their box. Have you ever been to Royal Ascot?"

"Only once. It was a memorable occasion."

"I'm sure that it was."

"You'll have a splendid time there."

"That's the value of staying in England for over six weeks. We get to take in so many of the major events. Don't we, Waldo?"

"What's that?" said her husband.

"I was talking about Royal Ascot."

"Yes, yes. That will be a treat. We're so grateful to Lord Eddington."

"It was Mr. Openshaw who introduced you to him," Isadora piped up, "and you didn't have a good word to say for the man at first."

"That's not true," scolded Singleton.

"Mother thought that he was uncouth."

"Don't be ridiculous, Isadora."

"That was the very word you used."

"I wouldn't say that of *anybody*," said her mother, quelling her with a glance. "How dare you even suggest it! Mr. and Mrs. Openshaw were charming people and it was a delight to meet them." She smiled at Genevieve. "Don't listen to her, Miss Masefield. I'm afraid that our daughter has a colorful imagination at times."

"That's not such a terrible vice," said Genevieve.

"It can lead to mistaken impressions."

Isadora was completely cowed. Genevieve gave her a friendly nudge to show that she was on the girl's side. Isadora rallied slightly. The menu was as tempting as ever and it took time for everyone to make a selection. Genevieve traded polite chat with the Singletons. It was twenty minutes or more before Isadora had the opportunity for a conversation with her friend that would not be overheard by her parents.

"I've got a message for you, Genevieve," she whispered.

"Have you?"

"I wasn't the only person who couldn't find you."

"Who else was there?"

"Guess."

"The Openshaws?"

Isadora frowned. "They don't even know you."

"They seem to know everyone else in first class."

"This was your secret admirer."

"I've told you before," said Genevieve, "Mr. Chase is not my admirer."

"I'm not talking about him, though I still believe that you're being chased by Stanley Chase as well." She giggled. "No, this was the famous cyclist."

"Theo Wright?"

"We met up in the lounge. I liked him enormously."

"I'm sure that he took to you as well, Isadora. He's very affable."

"Oh, I don't stand much of a chance beside you," said the other. "Theo has only got eyes for one person. He admitted it in so many words."

"Did he?" asked Genevieve, a trifle uneasy.

"He asked me to speak well of him to you."

"Oh, I'm sure it was only said in fun."

"It wasn't, Genevieve. He was in earnest, I can tell." She laughed gaily. "Isn't it funny? I'm the one who is sailing to England in the hope of finding a beau yet you've managed to get one without even trying."

"Theo Wright is not my beau," Genevieve said firmly.

"He'd like to be, I know that. I could hear it in his voice, Genevieve. He's not just an ardent admirer," said Isadora. "I think that Theo wants to marry you."

Genevieve felt a shiver run down her spine.

When Dillman returned to the purser's office, Paul Taggart was more anxious than ever.

"Well?" he asked hopefully.

"We've drawn a blank so far."

"Where *can* the fellow be?"

"Not on board the *Caronia*, I fear," Dillman said resignedly. "But we'll keep looking, Mr. Taggart. I promise you that."

The purser looked at his watch. "You should be having your lunch."

"That can wait. Everyone is in the restaurants. This is the perfect time to search some of the cabins more thoroughly. It's not just Sergeant Mulcaster we're after, remember. I'd like to find the stolen weapons as well."

"So would I, Mr. Dillman. This is turning out to be a nightmare crossing."

"Why? Has Mrs. Anstruther been to see you again?"

"Twice."

Dillman smiled. "She's letting you off lightly today, then."

"Why couldn't someone shove *her* overboard?" He checked himself. "I'm sorry, I didn't mean that. It was a dreadful thing to say. Mrs. Anstruther's problems are trivial compared to what we have to face."

"Quite."

"We're on the trail of an armed man, two of them, possibly." A thought struck him. "Don't you think that you should be issued with a firearm as well, Mr. Dillman?"

"Not when I'm dressed like this," said Dillman, indicating his tight-fitting suit. "A revolver would be rather difficult to conceal. Besides, I'm hoping that it won't come to a shoot-out."

"That's all we need!"

"How is Inspector Redfern?"

"I finally managed to persuade him to rest."

"He looked exhausted," said Dillman. "And that was a nasty head wound."

"The doctor's been back to check up on him."

"What about the prisoners?"

"Mr. Heritage has been moved to a cell. Miss Peterson remains where she is."

"Have they been told what happened?"

"No, Mr. Dillman. The inspector wants to keep it from them."

"Why?"

There was a gentle tap on the door. "Ask him yourself," said Taggart. "That's probably the inspector now. He did say he'd call on me as soon as he woke up." He raised his voice. "Come in!"

Dillman turned round, expecting to see Inspector Redfern, but it was a complete stranger who stepped tentatively into the office. The man was old and wizened. His suit was stained and crumpled. He ran his tongue nervously over his lips.

"Yes?" said the purser. "Can I help you, sir?"

Daniel Webb looked from one man to the other before speaking.

"How much do you pay for important information?" he asked.

EIGHT

The purser blinked his eyes in astonishment before staring hard at his unexpected visitor.

"Would you care to repeat that, sir?' he invited.

Daniel Webb looked at Dillman. "I'd rather do it in private."

"You can speak freely in front of Mr. Dillman. He's employed by Cunard."

"Oh, is he?"

"What's this about important information?"

"I may have seen something you ought to know about, sir."

"When?"

"Last night," said Webb. "On the main deck."

Taggart exchanged a glance with Dillman. "Go on, sir."

"Perhaps you'd like to sit down first," said Dillman, indicating the chair. "And it might help if we knew your name."

"Webb, sir. Daniel Webb." He sat down. "Steerage."

"And why have you come to me?" asked the purser.

"I may have something to sell."

"What does it concern?"

Webb gave a cackle. "Ah, you don't catch me like that. I'm

not giving it away free. The truth is that I need the money. Crossing the Atlantic is thirsty business."

Dillman had had time to appraise the old man. Webb did not look as if he could be of any use to them, but appearances could be deceptive. Dillman spoke quietly.

"Mr. Taggart is not authorized to buy information in the way that you suggest, Mr. Webb," he said, "but we may be able to come to an accommodation. Perhaps we could start by offering you a glass of whisky."

Webb's eyes ignited.

"Would that be acceptable to you?"

"Oh, yes."

"Mr. Taggart?"

"An excellent idea," said the purser, using a key to unlock a cabinet. "I do believe I could use a shot myself. What about you, Mr. Dillman?"

"No, thanks."

"How do you take it, Mr. Webb? With soda or water?"

"Neither," said Webb. "Give it to me as it comes."

The purser produced two glasses and a full bottle of whisky. Webb grinned as the drink was poured out. As soon as his glass was passed over, he raised it in thanks then took a sip. He emitted a long sigh of appreciation.

"Good stuff."

"I keep it for special occasions," said Taggart, adding water to his glass from a little jug before taking a first drink. "Boy! I needed that."

Dillman took charge. "Now, Mr. Webb," he said, "may I ask what you were doing on the main deck last night?"

"I felt sick," replied Webb. "Wanted some fresh air."

"What time would this be?"

"Late."

"How late?"

"Who knows?"

"It was a cold night. There couldn't have been many other people out on deck."

"I only saw those two."

"What two?"

Webb closed one eye. "Ah, you're trying to do it again, aren't you?" he said cagily. "You want to trick the information out of me for nothing."

"How do we know that it has any value?"

"Because of what that steward told me in steerage."

"And what was that?"

"Someone is missing."

"Did he give you any details?"

"No. But he was taking part in a search."

Webb exposed his few remaining teeth in a smile. There was a long pause.

"Listen," said the purser, losing patience, "we don't have time to play games with you, Mr. Webb. A serious assault was made on one of our passengers last night. The man who shared the cabin with him vanished completely. We suspect foul play. If you're holding back something that might actually help, then you're hampering the investigation and that's a crime in itself."

"I done nothing wrong," Webb said defensively.

"I'm sure that you haven't," Dillman agreed, "and we're grateful that you took the trouble of coming here. Mr. Taggart is not in a position to offer you any reward, but I am. Do you find that whisky to your taste?"

Webb drained his glass. "Very much."

"Tell us what you know and I'll buy you a whole bottle."

"Crikey!"

"But only if the information is genuine," warned Dillman.

"It is!" insisted Webb. He became uncertain. "At least, I think it is."

"How much had you drunk before you went on deck last night?" asked Taggart.

"Not enough."

"But you had been drinking?"

"What else can a man do on this damn ship?"

The purser was dubious. "I don't think that he can help us at all, Mr. Dillman."

"I can, I can," said Webb.

"Not if you were too drunk to remember what you saw."

"I can hold my beer, sir. Always could."

"Yet you claim that you felt sick."

"Well, yes. Maybe." Webb was confused. He eyed the bottle. "I don't suppose you could spare another glass of that, could you?"

"Not until you've told us what you know," said Dillman.

"Hurry up," urged Taggart. "We don't have time to waste."

"All right, all right," said Webb peevishly. "Don't rush me." He cleared his throat noisily. "At first, you see, I thought it was all a bad dream. Then the steward came into my cabin and I could see that something was up. I made him tell me. He reckoned that one of the passengers was missing."

"That's correct."

"So I got to thinking. Maybe my bad dream wasn't a bad dream, after all."

"Tell us about it," Dillman encouraged him.

"Well, sir, it's like this. When I got out on deck, I sat down to rest for a few minutes when I saw these two men. They were only a few yards away," he said, "so I had a good view of them both. One man was about my height, only broader. And a fair bit younger, I'd say, from the way he moved. The one who was pushing him was taller. He was holding something to the other man's head."

"Holding something?"

"That's right."

"A gun, perhaps?"

"I couldn't be sure," said Webb, running a hand across his unshaven chin. "But he was standing behind the first man and forcing him toward the rail."

"What happened then?" asked Dillman.

"The taller man hit him with whatever he had in his hand. I mean, he hit his head time and again. Knocked him to the deck then kept battering him until he stopped groaning. Next thing," he recalled, miming what he saw, "he struggles to pick the body up and pushes it over the side."

Taggart leaned forward. "Are you certain that's what happened?"

"Yes, sir."

"Why didn't you report it at once?"

"I must have fallen asleep. And had this bad dream."

"Or *thought* you did," corrected Dillman. "You're right, Mr. Webb. What you saw did happen. You're a valuable witness. Can you remember the place where it happened?"

"On the main deck."

"But at what particular spot? Clues may have been left there."

"Yes," said Taggart. "If he clubbed the man that hard, there would have been blood. Some of it may still be there."

Dillman was pessimistic. "Not in this rain, I'm afraid. But it's worth a look. Come on, Mr. Webb," he said, helping the old man up. "Let's see if we can find the spot where this occurred."

"Have I told you what you wanted to know?" asked Webb.

"Up to a point."

The old man grinned. "Does that mean I get the bottle of whisky?"

"All in good time," said Dillman. "Off we go."

John Heritage was not impressed with his new accommodations. The cell into which he had been moved had none of the comforts of a cabin in second class. It was small, bare, and featureless. Apart from the bunk, the only piece of furniture was a chair that was bolted to the ground. The iron walls were painted a dull cream and the door had bars in its tiny window. There was a stink of disinfectant. Like the other cells aboard, it was designed to hold unruly passengers or members of the crew who committed an offense. Heritage felt humiliated. He protested vehemently when Inspector Redfern visited him.

"I demand to be let out of here!"

"You're not in a position to make demands, Mr. Heritage."

"I'm not an animal that has to be caged."

"You're a murder suspect who has to be held in custody," said Redfern.

"What was wrong with my cabin? I was securely locked in there."

"We chose to move you."

"Why?" asked Heritage.

"That's our business."

A couple of hours' sleep had revived the inspector but there was still a dull ache at the back of his head. Ignoring the discomfort, he had first checked on his female suspect in the adjoining cabin then made his way to the cells. His wrists and ankles still tingled from his ordeal. The bandage around his head felt too tight.

Heritage tried to adopt a more reasonable approach.

"I'm not going to try to escape, Inspector," he said, "I promise you that."

"Where you would go?"

"Exactly. So why am being treated like this?"

"We make the decisions, Mr. Heritage, you simply abide by them."

"This is Sergeant Mulcaster's idea, isn't it?"

"Not at all."

"Left to him, I'd have a ball and chain as well. By the way," he said, "where is he? The sergeant usually comes in with my breakfast but the steward brought it today."

Redfern kept a straight face. "The sergeant is busy."

"You haven't let him question Miss Peterson alone, have you?" Heritage said in alarm. "You promised you wouldn't let him do that, Inspector. We both know how rough he can be. It would be a cruelty to her."

"I'm more concerned with the cruelty shown to your wife, Mr. Heritage."

"There was none."

"The coroner disagrees."

"Look," said Heritage, trying to control his rising temper, "let me go back to my cabin. I won't be any trouble to you."

"But you will be. You'll persist in telling lies."

"They're not lies."

"I'm fed up with listening to them."

"You can't just leave me here like this."

"A night or two in here might jog your memory."

"There's nothing wrong with it, Inspector."

"I think that there is," said Redfern calmly. "Tell me the truth and I'll consider moving you out of here. If you stick to the same story, you remain here."

"That's unjust!"

Redfern was appalled. "You dare to talk of justice?"

"All right," said Heritage, shrinking back, "I admit it was wrong to desert my wife like that. It was equally wrong to leave Stephen, my partner at the pharmacy, in the lurch. But I had no choice in the matter."

"Of course not. You had to cover your tracks."

"The pharmacy will survive without me."

"It's a pity that Mrs. Heritage didn't," said the Inspector. "As for your partner, Stephen Duckham, he was very hurt when he realized that you'd flown the coop and taken a lot of money out of the business account without even consulting him."

"I meant to pay it back in time."

"That's what they all say. You also cleared out your own bank account."

"We needed cash to set ourselves up in Ireland."

"You obviously didn't have to leave anything for your wife."

"Winifred had a small private income of her own."

"Then you slipped up badly," said Redfern. "When you killed her, you could have had access to her money as well. Why not take that?"

Heritage gave up. "Nothing that I say will convince you, will it?"

"Probably not. The one thing to your credit is that you confessed to having taken money from the business account that was not available for your personal use. In short, you robbed your partner behind his back. It's a lesser charge you'll have to face when we get back to England. That alone would merit a prison sentence."

"For me, perhaps, but not for Miss Peterson."

"Only a court can determine that."

"She wasn't involved in the deception."

"You'll have a hard job persuading a jury of that," warned the inspector. "Since she worked at the pharmacy as your assistant, Miss Peterson must have known about the financial side of the business. It may even have been her idea that you grabbed the money and made a run for it."

"No, Inspector!"

"Like you, she pulled the wool over Mr. Duckham's eyes. He was expecting her to turn up at the shop on Monday. Clever, that," said Redfern. "Making sure that you didn't give the game away by both of you telling him that you were taking a few days off. Imagine how your partner felt when he learned the pair of you had sailed to Ireland. Mr. Duckham had no idea there was any romantic entanglement."

"We were very discreet."

"Murdering your wife was not exactly an act of discretion, sir."

Heritage bit back a reply. He could see he was getting nowhere. Though he could never bring himself to like the man, he had come to have a grudging respect for Inspector Redfern. The detective was decent and straightforward. It was his companion who posed the problems. Heritage became thoughtful.

"What happened to your head, Inspector?" he asked.

"I told you. I had a slight accident."

"It looks as if it was more serious than that."

"Forget about me. You have enough worries of your own."

"You're such a careful man by nature," noted Heritage. "Except when you play chess, that is. You don't keep your wits about you then. But as a rule, I suspect you're the sort of person who never has accidents."

"Well, I did on this occasion."

"Was someone else involved?"

"That's nothing to do with you."

"It wouldn't be Sergeant Mulcaster, by any chance?"

"Good-bye," said Redfern, abruptly terminating the interview.

"Or maybe there's some other explanation," the prisoner speculated. "I thought it was odd when he didn't bring in my breakfast this morning. Then you came in with that bandage around your head."

"I'll look in on you later."

Heritage was suspicious. "Where exactly *is* Sergeant Mulcaster?"

"Perhaps you'll have come to your senses by then."

"What are you trying to hide, Inspector?"

Redfern shut the door firmly in his face.

It took Daniel Webb a long time to work out where he had slept the previous night.

"Are you sure it was here?" asked Dillman.

"It could have been."

"That's not good enough, Mr. Webb. You have to be certain."

"It was dark."

When he and Dillman first went out on the main deck, Webb was convinced that he had been on the starboard side of the ship when he witnessed the two men. It was only after a wasted quarter of an hour that he remembered he must have been on the port side. They began their search afresh. Dillman remained patient. The old man had brought them what might prove to be vital information about the disappearance of Sergeant Mulcaster. Irritating as he was, Daniel Webb had to be humored.

"It might have been here," Webb decided, pointing a gnarled finger. He changed his mind instantly. "Or perhaps it was a bit farther along."

"Which door did you come out of?"

"I thought it was the one we used ourselves."

"That was on the wrong side of the ship," Dillman reminded him. "We've just passed the exit directly opposite on this side and you ignored it. Why was that?"

"The rope, Mr. Dillman. There was no rope."

"This is the first I've heard of any rope."

"That's what I sat down on. A coil of rope."

"Why didn't you say so?"

"I've only just remembered."

"That gives us something to look for," said Dillman. "A coil of rope near one of the exits. When those men came through the door, they wouldn't have strolled along the deck together. They'd have gone straight to the rail."

"That's what happened."

"*Where*?"

"Let's find out."

They walked toward the prow of the ship until they reached the next door that gave access to the cabin area. Immediately beyond it, tucked a little way back, was a coil of thick rope. A smile of recognition spread over Webb's face.

"That's it, Mr. Dillman."

"You must have been uncomfortable if you slept on that."

"I was too drunk to care."

"And you're quite definite?"

Webb was decisive. "Yes." He scratched his head. "At least, I think so."

"Let's assume that you're right," said Dillman, moving to sit on the coil of rope. "Yes, you'd have had a good view from here of anyone coming through that door. If they went straight to the rail," he went on, getting up to cross to the bulwark, "they'd have ended up about here."

"A bit to the left," recalled Webb. "I could see them from an angle."

Dillman shifted his position. "About here?"

"Even farther over."

"Here, then?"

Dillman moved across to the designated area and earned a nod of approval. He crouched down to examine the deck. Steady rain had blown in for hours to clean the deck and obliterate any sign of blood, but it had not washed away a small, sodden object that Dillman picked up carefully between a finger and thumb.

"What is it?" asked Webb.

"Exactly what I was hoping to find."

He showed the abandoned cigarette to the old man.

Genevieve Masefield had some difficulty freeing herself from the attentions of Isadora Singleton without wounding the girl's feelings. Hoping to get back to her duties, she was met with a further delay. As she was leaving the first-class lounge, two men were coming toward it. When he saw her, the younger of them raised a hand. Stanley Chase gave her a warm greeting and introduced Frank Openshaw to her. The Yorkshireman's eyes lit up when he heard her name.

"Genevieve Masefield, eh?" he said. "You were mentioned in dispatches."

"Was I?" replied Genevieve. "By whom?"

"A charming young lady called Isadora Singleton. You might call her a belle from Boston. Never stopped singing your praises."

"I shouldn't pay too much attention to her, Mr. Openshaw."

"But I do, I do."

"Isadora tends to exaggerate."

"I disagree," said Openshaw. "If anything, she did the opposite. According to her, you're one of the most attractive ladies on the ship. I'd say that was being a trifle unfair to you. What do you think, Mr. Chase?"

"Miss Masefield already knows my opinion," Chase said gallantly. "I don't believe that there's anyone on the *Caronia* to compare with her."

"There you are, my dear. That's the opinion of a connoisseur.

Mr. Chase is an antiques dealer. He has an eye for quality."

Genevieve smiled. "I hope that he doesn't plan to sell me in his shop."

"It would be impossible to put a price on you," Chase said courteously. "Do you know, I've been so lucky on this voyage. First of all, I meet you, Miss Masefield. Then, today, I had the good fortune to sit opposite Mr. Openshaw and his wife. It was a meeting of true minds."

Openshaw chuckled. "What he means is that we're both interested in money."

"Making it or giving it away?" she asked.

"Both, in my case."

Chase was circumspect. "I'm no philanthropist, I'm afraid."

"It's not philanthropy, my friend," said Openshaw. "It's a form of advertisement. You have the satisfaction of helping those less fortunate than yourself, and the knowledge that you'll get beneficial publicity. Look what happened to the Openshaw Trust, for example. It provides accommodation for homeless people but it also broadcasts my name to the thousands who pass the building every day. Philanthropy is an investment."

"That's rather a cynical way of putting it, isn't it?" said Genevieve.

"I'm simply being honest."

" 'Frank by name and frank by nature,' " said Chase, quoting his friend's motto.

"That's me," Openshaw agreed with a chuckle. "But I'm so glad I finally met you, Miss Masefield. Isadora seemed bereft without you when she and her parents joined us for drinks yesterday evening."

"I'm surprised you remember either of our names," said Genevieve. "I hear that there were dozens of people invited."

"You'll be among them next time, and so will Mr. Chase," said Openshaw, turning to his companion. "But you've just put your finger on one of my secret weapons. I never forget a name. It's a gift that always impresses people. I may not see them for twenty years but I can always put a name to a face when I meet it again."

"That's a useful asset in business," noted Chase.

"Aye, it's a form of flattery."

Genevieve smiled. "I don't think I'll ever be in danger of forgetting *your* name, Mr. Openshaw. You're such a memorable person."

"I try to be, Miss Masefield. I sell myself, you see."

"We all do that to some degree or other," argued Chase. "Put it this way. I don't think I'd shift many antiques if I dressed in a cloth cap and a pair of dungarees."

"Now that's how *I* started my career," said Openshaw.

"You told me," Genevieve said politely. "I'll get out of the way so that you can astound Mr. Chase in the same way."

"Oh, he's already done that," explained Chase.

"Now I move on to the next stage," said Openshaw, slipping an arm around the other man's shoulders. "Having softened him up with the story of my life, I'm going to see if he'd like to invest in one of my companies."

The two men went off together. They hardly seemed kindred spirits, but Genevieve had seen less likely partnerships on board. Stanley Chase was an educated man with refined tastes. He might be expected to steer clear of such an unashamed vulgarian as Frank Openshaw. The same could be said of the Singletons yet they had been won over by the promise of an introduction to representatives of the British aristocracy. Such a promise would be unlikely to lure Chase. As she strolled toward the purser's office, Genevieve wondered what it was that had interested the quiet antiques dealer in the gregarious financier.

Inspector Redfern examined the cigarette butt with great solemnity. He gave a nod.

"Are you sure?" asked Dillman.

"This is the brand that he smoked."

"It could have been dropped by someone else."

"How many people on the main deck last night were smoking an expensive Balkan cigarette?" said Redfern, putting the butt in the ashtray on the table. "It was Ronnie's one indulgence. No wife and children to support, you see. He could afford it. I'm a pipe man myself. Ronnie—Sergeant Mulcaster—swore by these."

"Then I'm afraid that he's smoked his last one."

"Where did you find it?"

Dillman had called at the inspector's cabin to report the find. He had hoped the cigarette might be a brand that Mulcaster never touched, but it was not the case. He gave Redfern a concise account of how he came to pick up the discarded butt. For the sake of brevity, he omitted details of the early blundering efforts of Daniel Webb to locate the spot where he had witnessed the murder.

"Where is this fellow now, Mr. Dillman?" asked Redfern.

"He's gone back to his cabin."

"I'd like to speak to him myself."

"You'll have to wait before you can do that."

"Why?"

"Mr. Webb was not alone when he went back to his bunk."

Redfern was shocked. "He's taken a woman there at *his* age?"

"Not a woman," said Dillman. "A bottle of whisky. I promised to buy it for him if he gave us crucial evidence—and he certainly did that. We can forget about him for the rest of the day. He'll be drunk already."

"Is that all we have? The word of an old soak?"

"It's given us our one definite clue, Inspector."

"Yes," sighed the other, looking at the cigarette butt. "Poor Ronnie!"

"My guess is that it dropped from his lips when he was hit from behind. I know that he enjoyed a smoke," said Dillman. "I bumped into him on the main deck myself on our first night at sea. He barely took the cigarette out of his mouth."

"He got through twenty a day. You can imagine how many

packets we brought with us. We were lucky not to be arrested for tobacco smuggling."

"There is one consolation, Inspector."

"Is there?"

"I don't think he'd have suffered for long. According to Mr. Webb, the attacker knocked him out with a series of savage blows. It took much less than a minute. After he hit the water, Sergeant Mulcaster probably never even regained consciousness."

"I don't find much consolation in that, Mr. Dillman. The stark fact is—if our supposition is correct—that a serving detective was bludgeoned to death before being tossed over the side of the ship. We don't even have a body as visible proof of the crime."

"We have Daniel Webb."

"It's not the same. We're severely handicapped."

"No body, no case."

"Oh, we have a case," said Redfern, "but it's been made that much more difficult. I've already got two murder suspects in custody. I never thought I'd be investigating the killing of my sergeant as well."

"Count on me for whatever help you need."

"Thanks. This time, I won't be too churlish to accept."

"Do you have any theories?"

"None, Mr. Dillman. I'm trying to get used to the idea that Ronnie is dead." He walked around the cabin. "He was such a presence here. Full of life."

"Perhaps that was his downfall, Inspector."

"In what way?"

"I was standing by the gangway when you came aboard," said Dillman. "Sergeant Mulcaster did go out of his way to be seen. There was no need to tote that shotgun."

"It wasn't our idea. The newspapers wanted photographs of the prisoners being escorted aboard. They begged us to have a weapon in sight. The New York Police Department didn't wish to miss out on publicity, either, so they assigned those two officers you saw. It was all done for the camera."

"I thought it looked staged."

"We deliberately left it until the last moment to board the ship so that we wouldn't cause too much disruption."

"You were still seen," Dillman reminded him. "That's what I keep coming back to. Someone may have recognized you. Someone with a reason to dislike Scotland Yard detectives."

"British prisons are full of people like that."

"We may have one or two aboard, Inspector."

"But we took care to keep our heads down, Mr. Dillman. Neither of us went anywhere near the public rooms. I made sure of that."

"Someone found out about this cabin."

"But why kill Sergeant Mulcaster and not me?" wondered Redfern. "That man had me at his mercy. He could easily have smashed my head in. Instead of that, he knocks me out and ties me up."

"Leaving the field clear for the attack on your colleague."

"But I had no intention of going up on deck."

"The attacker didn't know that," reasoned Dillman. "What was certain was that you'd soon have started to worry about the sergeant's absence. You knew precisely how much time it took him to smoke a cigarette. Before long, you'd have gone looking for him."

"True."

"The villain was taking no chance. He was a belt-and-suspenders man. With you out of action, it would be a whole night before Sergeant Mulcaster's disappearance was reported. By that time, the killer had merged back into our passenger list."

"It's frightening," confessed Redfern.

"We won't let him get away with it."

"Look at the size of the ship, Mr. Dillman."

"I know, sir. It won't be easy to track our man down."

"Where do we look?"

"Everywhere."

There was no rest from the training schedule. While other passengers relaxed or spent the afternoon in various leisure pursuits, Theodore Wright was pounding his way around the boat deck, grateful the rain had stopped but wishing he could catch a glimpse of either Genevieve Masefield or Isadora Singleton to relieve the boredom of his run. His routine was well known by now and other passengers waved to him as he passed. Some even gave him a round of applause to encourage him. Wright acknowledged them with a wave but he was disappointed not to see a sign of the two passengers he liked most. As he made his final circuit, a tall, graceful woman stepped out on deck some thirty yards ahead of him, wearing a wide-brimmed straw hat covered in flowers. Thinking it was Genevieve, he accelerated at once then saw he was mistaken. Lifting her head, the woman gave him an unfriendly glare but Wright did not even see it. His eyes were fixed on her hat.

Five minutes later, he was lying facedown on his bunk while his coach massaged his legs. Wes Odell worked slowly, using his fingers to explore any tightening in the calf and thigh muscles. He was a skilled masseur whose preparation of the cyclist enabled Wright to win a sequence of races without once suffering from cramp. The coach took the opportunity to raise a delicate subject.

"Wait until after the race, Theo," he advised.

"What do you mean?"

"That's the time to celebrate. When you've taught Gaston Vannier that he ought to keep his mouth shut. Win the race first and then start worrying about finding yourself a girlfriend to take out for dinner."

"It's not a girlfriend I'm looking for, Wes."

"Then what is it?"

"You wouldn't understand," said Wright.

"Try me."

"Well, I don't want to push those pedals for the rest of my days."

"Nobody's asking you to, Theo."

Wright laughed. "You would. Given the chance, you'd keep me in the saddle until I was sixty. I'm looking ahead, Wes. I have to retire someday."

"When you've proved that you're the best."

"I *am* the best."

"Only back home," said Odell, pouring something onto his palms from a jug before continuing his massage. "You haven't conquered France yet—or England, for that matter. You want to finish at the top, don't you?"

"Definitely. I aim to retire unbeaten."

"Then let's have a final push for the next year or two. Win the Bordeaux-to-Paris and the whole of Europe will know about Theo Wright. That's when we cash in, don't you see? Make your name then reap the rewards."

Wright was hesitant. "For two more years?"

"Maybe more, maybe less."

"It certainly won't be more, Wes."

"Don't be too hasty," said Odell, moving his hands from one leg to another. "You've put the hard work in. Reap the benefits. When you've made your name in France, the offers will come flooding in. Everyone will want you to take part in their races because Theo Wright will sell tickets. They'll pay you appearance money. We'll be able to name our own price. Just think how much we could clean up."

"You always said we weren't in this for the dough."

"We're not, Theo—but we have to eat."

"I want to move into designing bicycles," said Wright. "Nobody knows as much about them as me. That's where my future lies—on the drafting board. But I want a private life as well—a wife, kids, a proper home. I'm fed up with traveling, Wes."

"It will all come in the fullness of time."

"I may not be able to wait that long."

Odell took a stand. "We've got a contract, remember," he asserted.

"It doesn't bind me hand and foot forever."

"No, but it does give me certain rights."

"I don't recall any mention of a right to control what I do when I'm not in the saddle," said Wright, turning over and sitting up. "So let's get one thing clear, shall we? If I fall for someone, that's my business. A long as it doesn't get in the way of my cycling, I'll do what I damn well like. Okay?" He saw the coach's shining palms. "Hey, what did you put on my legs today? It's not the usual stuff."

"It's a new ointment I'm trying. How does it feel?"

"Great! It's really great."

"Good."

"It doesn't smell as strong as the liniment."

"We'll see how it goes."

Wiping his hands on a towel, Odell turned away from him to hide the scowl on his face. He was seething with resentment. When they had stepped onto the vessel, Theodore Wright had been completely under his control. Power had shifted slightly. The cyclist wanted to make his own decisions now. The problem had to be addressed.

Although he was now engaged in a murder investigation, Dillman could not neglect his more routine duties. When another passenger in second class reported the theft of a wallet, the detective wondered if it had been the work of the same pickpocket. After taking a statement from the victim, he came to the conclusion that one man had been responsible for both of the crimes that had come to light. Convinced they took place in one of the public rooms, Dillman walked toward the second-class lounge. As he turned a corner, he caught sight of a familiar profile. Ramsey Leach came up some steps before walking jauntily along the corridor toward him. When he saw Dillman, the undertaker's smile faded.

"Hello, Mr. Leach," said Dillman, coming to a halt.

"Good afternoon."

"What are you doing down here?"

"I got lost, Mr. Dillman."

"I should have thought you'd have found your way around the ship by now."

"Yes," said Leach with a pained smile. "I took a wrong turning somewhere."

"Remember the decks in order of descent."

"Is that the way to do it?"

"I think so. Boat, promenade, shelter, upper, main, lower, orlop. There's also the lower orlop, of course, but you don't need to go anywhere near that."

"No, Mr. Dillman."

"I haven't seen much of you since the first day."

"Oh, I've noticed you from time to time."

"What about Mr. Openshaw?"

"I've kept well out of his way," said Leach with a faint smile. "He's a rough diamond and I'm never easy in their company. I kept feeling sorry for his wife."

"Mrs. Openshaw?"

"Yes. I wondered how many times she'd heard the story of his life. As for his boast of being 'Frank by name and frank by nature,' she must wish that her husband could find something new to say."

"Frank Openshaw is harmless enough."

"I agree, Mr. Dillman, and I mean no criticism of him. What he's done is truly remarkable. He's given generously to various charities as well. I take my hat off to him. But I don't really want to sit opposite him again," he confessed. "In my profession, people tend to talk very quietly. Frank Openshaw is too deafening for me."

"He's loud," agreed Dillman, "but not offensively so. And I found Mrs. Openshaw delightful. My only complaint about the meal we shared with them is that you and I didn't get a chance to have a proper conversation."

"I'm not a very sociable being."

"Nevertheless, I'd like to have heard what you thought of America."

"It was astounding. I spent the whole time with my jaw agape."

"We do like to do things on a massive scale."

"It was the pace of life that I noticed. So much faster than in England." He gave another pale smile. "I suppose I've been spoiled. In my daily work, everything moves very sedately. I prefer it that way." He stepped past Dillman. "But I won't hold you up."

"You're not doing so, Mr. Leach. I was going to ask what brought you across the Atlantic in the first place."

"Curiosity, Mr. Dillman."

"Where exactly did you go?"

Leach looked uneasy. "I haven't time to discuss that now, I'm afraid," he said, moving away. "Do excuse me. I'll make sure that I don't go astray again."

Dillman watched him scurry along the corridor. For a man who went through life at a funereal tread, Ramsey Leach was going at a surprising speed.

Genevieve Masefield's pace was steady rather than fast. She seemed to glide along. After visiting the purser and hearing about the evidence provided by Daniel Webb, she had to return briefly to her cabin. Before she could open the door, however, she saw a steward walking purposefully toward her.

"Miss Masefield?" he asked.

"Yes," she replied.

"These are for you."

He handed her a large bunch of flowers and walked away. She was mystified.

NINE

Carrie Peterson sensed something had happened. They had left her alone for too long. In the past, Inspector Redfern had always brought her meals in. He and Sergeant Mulcaster had questioned her regularly as they tried to catch her out and wrest a confession from her. By applying more pressure each day, they hoped to break her resistance. Yet there had been little sign of them so far. Inspector Redfern had made only a brief appearance to check on her, not even staying long enough for her to ask why his head was bandaged. Mulcaster never turned up at all. It was puzzling. Something unusual had occurred and she was bound to fear that it was connected with her lover. Had they used violence against him? Since their arrest, Mulcaster had often seemed on the verge of doing so. Carrie was disturbed. Was the inspector's injury the result of a tussle in which John Heritage had fought back?

Her anxiety slowly intensified. Her lover would stand no chance against the combined strength of two detectives. The thought they might have tried to beat information out of him brought her out in a cold sweat. The longer they left her alone, the greater her fears became. Her whole body began to tremble.

Unable to stand the suspense any longer, Carrie rushed to the door and started to pound on it with her fists.

"Don't touch him!" she yelled. "Leave John alone."

The noise brought an instant response. Inspector Redfern came out of the next cabin to unlock her door. Bursting in, he eased her back to the center of the room.

"What on earth do you think you're doing?" he asked.

"I want you to stop hitting John."

"We haven't touched him, Miss Peterson."

"Are you sure?" she demanded.

"Completely. Now, let's have no more outbursts like that," he said sternly. "You'll disturb the other passengers and we can't allow that. If you can't behave, we shall have to place you under restraint. Do you understand?"

"I was worried about John."

"Without cause."

"I know that Sergeant Mulcaster threatened to punch him."

"Mr. Heritage is unharmed."

"You would say that, Inspector. Let me see him. Show him to me."

"No," said Redfern.

"A glance is all I ask. Just to reassure myself. Let me peep into his cabin."

"He's not there anymore, Miss Peterson."

She became alarmed. "Where is he?"

"Mr. Heritage has been moved elsewhere."

"Why?"

"That's my business."

"Have you taken him somewhere more private so I won't hear his screams of pain while you hit him? Is that what you've done?"

"Of course not," replied Redfern, raising both hands to calm her. "We'd never do anything like that. Contrary to what you might imagine, we take care of our suspects. We treat them with a degree of respect, however dreadful their crimes."

"John hasn't committed a crime."

"He stole money from the business account, Miss Peterson. That was certainly a crime. Ask his partner. Stephen Duckham was in a terrible state when he learned what the pair of you had done."

She looked surprised. "I know nothing about any business account."

"Where do you think the money came from to buy your tickets to Ireland?"

"From our savings. John and I saved up for months."

"That obviously wasn't enough," said Redfern, "so Mr. Heritage plundered the pharmacy account. I can see why Mr. Duckham was so distraught. That was the money used to buy fresh supplies of drugs."

"I don't believe you. John would never do a thing like that."

"He deserted his partner without warning. So did you."

"That was different," she argued.

"Is it? How do you imagine Mr. Duckham felt when he saw that the pair of you had disappeared together? He couldn't run the pharmacy on his own, especially as the funds kept for purchasing stock had been raided."

Her mood changed. "Stephen deserved it," she said coldly.

"Nobody deserves to be treated like that."

"He did. It was John who did most of the work at the pharmacy, helped by me. Stephen Duckham was a dreadful man. Because he was the senior partner, he used to push us both around at will. In my case," she added, wincing at the memory, "he did rather more than push."

"I don't understand."

"He caught me on my own in the storeroom, Inspector. He began to take liberties. I begged him to stop but he kept on molesting me. If he hadn't heard John coming in from the shop, I don't know what would have happened."

"Did you complain to Mr. Heritage?"

"Not at first," she said, shaking her head. "I was too embarrassed. Besides, it would have been my word against that of Mr. Duckham. I didn't think anyone would believe me." She smiled reflectively. "But John did. He sensed that something untoward had happened. He pretended not to notice it but he made sure that he walked home with me that evening so he could get the story out of me."

"Was he shocked?"

"No, Inspector. That was the awful thing. Apparently it was not the first time Stephen Duckham had tried to take advantage of a female employee. The young lady before me had resigned because of him."

"What did Mr. Heritage do?"

"He promised to look after me in future."

"Didn't he challenge his partner?"

"John didn't want to do that in case it caused trouble. When all was said and done, he and Mr. Duckham had to go on working together. And he guaranteed *my* safety," she stressed, "so I was prepared to stay in my post. In fact," she admitted, "after the talk we had that evening, nothing would have made me leave. That was how it started."

"Your romance with Mr. Heritage?"

"He came to my rescue."

"I can't say that he looks much like a knight in shining armor to me," Redfern said doubtfully. "I presume you were fully aware that Mr. Heritage was a married man at the time. Did that fact carry no weight?"

"Naturally, Inspector. I agonized over it for months."

"What about him?"

She hesitated. "John was not well treated at home," she said at length.

"Is that why the two of you conspired to kill Mrs. Heritage?"

"She didn't deserve John."

His ears pricked up. "So you *were* responsible for her death?"

"I didn't say that, Inspector. Don't ask me to grieve for her, that's all."

"Mr. Heritage shows no remorse, either."

"Why should he?"

"A wife is a wife, Miss Peterson."

A strange look came into her eye. She gave a mocking smile.

"But he doesn't have a wife anymore," she said quietly. "Does he?"

As she arranged the flowers carefully in the vase, Genevieve speculated on who might have sent them. The mixed bouquet was expensive. Evidently it had come as a gesture of affection, yet there was no card from the sender. She wondered why. Did he wish to remain anonymous until he saw how she reacted, or did he assume that she would guess instantly who had bought the flowers? It was puzzling and it took some of the edge off the pleasure she had experienced at receiving the gift. Was there a hidden meaning in it? What would she be required to do in return? By the time she had finished arranging the flowers, she felt quite unsettled.

Only two names suggested themselves. The obvious one was that of Theodore Wright, the friendly cyclist whom she had met during his training run on deck. She was fond of him and knew that he liked her, but they had seen relatively little of each other. Then she recalled the remark he had made about her to Isadora Singleton. When the girl had teased her about Wright's passion for her, Genevieve had not taken it too seriously. A bouquet of such size and cost, however, could not be ignored. If it had been bought by Wright, then he had more than a passing interest in her. Genevieve was worried. It was awkward enough to have Isadora on her tail all the time. Pursued by a doting admirer as well, her work on the *Caronia* would be badly restricted. She fervently hoped that Theodore Wright was not the sender. It would cause complications.

The other person who came into her mind was Stanley Chase, yet they had spent even less time together. Attentive to her over a meal, he had given no indication of any deeper feelings for her. Indeed, it was he who had announced that she had made such an impact on Theodore Wright, and he had done so without a trace of jealousy. At the same time—and Isadora had observed it as well—Chase did look at her with a distinct sparkle in his eye. When she encountered him in the company of Frank Openshaw, he had been very amiable, quick to confirm, albeit lightheartedly, that he found her the most enchanting woman on the vessel. What had sounded like a polite compliment now took on a different meaning. As she picked her way back through the few conversations she had had with him, Genevieve came to see that Stanley Chase could not easily be dismissed as a possible suitor.

In some ways he was the more likely person. Theodore Wright might have become enamored but he would hardly express his affections with a bouquet of flowers. He was such a direct and honest young man that he would be inclined to declare himself openly. Chase, on the other hand, was controlled by English reserve. He would never blurt out anything that concerned his innermost feelings. Flowers would be his preferred approach. Genevieve could see they had been carefully chosen and Wright did not look like a man with any floral expertise. Stanley Chase, however, would know the exquisite appeal of early red and white roses, nestling beside lilies, lilac, and carnations, the whole bunch surrounded by the most delicate strands of gypsophilia. It was a gift that an English gentleman would send to a lady. That thought caused Genevieve even more disquiet. While she found Chase a congenial companion, she was very uneasy at the notion of any closer relationship.

She made a few last adjustments to the flowers then stood back to enjoy them afresh. Theodore Wright or Stanley Chase? She could not make up her mind between them. No other passengers came to mind. Waldo Singleton and Frank Openshaw were the only other two men with whom she had had any real contact and neither of them was a possible contender. It came down to a choice between two people. After sifting through the evidence, she decided that Chase was the anonymous sender, if only because a romantic gesture from him would be more likely to take that form. Yet even as she ousted Wright from the running, she chided herself for making such a simplistic judgment. The American male was just as capable of surprising her in that delightful way as his English counterpart. As soon as she remembered that, Genevieve realized she had omitted the one desirable name from her list of suspects.

"Oh, George!" she exclaimed, sniffing the flowers once more. "You darling!"

Unaware that he was provoking such fond thoughts, Dillman was let into the cabin by the purser. Concern had darkened the bags under Paul Taggart's eyes. The dramatic events aboard his ship were starting to take their toll.

"What's the trouble?" asked Dillman.

"Inspector Redfern has had something of a relapse."

"A relapse?"

"The doctor thinks that it's delayed concussion," Taggart said quietly. "He's ordered the inspector to rest and given him some sleeping tablets. You'd better speak to him before he dozes off."

"Right."

"I'll leave you to it, Mr. Dillman. If you should need me, I'll be in my office."

The purser let himself out and Dillman went through into the bedroom. It was identical in size and shape to the one that he occupied himself, in first class, but it was not as well appointed and the decor was far less elaborate. Inspector Redfern occupied the bunk along the right-hand wall. Propped up on a pillow, armed folded in defiance, he was wearing a striped dressing gown. Dillman could see his frustration.

"How are you, Inspector?" he inquired.

"I'm fine in myself, Mr. Dillman. It's this headache of mine."

"You may have tried to get back into action too soon."

"I hate the thought of lying here when there's so much to be done."

"Leave that to us."

"That's what Mr. Taggart said—and the doctor. They ganged up on me. All that happened was that I had these dizzy spells. They soon passed."

"Take no chances, Inspector. Nobody else who spent the night as you did would even dream of getting up."

"I had to keep an eye on the suspects."

"Let someone else do that for you, Inspector."

Redfern heaved a sigh of reluctance. "I may have to," he conceded. "I owe you something of an apology, Mr. Dillman. The purser has been telling me about the reputation you've built up on Cunard liners. It isn't just petty crime that you deal with. According to Mr. Taggart, you've solved a murder case before."

"On more than one occasion," Dillman said modestly.

"It seems that Miss Masefield has earned her share of plaudits as well."

"We work as a team, Inspector."

"Well, I'm not going to keep you both at arm's length anymore," decided Redfern. "When Sergeant Mulcaster was alive, it was different. Two of us could handle our prisoners without any difficulty. Ronnie was incensed when you offered a helping hand. Wrongly, it seems now. But I'm to blame as well. I let silly professional pride get in the way as well. I'm sorry, Mr. Dillman."

"No apology is called for."

"I think that it is."

"Then I accept it willingly."

"Do you still want to be involved?"

"Very much, Inspector."

"I'd understand if you gave me a dusty answer. It'd be no more than I deserved."

"Forget what happened," advised Dillman. "Sergeant Mulcaster's death changes everything. As far as I'm concerned, we start with a clean slate.

"Good." Redfern yawned. "I'm starting to fade already," he complained.

"What would you like us to do?"

"Have free access to both of them. I spoke to John Heritage earlier but made little progress. He's a devious man, difficult to pin down. He's also hopping mad because I asked the master-at-arms to transfer him to a cell."

"Was that necessary?"

"I felt so at the time."

"What about Miss Peterson?"

"She's the one who baffles me," said Redfern, yawning again. "One minute she looks as innocent as the driven snow; the next, she makes a remark that makes me think she's every bit as guilty as him."

"I'll ask Genevieve to interview her."

"Warn her beforehand. Carrie Peterson is a creature of moods."

"I'll see what I can get out of Mr. Heritage."

"Don't play chess with him, whatever you do. He destroyed me. Oh, and don't mention what happened to Sergeant Mulcaster," he ordered. "There's no need for them to know. They'd only take pleasure from the information."

"They're bound to ask where he is, Inspector."

"Fob them off as best you can."

"It would be helpful to know more details of the case."

The inspector's eyes began to flicker. "Of course, Mr. Dillman," he said drowsily. "You can't work in the dark. There's a dossier on the table in the other room."

"I'll find it. You get some sleep."

"Wake me if there are any developments."

Dillman was firm. "No, Inspector. There's nothing you'd be able to do in that state. Thank you for trusting in us," he said. "We'll try not to let you down."

"I could never ride anything like that!" exclaimed Isadora Singleton with a giggle.

"You can, if I hold you on."

"It's far too big, Theo."

"The saddle is as low as it can get."

"Yes," she pointed out, "but even so, it's not designed for a lady."

"I'm sorry about that, Isadora," said Wright. "It's the one I use in races. I'm not likely to win any of those on a lady's bicycle, am I?"

"I'd love to see you try!" she said, shaking with mirth.

Isadora had come for her first lesson with some misgivings. Excited by the idea of learning to ride, she wondered if it was too perilous a venture to undertake, and she was terrified that her parents would find out she was alone with a young man. At Wright's suggestion, they met in the storeroom where his machines were kept. Both bicycles had triangular steel frames and large wheels with dozens of spokes in them. The pneumatic tires were the best available. What frightened Isadora most were the dropped handlebars. She did not believe she could ever guide the machine with them.

"It's built for speed, strength, and lightness," explained Wright, stroking the crossbar with pride. "When bicycles were first made, they were as heavy as lead. Nobody could have ridden one of those from Bordeaux to Paris. They've improved a great deal over the years. This one, as you see, is stripped down to essentials."

"It's not very pretty."

"It's not meant to be, Isadora."

"Some of my friends have very pretty bicycles."

"This one has a pretty rider," he joked, cocking his leg over the back wheel and sitting in the saddle. "It'll have an even prettier one when we get you on here."

"I'd be afraid to fall off."

"Not when I'm here to catch you. Watch me. Balance is the key to cycling."

After twisting the front wheel at an angle, he put both feet on the pedals, keeping his balance by making minor adjustments with the handlebars. Isadora was so impressed that she clapped her hands with glee. She had never seen such a clever balancing act in so confined a space. Eventually Wright put one toe to the floor to steady himself.

"Now it's your turn," he said.

"I could never do that."

"I'm not asking you to, Isadora. I just want you to see what it's like to sit in the saddle. Come on," he said, dismounting. "I'll hold you on."

Her face clouded. "Oh, I'm not so sure about that, Theo."

"Why not?"

"Maybe this is not such a good idea."

Doubts afflicted her. She was less worried about sitting on the bicycle than being held in position by someone whom, when she thought about it, she had only known for a very short time. Her parents would be horrified and all her social instincts told her to thank Wright for his offer then bring the private lesson to a close. At the same time, however, she felt the exhilaration of doing something bold and forbidden, something that she had never foreseen when she stepped aboard the ship. Isadora was also reassured by Wright's friendly grin. His manner had been respectful throughout. She reminded herself that he was no ordinary cyclist. Isadora would be given her first tuition by no less a person than the American champion. It was an honor.

"Just for a second, then," she consented.

"Swell!"

"You'll have to turn round, Theo."

"What?" He realized what she meant. "Oh, sure."

Wright turned his back so that she could hitch up her long skirt with one hand. Holding the bicycle with the other, she cocked her leg over the machine and felt for the saddle. It was hard and uncomfortable.

"How are you doing, Isadora?" he asked.

"Not too well. See for yourself."

He turned round and saw that her toes were fully extended to touch the floor. Even though it was stationary, she was very wary of the machine. He bent down to flip the hem of her long skirt away from the chain.

"You don't want to get oil on that lovely dress."

"Mother would never forgive me."

"Now, hold still," he advised.

"What are you going to do?"

"Prove something to you, Isadora." He took a firm grip on the saddle and the handlebars before grinning at her. "Take your feet off the floor now."

"I daren't do that, Theo."

"Go on. I've got a firm grip."

"It won't be safe."

"Just try—that's all I ask."

Isadora lifted one foot off the ground and put it on a pedal. Feeling as stable as she had before, she experimented by lifting her other toe an inch off the ground. Wright held the machine so tightly that it did not budge. Isadora was encouraged enough to risk putting her other foot on a pedal. She let out a cry of triumph.

"I can ride!" she cried. "I'm riding a bicycle at last."

Wright laughed. "There's a little more to it than that," he warned.

Genevieve Masefield had convinced herself that Dillman must have sent the flowers. Before she could thank him, however, she needed confirmation. There was no florist aboard but the *Caronia* did have a large supply of flowers to be used as decoration on the tables in the first- and second-class restaurants. Evidently, her bouquet must have come from that source. She went to find out who had ordered them. Her journey took her past the lounge. Genevieve paused at the door when she saw that one of her potential admirers was there. Listening earnestly to what Frank Openshaw was saying, Stanley Chase gave an understanding nod from time to time. He did not look in her direction and Genevieve decided that he did not need to do so. Something about him told her he was probably not the man she was after. At heart, she guessed, he was a shrewd businessman who would rather listen to an investment opportunity than take a romantic interest in a woman on a transatlantic voyage. Genevieve turned away. Before she could go off to track down the person who did send the flowers, however, she was confronted by a smiling Cecilia Robart.

"Good afternoon, Miss Masefield," she said.

"Oh, hello, Mrs. Robart."

"How many other crimes have you solved?"

"None so far," said Genevieve, noting her gold earrings. "Fortunately, we've had no more reports of theft as yet."

"I'm sorry that you got one from me. As you see, I'm wearing the earrings," said Cecilia Robart, brushing one of them with a finger. "I'm so careful with them now."

"Good."

"Were you looking for someone in the lounge?"

"No, no, Mrs. Robart."

"I wondered if you had colleagues aboard. I suppose that you work in a team."

"If only we did," said Genevieve, careful to give nothing away. "It would make my life easier. No, I work alone, I'm afraid. Luckily, there are not too many calls on my time. Most passengers are very law-abiding."

"That's what Sir Harry was saying last night."

"Sir Harry?"

"Sir Harry Fox-Holroyd. I sat next to him and his wife at dinner. They were delightful company," she said. "Very unassuming. Anyway, Sir Harry was talking about the essential honesty in the Anglo-Saxon character. I agreed with him. He made an interesting point."

"Oh?"

"Well, he admitted freely that we do have our criminal element in England, but it's not a large one. The question we ought to be asking, Sir Harry said, was not why the small minority turned to crime but why the vast majority would never dream of it in a million years." Mrs. Robart laughed. "I know that I wouldn't, and it's not simply out of fear of the consequences. It just seems so, well, foreign to our nature. Sir Harry was right about that."

"Unfortunately, it's not foreign to everyone's nature," said Genevieve.

"Quite. Look at those two killers we have aboard."

"They're only suspects, Mrs. Robart."

"Yes, I know," said the other woman. "And I'm ashamed that I had such silly fears earlier on. When there are Scotland Yard detectives aboard, we've nothing at all to worry about. Sir Harry reassured us about that," she went on. "He spoke very highly of Scotland Yard. Apparently they had a robbery at their London home and the villains were caught within a matter of weeks."

"Was the stolen property recovered?"

"Oh, yes. The thieves hadn't managed to sell the jewelry." She laughed again. "Scotland Yard is almost as efficient as you, Miss Masefield. Except that theirs was a real crime, of course, and the one I reported was not. Oh, I can't tell you how grateful I am to you," she continued, putting a hand on Genevieve's arm. "I got so flustered when I thought I'd lost my precious earrings. You put my mind at rest."

"Good."

"I know you wouldn't take any reward but I'll find a way to thank you somehow."

After gently squeezing her arm, Cecilia Robart walked into the lounge to join two other ladies for afternoon tea. Genevieve was forced to revise her judgment. She had to accept the possibility that the flowers had not, in fact, been sent by any of the three men she had considered. They might have been a gift from a woman. She could still feel the touch of Mrs. Robart's hand on her arm. The thought that it was she who might be the anonymous sender was troubling.

Given permission to speak to the prisoners, Dillman did not waste any time. Instead of interviewing John Heritage in his cell, however, he borrowed the office used by the master-at-arms. After introducing himself, Dillman explained why he was there. Heritage was pleased by what he saw as more humane treatment.

"Thank you, Mr. Dillman," he said. "I appreciate this."

"That cell is rather cramped for two people at the same time."

"Inspector Redfern didn't think so."

"I prefer to do things my way."

"But why has he sent you and not Sergeant Mulcaster? Does the inspector think that you'll be able to wheedle things out of me?"

"Not at all," Dillman said easily. "For obvious reasons, I took a professional interest in the case and the inspector was kind enough to allow me to speak to you. I'm not here to interrogate you, Mr. Heritage. I'm like a doctor who's been called in to offer a second opinion. And you're under no compulsion to answer my questions," he added. "If you'd rather go back to your cell, just say the word."

"No, no, I'll stay here."

"It might be to your advantage."

"In what way?"

"Well," said Dillman, "I'm not as familiar with the details of the case as Inspector Redfern and Sergeant Mulcaster. On the basis of what they know, they have no doubts at all about your guilt."

"What about you?"

"I prefer to keep an open mind."

Heritage was skeptical. "You're still on their side, though, aren't you?"

"I'm on nobody's side. If what you say convinces me that you're guilty, then that's what I'll report. But if, on the other hand," emphasized Dillman, "I come to believe in your innocence, I'll tell the inspector why."

"Is that what you're pretending to be—a defense barrister?"

"I'm not pretending to be anything," Dillman said earnestly. "I don't blame you for being suspicious. I'd feel the same in your position. After all, I'm an American. I'm not too familiar with the British legal system. But I'm here to listen, Mr. Heritage. So," he offered, spreading his arms, "take me or leave me."

Heritage studied him for a moment. Dillman seemed intel-

144

ligent and personable. He had none of the faint menace that hung around Sergeant Mulcaster nor the tenacious formality of Inspector Redfern. Nothing could be lost by talking to him. While the prisoner was making up his mind, Dillman was able to appraise him in turn. Being in custody had made Heritage look older. His eyes were ringed with fatigue, his forehead more deeply etched, and his beard more salted with gray. There was little in his appearance to suggest why Carrie Peterson had been attracted to him.

"Very well," said Heritage at length. "Ask what you will."

"Thank you."

"But before you ask the obvious question—no, we did not kill my wife."

"That wasn't what I was going to ask you," said Dillman. "I'm more interested to know if you were surprised when the police followed you to Ireland."

"Extremely surprised."

"Why?"

"Because we'd been careful to leave no trail."

"There's always a trail of some kind, Mr. Heritage."

"We thought they'd have no reason to follow us."

"A dead body is fairly strong motivation," argued Dillman, "even if you were not responsible for the murder. When a wife dies, it falls to the husband to identify the body. They were bound to come looking for you. Then, of course, there was the matter of the money that you stole from the pharmacy account."

Heritage was bitter. "I was owed that, Mr. Dillman," he said. "It was small recompense for all the misery I'd had to put up with from my partner. I had no qualms at all about raiding the account. I was fairly certain that Stephen had been dipping into it himself without telling me."

"Did Miss Peterson know where the money came from?"

"That's a private matter."

"In other words, you didn't tell her."

"I've given you my answer."

"Did you make all the travel arrangements?"

"Of course."

"Why did you choose Ireland?"

"Carrie has relatives there."

"That was a mistake, Mr. Heritage," said Dillman. "Relatives constitute a trail. So do close friends. The police always start with them when they're hunting missing persons. To come back to your wife," he continued, watching the other man closely. "If you didn't kill her, she must have been alive when you left the house."

"She was, Mr. Dillman."

"How do you know?"

"Because I spoke to her. I told Winifred that I was going for a long walk." He rubbed his beard. "What I didn't say, of course, was that I wasn't coming back. I'd packed my things a day earlier and left them at Carrie's flat."

"How did you feel when you walked out of the house?"

"Relieved."

"And vengeful?"

"Oh, yes," confessed the other. "I was getting my revenge."

"Your wife died in agony that same day, Mr. Heritage. Are you sure your revenge didn't take a more deadly turn?"

"Quite sure."

"Then why did you take home that poison from the pharmacy?"

Heritage lowered his head. "It doesn't matter now," he mumbled.

"But it does," insisted Dillman. "It's a crucial factor. You had motive, means, and opportunity to kill your wife. What puzzles me is why you recorded the purchase of that poison in the record book at the pharmacy. Surely you could have taken it without anyone ever knowing." There was a strained silence. "Well?"

"I *wanted* her to know," said Heritage.

"Miss Peterson?"

"No, my wife."

"I don't follow."

"The poison was not for Winifred at all."

Dillman was shocked. "You intended to commit suicide?"

"It seemed like the only way out at the time," Heritage said gloomily. "In view of what's happened since, I'm beginning to wish I'd had the courage to go through with it."

When she found the store where the flowers were kept, a steward in a blue apron was arranging displays in a series of small vases. He gave a polite smile.

"Can I help you, madam?"

"I hope so," said Genevieve. "Earlier on, I received a bouquet of flowers. They could only have come from here. I'd like to know who sent them."

"I'm afraid I can't tell you that," said the man.

"Why not?"

"Because I gave my word to the customer."

"Was it a lady called Mrs. Robart, by any chance?"

"The customer didn't give me a name."

"Just tell me if it was a man or a woman," said Genevieve. "That's all I ask."

The steward wavered. "Well . . ."

"*Please*—this is important to me."

"It was a gentleman," he admitted, "but that's all I'm prepared to say."

Genevieve thanked him and left him to get on with his work. She was relieved to be able to eliminate Cecilia Robart from consideration but would clearly have to wait before the true identity of the sender was revealed. As she walked away, she chided herself for taking time off to do some private detection. A murder had been committed and there was a strong suspicion that drugs were being smuggled across the Atlantic on the *Caronia*. With such serious crimes to address, she felt slightly ashamed of herself. Her main task was to help in the search for the man who killed Sergeant Mulcaster and dumped his body into the sea.

Before she was able to do that, however, she was accosted

on the staircase by Wes Odell. He was not in the mood for pleasantries.

"I need to speak to you, Miss Masefield," he announced.

"Can't it wait?"

"No, it can't."

"I'm frightfully busy at the moment."

"Been looking for you all afternoon. I'm not going to let go of you now."

"If you insist," she said with a shrug. "What seems to be the problem?"

"You are, Miss Masefield."

"I beg your pardon!"

"You're distracting Theo."

"Not intentionally, I can promise you."

"That makes no difference," said Odell. "Since he met you, his mind is not as completely on his cycling as it should be. Theo claims that it is, but I know him too well. So let's get one thing straight, shall we?" he affirmed. "His career comes first."

"I wouldn't try to contradict that."

"Then play along with me."

"What do you mean, Mr. Odell?"

"Keep out of Theo's way. Give the kid the cold shoulder."

"I'll do nothing of the kind," said Genevieve, offended by the notion. "I'm free to speak to anyone I choose and I certainly won't have you exerting any control over my private life."

His eyes flashed. "Don't cross me, Miss Masefield."

"It appears I've already done that without even realizing it."

"There's too much at stake here."

"That doesn't give you the right to make demands of me."

"Do you know how long it takes to train a champion?"

"Mr. Odell—"

"Do you know how much I've invested in Theo Wright?" he asked, jabbing a finger at her. "Years of time and tons of money. That kid was a raw novice when I took him on. He didn't even have enough dough to look after himself properly. But he had terrific promise. I backed that promise."

"I'm pleased for both of you."

"Then don't stand in our way."

"That's not what I'm doing, Mr. Odell."

"I want a return on my investment," he asserted. "I've been building him up steadily for this race in France. It's the most important test of his career. Theo has got the talent to win—but only if he commits himself heart and soul to the race."

"I can't imagine him doing anything else. He's very single-minded."

"He was until you came on the scene, Miss Masefield."

"I'm just one passenger among over two thousand."

"You're the only one that matters to him."

"I can't believe that," said Genevieve, anxious to detach herself. "However, I refuse to discuss this any further. Theo and I are friends, but that's as far as it goes and as far as it ever could go. Does that satisfy you?"

"No," he said stubbornly.

"Well, it's all that you're going to get, Mr. Odell."

"I want more than that."

"Excuse me," she said, trying to walk past him.

He blocked her path. "You're going nowhere till we've got this sorted out."

"It *is* sorted out."

"I want your word that you'll lie low for a while."

"Lie low?" echoed Genevieve, insulted by the suggestion. "Who on earth do you think you are, Mr. Odell? You can't tell me what to do."

"You're a threat to Theo."

"That's a matter between you and him."

"No, it's between the two of us, Miss Masefield. I've spoken to Theo. He won't even talk about the subject. That shows how bad it is."

"It's not my fault."

"That's a matter of opinion," he said resentfully. "You gave the guy plenty of encouragement over a meal yesterday."

Genevieve was roused. "I did nothing of the kind, I assure

you. If you interpret polite conversation as encouragement, Mr. Odell, then you need to have some lessons in social behavior. Now, please get out of my way."

"One last warning."

"No," she replied with dignity. "I won't hear another word."

She glared at him. He moved reluctantly out of her way and she swept past him.

"Just wait," he called after her. "You'll be sorry you didn't play ball."

The talk with John Heritage had been enlightening. Dillman learned that the case was far more complex than he had imagined when he studied the dossier loaned to him by Inspector Redfern. Circumstantial evidence was still heavily weighted against the suspect, and Dillman was by no means persuaded of his innocence, yet he felt he had seen a side of Heritage that had been invisible to the detectives who had arrested him. After admitting that he had contemplated suicide, the man had broken down and cried. It was a touching scene. Sitting in silence, Dillman gave him plenty of time to recover. What he could not decide was whether the tears were genuine or a display of emotion calculated to win his sympathy. Heritage dabbed at his eyes with a handkerchief.

"I'm sorry, Mr. Dillman," he said. "Do forgive me."

"There's nothing to forgive."

"I've been under such terrible pressure these last few days."

"I know, Mr. Heritage."

"Have you ever had the police chasing you?"

"No," said Dillman. "I've usually done the chasing. It's very stressful for the suspect. I've seen more than one collapse with a heart attack when cornered."

"I'm surprised I didn't do the same," Heritage said ruefully. "We thought we were safe when we got to Ireland. When we managed to get a passage to America, we were absolutely certain that we were. You can guess how we felt when we they arrested us on board ship."

"Was Sergeant Mulcaster carrying a shotgun at the time?"

"Yes, Mr. Dillman. I still have the bruise on my chest where he prodded me with it. But it was the way he grabbed Carrie that really upset me. There was no need for it at all. It was gratuitous violence."

"Go back to what you were telling me."

"About the poison?"

"Does Inspector Redfern know why you bought it?"

Redfern shook his head. "No. I kept that from him."

"Why?"

"For two reasons," said the other man. "First, I don't think he'd have believed me. Second—and more to the point—I was too ashamed to talk about it. Except to Carrie. It was before we had decided to run away together. My wife had refused to give me a divorce and the situation seemed utterly hopeless."

"Killing yourself would have solved nothing."

"I realize that now."

"You'd have had two women grieving over you."

"One," Heritage said bluntly. "Carrie Peterson. It was because of her that I drew back." Hatred came into his voice. "Winifred never would have mourned me. She'd have been glad, Mr. Dillman. It would have meant that she'd won."

"Won what?"

"It doesn't matter."

"I think it does."

But Heritage was not prepared to say anything more about his marriage. After a few more questions, Dillman elected to bring the interview to an end. He needed to assimilate what he had already gathered.

"Perhaps we can talk again sometime," he suggested.

Heritage was guarded. "If you wish—but don't expect a confession."

"I've already had one. Of a kind."

He got up from his chair and the prisoner followed suit. As they moved to the door, Heritage remembered something. He looked Dillman in the eye.

"What happened to Inspector Redfern's head?" he asked.

"He had an accident."

"Is that the truth?"

"As far as I know, Mr. Heritage."

"What about Sergeant Mulcaster? Why hasn't he come today?"

"Would you rather be questioned by him?"

"Not at all," said Heritage. "I won't pretend that I enjoyed this chat with you but it was far more pleasurable than a grilling by Sergeant Mulcaster. He's a vicious bully. I was lucky that he didn't beat me to a pulp. He was more than capable of it. The sergeant used to boast about what he'd done to other people he caught."

"Indeed?"

"He was trying to scare me, Mr. Dillman. Thank heaven that Inspector Redfern kept him under control or I might have finished up like Nicholls."

"Who?"

"Sidney Nicholls," explained Heritage. "The sergeant claims he resisted arrest and that gave him the license to tear the man apart. He boasted to me that he put Nicholls in hospital for a fortnight."

"What was the man's crime?"

"Drug trafficking."

TEN

Frank Openshaw liked to collect people around him so that he could hold court. There was more to it than the simple desire to impress them with the story of his life. Though many of the guests would be invited purely on a social basis, there would always be a smattering of those whom he hoped to involve in one of his many business ventures. Hospitable by nature, he also expected a return on his money. When he and his wife returned to their cabin that afternoon, they went through the guest list for their next gathering. Those who had come on the previous evening were discounted. Twenty new people had been invited to join them for drinks before dinner. The list was not entirely made up of his choices. Kitty Openshaw had contributed a couple of names herself.

"These are mine," she said, handing him a slip of paper.

He glanced at the names. "Who is Iris Cooney?"

"A lovely American lady, who visits her son in London every two years. She uses a walking stick but she refuses to let arthritis hold her back. Mrs. Cooney sat next to me in the hairdressing salon."

"Is she traveling alone?"

"Her husband passed away ten years ago."

"Does she have any brass?"

"Frank!" scolded his wife.

"Some of these American widows have more money than they know what to do with," he said airily. "Look at that woman we met on the *Mauretania* when we sailed to New York. She was worth millions."

"Well, I didn't ask Mrs. Cooney about her money. It's not the polite thing to do."

"But you must have got some idea, Kitty. That's the wonderful thing about brass. You can *smell* it on people. You can see it in the way they dress and the manner in which they talk to other people. That's why I invited Stanley Chase."

"Oh, I liked him."

"So did I."

"Such nice manners."

"And such a thick wallet," he said with a chuckle. "I sensed that as soon as he sat down opposite us. There's big money in antiques. Look at his card," he went on, taking it from his waistcoat pocket. "He has a business in the King's Road, Chelsea, and a house in Knightsbridge. Property is not cheap in either of those places, I can tell you. He also has a cottage in the south of France. Chase must be making a small fortune."

"I wouldn't know about that. I just thought he was a gentleman."

"Who's this other person you've invited?"

"Pamela Clyne."

"Another rich American widow?"

"Far from it," said Kitty. "She's English. Miss Clyne is a friend of Iris Cooney's. I had tea with them this afternoon. It was one of those awkward situations, Frank. I couldn't invite the one without the other."

"All the more, the merrier."

"The truth is that I felt sorry for Pamela Clyne. Apart from Mrs. Cooney, she doesn't seem to know anyone else on board. She's one of those very shy women from down south."

"Wouldn't last two minutes in Yorkshire, then," he said briskly. "If you don't speak up for yourself there, you're nowt. Pamela Clyne, eh? What's her story?"

"I'm not sure that she has one."

"Every woman has a story."

She clicked her tongue. "You always say that."

"It's true, Kitty."

"Not in Miss Clyne's case," said his wife. "She doesn't seem to have done anything or been anywhere. The trip to America was obviously the biggest thing in her life and she's still a bit overwhelmed. Just like me after my first trip."

"You've made a few since then."

"Thanks to you, Frank."

"Stick with me and I'll show you the world. That's what I said."

"You've been as good as your word."

"I always am." He gave her a peck on the cheek. "Right, then. All we have to do is to add your names to my list and we're done."

"Who have you invited?"

"All kinds of interesting people."

"Such as?"

"A bank manager from London, and his wife."

She smiled indulgently. "Trust you!"

"He could come in useful. You never know."

"Who else?"

"The finest professional cyclist in America."

"I didn't know there were such things."

"Well, there are and he makes a very decent living out of it. According to his coach, Mr. Odell, the lad is more or less certain to win a famous race in France and pick up a large check for his pains. Odell will make a tidy packet as well."

"Will he? How?"

"Betting, Kitty. He's going to back his lad heavily and make a killing."

"I've never seen the point of riding a bicycle round and round a track," she said. "It's a bit like those white mice you see turning a wheel."

"Theo Wright is a road racer," he explained. "He's going to cycle from Bordeaux to Paris. Take him the best part of a day, that will. Bound to be saddlesore after that."

She was taken aback. "Can anyone cycle for that long?"

"The lad has won six day-races before now, love."

"Well, I never!"

"Anyway, I invited him and his coach this evening—but I told them to leave the bicycle behind. Theo had one stipulation, though."

"What was that?"

"He took me aside to whisper it," said Openshaw, lowering his voice. "Wanted me to invite a certain young lass as well."

"Why?"

He nudged her softly. "Why do you think, Kitty?"

"Is he sweet on her?"

"As sweet as I was on you at his age."

"And have you invited her?"

"That was the funny thing," he said with a ripe chuckle. "I'd already penciled her name in. Met the lass in question earlier on. Stanley Chase introduced me to her. I can see why Theo Wright is so keen to chat with her over a glass of champagne."

"Oh?"

"She's right gorgeous, Kitty."

"What's her name?"

"Miss Masefield," he said. "Miss Genevieve Masefield."

Genevieve arrived at the purser's office to find both Dillman and Paul Taggart there. The moment she saw Dillman, she knew he had not sent the bouquet to her. He was too preoccupied. His expression was solemn, his mind focused wholly on his work. Involved in a murder investigation, he would have had neither time nor inclination to pick out the flowers. Though he had a strong romantic streak in his nature, she had to accept that it had been subordinated to other things. Hiding her disappointment, she crossed his name off her mental list.

"I got your note, George," she said. "What's happened?"

"Quite a lot. We've got a job for you."

"Well?"

"I'd like you to speak to Carrie Peterson."

"But Inspector Redfern was against the idea."

"That was before he lost Sergeant Mulcaster," said the purser. "The blow the inspector took to the head has left him with a concussion. The doctor insisted on rest. Inspector Redfern is sleeping in his cabin right now."

"Before he nodded off," added Dillman, "he gave us his blessing."

She was pleased. "We can interview the prisoners?"

"Yes, Genevieve. I've already spoken to John Heritage."

"How did he seem?"

"Grateful to talk to someone who didn't hassle him."

"Sergeant Mulcaster didn't believe in the kid-glove approach," observed Taggart.

"What did you find out, George?" she asked.

Dillman told them the salient facts about his visit to John Heritage but admitted he was no nearer deciding if the man was guilty or innocent of the crime with which he was charged. He picked out one significant piece of information.

"Sergeant Mulcaster boasted about his rough treatment of suspects," he said. "I'd like you to find out what Carrie Peterson has to say about him. Apparently he was less than courteous when they arrested her."

"Did you tell Mr. Heritage what has happened to the sergeant?" asked Genevieve.

"No. The inspector wants that information suppressed."

"I'm all in favor of that," Taggart said seriously. "If the rest of the passengers knew that a Scotland Yard detective was thrown overboard last night, there'd be general hysteria. That kind of thing gives them the shakes."

"Inspector Redfern had another reason for keeping it from the prisoners," said Dillman "and I agree with him. Tread carefully, Genevieve. You're not there to trick a confession out of her. Just listen to what she has to say, especially about the sergeant."

"When can I see her?" she asked.

"As soon as you like."

"I'll go there at once."

"Not before you've read this," said Dillman, handing her a dossier.

"What is it, George?"

"The inspector kindly loaned this to me. It will explain why he's so adamant that he has two cold-blooded murderers in custody. It's also got some background material about Carrie Peterson that you need to know."

"Thanks."

Dillman looked at her properly for the first time and smiled.

"What have you been up to since we last met, Genevieve?" he asked.

"Routine patrol, for the most part."

"Has anything come to light?"

"Not as yet. I'm slowly widening my field of contacts. They include a man whose name you've already mentioned to me, George."

"Oh, who's that?"

"Frank Openshaw."

" 'Frank by name, and frank by nature,' " he recalled.

"That's the one."

"I know Mr. Openshaw," said Taggart. "He and his wife have sailed on the *Caronia* before. He's a wealthy financier. Very popular with the stewards because he gives such handsome tips."

"He's certainly a generous host," said Genevieve. "When I slipped back to my cabin, I found an invitation to join them for drinks before dinner this evening. And I know for a fact that the Openshaws had a similar party yesterday."

"They'll have one every evening. They have in the past, anyway."

Dillman nodded. "Frank Openshaw is a man who likes an audience."

"Well, I'll be part of it this evening," said Genevieve. "It's the sort of occasion when you can pick up useful information. Anyway," she went on, holding up the dossier, "I'll study this before going to see Carrie Peterson. How do you think she'll react?"

"Positively, I hope," said Dillman. "If she asks about the bandaging around the inspector's head, tell her he had an accident but that you don't know the details."

"She's bound to wonder about Mr. Heritage."

"Assure her that he's fine."

"Right."

"Do all you can to win her confidence."

"I will, George. If you'll excuse me, I'll get on with it."

After an exchange of farewells, she slipped out of the office.

"What do you expect to get out of Carrie Peterson?" asked Taggart.

"I don't know," replied Dillman. "From what the inspector told me, she's a rather strange young lady. That's why I think Genevieve ought to handle her."

"Any special reason why you want her to ask about Sergeant Mulcaster?"

"Yes, Mr. Taggart. Something that John Heritage told me rang a tiny bell at the back of my mind. The late Sergeant Mulcaster had many virtues but patience was not one of them. You could see the aggression bubbling away below the surface."

"I noticed that."

"Unhappily, it was not always held in check. According to Mr. Heritage, one of the men the sergeant arrested took a dreadful beating and finished up in hospital. That sort of thing gets a detective a bad name."

"It could have been an isolated incident."

"I doubt it somehow."

"And if it wasn't?"

"Then it might provide us with a motive for his murder,"

said Dillman. "The sergeant clearly enjoyed the reputation he'd gained for robust policing. People on the other side of the law might not be so impressed."

"Only if they'd come across him."

"Oh, I suspect that Sergeant Mulcaster's name was known far and wide. He's like Frank Openshaw in that respect. He likes to draw attention to himself." He pursed his lips for a moment. "It's only a theory, of course, but the more we know about the sergeant, the closer we'll get to understanding why he was killed."

"Sounds sensible."

"It's a starting point, Mr. Taggart."

"I agree." Taggart remembered something. "What about our pickpocket?"

"I've had too much to do to give him my full attention," confessed Dillman, "but I haven't forgotten him. He's obviously a pro and that means he doesn't rush things. He's targeted two men and relieved them of their wallets so skillfully that they didn't feel a thing. My guess is that he'll wait to see the response before he dips his hand in someone's pocket again. Guys like that have a sixth sense about ship's detectives."

"How do you hope to catch him?"

"You'll see." He moved to the door. "I'll get out of your way, Mr. Taggart."

"No, hold on a minute," said the purser, sorting through some papers on his desk. "I've been doing a little detective work on my own account."

"Good for you!"

"I could be barking up the wrong tree, of course."

"We all do that from time to time. What have you found?"

"Well," said Taggart, "I was checking through the manifest. The obvious way to smuggle drugs is to conceal them inside freight. That's why it's examined so carefully before it's allowed on board. The vast bulk of it is patently legitimate. You only have to look at the names of the people involved. But one or two items in the cargo hold did catch my eye."

"For instance?"

"This one here," Taggart pointed a finger at the manifest. "It's such an unusual item for us to carry. Empty, that is. We've had a few occupied ones aboard before now. Someone being returned to his own country and so on."

"What exactly are you talking about?"

"A funeral casket."

"Now I'm with you."

"I got to thinking how easy it'd be to hide drugs in that."

"Very easy."

"The guy who brought it on board is English, so I guess he'd call it a coffin."

Dillman felt a shock of recognition. "I think I know who he is."

"Who?"

"Mr. Ramsey Leach."

"How did you guess?"

Wes Odell's search led him eventually onto the promenade deck. Theodore Wright was leaning against the rail, chatting with a short, swarthy man of middle years with a neat mustache. Odell was glad that he had found the cyclist at last.

"Where have you been, Theo?" he complained.

"Talking to a supporter of my rival."

"What rival?"

"Vannier, of course."

"The best cyclist in the world," said the other man, with a heavy French accent. He thrust out a hand. "Michel Fontaine," he declared.

Odell shook his hand. "Wes Odell. I'm Theo's coach."

"He knows all about us, Wes," Wright said with a grin. "Mr. Fontaine recognized me from a picture he'd seen in a French newspaper. We're *famous*."

"Before the race, maybe," argued Fontaine. "Afterwards, you'll be forgotten."

"Not if I win."

"Gaston Vannier will win. He always does."

"Only because he hasn't come up against Theo before," said Odell.

"What chance does this boy have? Look at him. While you cross the ocean on a liner, Gaston will be training on the roads between Bordeaux and Paris. He knows them better than anybody." He gave a smile of mock sympathy. "You have never even been to the country before."

"One road is much like another," said Wright.

"You have no chance, *mon ami*."

Odell was getting angry. "Don't listen to him, Theo."

"All that he will see is the back of Gaston's jersey."

"Says who? What do you know about cycling?"

"Very little," replied Fontaine genially, "but I read the papers. All the experts say the same thing. Gaston Vannier cannot lose. He has one big advantage."

"What's that?" asked Wright.

"He is French."

Fontaine laughed merrily then strolled off down the deck. Odell wanted to go after him to continue the argument but Wright took no offense from the remarks.

"At least they know that we're coming, Wes."

"They'll know you've been there when you win the race."

"French guys are very patriotic. I won't be popular."

"You'll have a *name*, Theo. And that will open doors for us. Anyway," he said, "what have you been doing all afternoon? I couldn't find you anywhere."

Wright was evasive. "I was around."

"You weren't with that English dame, were you?"

"If only I had been!"

"Theo!"

"Genevieve is a friend."

"You can't afford to have friends—not that kind, anyway."

"I'll decide that."

"Not as long as I'm your coach." Odell saw Theo's jaw

162

tighten, and backed off. He tried a more relaxed approach. "How do you feel?"

"I felt great until you started to hassle me."

"No stiffness in the legs?"

"Not after that massage you gave me."

"Good."

"What was in that stuff, Wes? It put a kind of zing into me."

"Oh, it's just an ointment I made. We'll use it again."

"That's okay by me." Wright shrugged his shoulders. "So why have you been chasing me this afternoon?"

"For a chat, that's all."

"We never stop chatting, Wes."

"I wanted a word about that guy with the loud voice."

"Frank Openshaw?"

"Yes," said Odell. "That's him. I'm worried about that invitation to have a drink in his cabin this evening. Maybe we should give it a miss, Theo."

"Not on your life!"

"We got nothing in common with guys like that."

"There'll be lots of other people there as well."

"So? He won't notice if we don't turn up."

"But I want to go, Wes. We can't just stay away. What will Mr. Openshaw think?"

"We can send him an apology."

"But we've already accepted his invitation."

"You accepted it, Theo," said Odell. "I just went along with the idea. The more I think about it, the more I worry. It could be dangerous."

"Dangerous?"

"All that booze floating around. You're not supposed to touch alcohol."

"They'll have soft drinks as well," reasoned the cyclist. "Besides, there's plenty of booze floating around in the restaurant during lunch and dinner. Yet I haven't been tempted to touch a drop. Come clean, Wes," he advised. "What's the real reason you don't want to show up this evening?"

"I think we'd be out of place."

"Not with a guy like Frank Openshaw. He's as straight as they come. I took to him. He's like me. Born at the bottom of the heap and dragged himself up by sheer hard work. I'd have thought you'd admire him for that."

"I do. It's the others I worry about."

"What others?"

"Some of the stuffed shirts aboard. They'll all be there."

"Who cares? I'm not being scared off by anybody. I'm surprised at you, Wes," he said. "You always tell me to hold my head up. We don't need to kowtow to anyone, you say. Lost your nerve all of a sudden?"

"No, Theo."

"Then why all this worry about a drink with friends?" He saw the look in the coach's eye and understood. "Ah, now I get it!"

"*She'll* be there, won't she?"

"No idea."

"But she could be," said Odell, with rancor. "She's the kind of woman who gets herself invited to things like this. It's her world."

"Why don't we keep Genevieve's name out of this?"

"You know damn well why not."

"Wes—"

"She's bad news, kid. Take my word for it."

"Look," said Wright, trying to keep calm. "When it comes to cycling, I worship you as a god. There's nobody to touch you. Away from it, though, I make my own decisions and you'd better get used to the idea."

"Not if one of those decisions costs us that race in France."

"It won't do that."

"Stay away from her, Theo," urged the coach. "Let's skip that party this evening."

"No, Wes."

"I got this feeling about it."

"So have I. It's going to be good fun."

164

"Pull out, Theo."

"But I've no reason to."

"I'm asking you, as a favor to me. I won't be turning up, I know that."

"You can please yourself," said Wright. "Whatever happens, I'm going."

Carrie Peterson was astonished when her visitor explained who she was. The prisoner stared at Genevieve Masefield with a surprise that was tinged with disbelief.

"You're a *detective?*" she asked.

"Employed by the Cunard Line."

"I didn't realize a woman could do a job like that."

Genevieve smiled. "We can go to places that men can't always reach. When it comes to a difficult arrest, of course," she said, "some male assistance is welcome."

"I know all about being arrested," said Carrie, scowling. "Sergeant Mulcaster left bruises all down my arm." She was suspicious. "Why isn't he here with you?"

"Inspector Redfern thought you might prefer to talk to me."

"I'd rather talk to anyone but the sergeant."

"If nothing else, I can break the monotony for you. Of course, you're under no obligation to speak to me, Miss Peterson. Say the word and I'll disappear."

The other woman scrutinized her in silence for a long time.

"How is John?" she said at length.

"He's fine, I promise you."

"Have you seen him yourself?"

"No, but a colleague of mine had a long talk with him earlier. Mr. Heritage is bearing up very well under the circumstances."

"Well, I'm not," said Carrie.

"I'm sorry to hear that."

"They shouldn't treat me like this. I've done nothing wrong."

The strain showed in her face and in the sag of her shoulders. Carrie Peterson looked weary and hunted. There was an edge of desperation in her voice. Genevieve schooled herself not to feel sorry for the woman. Objectivity was essential.

"May I sit down?" she asked.

Carrie nodded.

"Thank you."

Genevieve took a seat but the other woman remained on her feet, still watchful.

"What exactly is going on, Miss Masefield?"

" 'Going on'?"

"Yes. Inspector Redfern has a bandage around his head, Sergeant Mulcaster hasn't looked in all day, and now you turn up out of the blue. It smells fishy to me."

"Does it?"

"Why should you be involved at all?"

"I explained that."

"There something you're not telling me, isn't there?"

"Miss Peterson," said Genevieve calmly, "I simply came here to listen to you. It's all I'm authorized to do. I understand that you've been troubled by the way you've been questioned so far. It must have been frightening, coming as it did on top of the shock of the arrest."

"I've been terrified."

"Tell me why."

Carrie Peterson needed some time before she decided she could trust her visitor. When she spoke again, she gave a detailed, if halting, account of her arrest and of the statements she'd given the detectives during her time on the vessel.

"I've told them the truth," she pleaded. "We're completely innocent."

"That remains to be seen."

"Neither of us has ever been in trouble with the police before, Miss Masefield. We led respectable lives. We worked hard at the pharmacy. John and I caused no trouble to anybody."

"You made up for that when you left," Genevieve reminded her. "I gather that Mr. Duckham was distraught when the pair of you walked out on him without warning."

"It was the only way we could do it, don't you see?"

"Frankly, no."

"Our hand was forced."

"Did Mr. Heritage have to raid the shop account like that?"

"That's what the inspector asked me," said Carrie. "To be honest, it was the first I'd heard of it. If it happened, John must have had a good reason to do it." Her voice darkened. "He suspected for a long time that his partner was taking money out of the account on the quiet. That'd be typical of Stephen Duckham! I shed no tears for him."

"What Mr. Heritage did was a crime."

"I don't see it that way."

"And what about the death of Mrs. Heritage?"

"We knew nothing about that until the police arrested us."

"Then why did you run away?" asked Genevieve. "If you were not implicated in Mrs. Heritage's murder, why jump on a ship and sail to America?"

"It was our only chance," said Carrie, sitting opposite her and leaning forward in her chair. "We knew that John's wife would try to find us but we never imagined they'd follow us to Ireland. When we realized the police were on our tail, we thought Mrs. Heritage had sent them. So we booked passages on the first ship we could find."

Genevieve pondered. "You didn't like Mrs. Heritage, did you?"

"I *despised* her."

"Why?"

"Because of the terrible way that she treated him."

"Is that what he told you?"

"I saw it with my own eyes, Miss Masefield, believe me. Winifred Heritage was a witch. While he was in that house, John led a dog's life."

"It's one that he chose himself, Miss Peterson."

"That's what he always used to say," recalled Carrie. "John admitted that it was his own fault for marrying her. He's a religious man. He took his marriage vows seriously."

"Until he met you."

"He wrestled with his conscience for months about us."

"What about you?"

"I did the same, of course. What sort of people do you think we are?" asked Carrie with indignation. "I'd been brought up to believe that marriage was for life. The last thing I wanted to do was to break up a home." She screwed up her face. "Then I met Mrs. Heritage and I changed my mind. It would have been cruel to leave him under the thumb of a woman like that."

"Like what?"

"Have you ever been treated with total contempt by anyone, Miss Masefield?"

"No, I don't think I have."

"John had to put up with that day after day. Sneers, insults, demands. It was the same at work," she said. "Because he was the senior partner, Mr. Duckham used to tease and bully John. It was embarrassing to watch."

"Why did Mr. Heritage put up with it?"

"Because he had no choice at first."

"And then?"

"He saw a way out," she said simply. "With me."

"Whose idea was it to go to Ireland?"

"Mine. I had relatives in Cork."

"What about your family in England?"

"I have none, to speak of. My parents both died."

"You must have had lots of friends?"

"I just had to forget about those, Miss Masefield."

"It was such a huge step for the both of you to take," said Genevieve. "Running away from everything like that. You must have thought about it for a long time."

"We did."

"Were there no misgivings?"

"None at all."

"Did you never pause to consider the damage you'd leave behind?"

"No," Carrie Peterson said with a defiant smile. "We're in love."

After sleeping for a couple off hours, Inspector Redfern awoke in his cabin. His head was still throbbing but there was far less pain. Anxious to get back to work, he struggled out of bed then summoned a steward to fetch some hot water. While the man was away, Redfern peeled off the bandaging and examined himself in the mirror. His face was drawn, his eyes bloodshot. His forehead still bore the imprint of the bandage. The hot water finally arrived and he was able to wash and shave. He felt much better as a result. Redfern had just finished dressing when there was a light tap on the door. He opened it to find Dillman outside. The visitor was invited in.

"I wasn't sure if you were awake," said Dillman. "That's why I didn't knock hard." He peered considerately at the other man. "How are you feeling now, Inspector?"

"Better."

"Good."

"Any news?"

"I came to tell you about my conversation with Mr. Heritage."

"How did you find him?"

"Bitter and unhappy."

"Criminals are always like that after arrest," said Redfern. "They always blame us for daring to catch them. And even if you nab them with a smoking gun in their hand, they always swear that they're innocent. In twenty-five years of arresting villains, I've never had one with the guts to admit his guilt straight away."

"Mr. Heritage is still protesting *his* innocence."

"He would."

"I expect that Carrie Peterson will do the same."

"What did Miss Masefield get out of her?"

"I don't know, Inspector. Genevieve is in there with her now. I daresay she'll report to you when the interview is finished." He produced a small notebook from his inside pocket. "But let me tell you about Mr. Heritage. I jotted this down after I'd left him. I didn't want him to think he was being grilled."

"Go ahead, Mr. Dillman."

Redfern sat down to listen. He was impressed by Dillman's lucid account of the meeting with the prisoner and interested to hear the new facts that had come to light. On one point, however, he remained skeptical.

"I refuse to believe that John Heritage bought that poison because he was contemplating suicide."

"That's how he thought you'd feel," said Dillman.

"To begin with, I don't think he's the type."

"Why not?"

"Look at the fellow, Mr. Dillman. He was locked into an unhappy marriage for all those years. His partner, Stephen Duckham, seems to have taken advantage of him at every stage. Heritage became resigned to it all," said Redfern. "You don't put up with that kind of misery for all those years then decide one day that you can't stand it. He *could* stand it. That's obvious."

"You're forgetting the crucial factor."

"Am I?"

"Carrie Peterson. When she came into his life," said Dillman, "everything was transformed. He suddenly had a vision of a better life with her. He just couldn't go on as he was. The low point came when his wife refused to give him a divorce. My guess is that that was when he had these suicidal thoughts."

"Thoughts, maybe. But would he have the courage to act on them?"

"You need desperation rather than courage, Inspector. He certainly had that."

"What about Miss Peterson? He claims to love her."

"I don't think we can doubt that."

"Would any man commit suicide in that situation? He'd be leaving her in the most appalling predicament. Heritage would never have done that to Carrie Peterson."

"Probably not."

"There's another point, Mr. Dillman. According to the pathology report, the poisons he bought were used to make a lethal compound. Winifred Heritage died in agony. Her husband was a pharmacist," said Redfern. "If he was planning to kill himself, surely he'd have chosen a less painful method."

Dillman nodded. "What puzzled me is the record book, Inspector."

"Why?"

"When he bought the poison, Heritage noted it down with care. When you found his wife dead, all you had to do was to look in the record book at the pharmacy, and there was your proof." Dillman shrugged. "Mr. Heritage is an intelligent man. He would have diverted suspicion away from himself, not paint a large red arrow for the police to follow. It doesn't make sense."

"It does when you really get to know him."

"What do you mean?"

"I've played chess with him, remember? His true character began to emerge then. He was toying with me, laughing into his beard every time I made a mistake. I think he *wanted* us to know that he'd murdered his wife," said Redfern, "because he never thought we'd track him to Ireland. Don't you see, Mr. Dillman? He was taunting us."

"There's a big difference between a game of chess and a murder."

"Both involve cunning and forethought."

"True."

"Be frank with me. You've met the man. Do you think he's capable of murder?"

"Yes," decided Dillman. "He's *capable* of it, but that doesn't mean he actually committed it." He put his notebook away. "Does the name of Sidney Nicholls mean anything to you?"

Redfern's face hardened. "Why do you ask?"

"Because he was mentioned by Sergeant Mulcaster on more than one occasion, it seems. When he questioned Mr. Heritage, the sergeant used to boast about some of the arrests he'd made. I don't want to speak ill of the dead," said Dillman, "but your colleague does seem to have exceeded the bounds of reasonable force at times."

"Ronnie Mulcaster was a good detective."

"I'm sure that he was."

"I don't need to tell you how aggressive some criminals can get."

"Was this Sidney Nicholls one of them?"

"According to Sergeant Mulcaster," said Redfern. "He was working with someone else in those days. Nicholls was the worst kind of villain. He was completely unscrupulous. We'd been after him for years."

"He was involved in drug trafficking, I believe."

"And prostitution. Sidney Nicholls was scum, Mr. Dillman. When Ronnie finally caught up with him, Nicholls gave him a lot of verbal abuse. Ronnie saw red and gave him the hiding that he deserved."

"In other words, he lost his temper."

"He was provoked," Redfern said defensively.

"What did his superiors do?"

"They gave him a reprimand."

"Is that all? It sounds to me as if Sergeant Mulcaster went too far."

"Nicholls was asking for it, Mr. Dillman."

"Would *you* have responded like that, Inspector?"

"No," Redfern admitted. "I'd have exercised restraint."

"What happened when Sergeant Mulcaster was reprimanded?"

"I spoke up for him, Mr. Dillman. I asked for him to be transferred to me."

"When was this?"

"A few years ago."

"Did the sergeant do anything like that again?"

"Nothing as bad as that."

"But there were other occasions when he became over-zealous?"

"Look, why are we talking about him like this?" Redfern said angrily. "Ronnie Mulcaster had an excellent record as a detective. He got results and that's what matters. You ought to be searching for his killer, not running the man down. Why dredge up the name of a villain like Sidney Nicholls?"

"Because I think he may be relevant here."

"How?"

"Indirectly," said Dillman. "He may be part of the reason that you were spared and Sergeant Mulcaster was murdered. What you've just told me has made me even more convinced of it. We have a clear motive, Inspector."

"Do we?"

"Revenge."

Locked in his cell again, John Heritage had plenty of time to brood. He wondered what sort of an impression he had made on Dillman. The detective was not an official part of the investigation but he was a means by which Inspector Redfern could be influenced. Heritage had reservations about his visitor. Dillman had been polite, efficient, and highly plausible but his reason for being there was never exactly clear. Heritage had been on guard throughout, sensing that the American was there to use a friendly chat as a subtle means of cross-examination. It was a more pleasant way of being questioned than either of the Scotland Yard detectives could devise, and it got him, albeit briefly, out of the narrow confines of his cell. For that alone, he was grateful to Dillman. Whether or not he could count on him as a possible ally was uncertain. Heritage reminded himself that, in essence, his visitor was a policeman. None of them could be trusted.

While his chief concern was the fate of Carrie Peterson, he also speculated on the whereabouts of Sergeant Mulcaster. It was late afternoon and still he had seen no sign of the man. That was highly unusual. Mulcaster was the sort of person who would be sure to call on him, if only to gloat through the bars in the window. Heritage suspected it was on the sergeant's advice that he had been moved from his cabin. By depriving him of any comforts, they were hoping to weaken his resistance.

That seemed to be their strategy. Ignoring him throughout the day might also be deliberate. It left him vulnerable to the more relaxed interrogation by Dillman and allowed the two detectives to concentrate instead on Carrie Peterson. It was impossible to know how she would cope under the strain. Unable to help her or even to make contact with her, Heritage felt sad and frustrated. The blame lay firmly on him and he was beset by recriminations.

It was the commotion that interrupted his brooding. An old man's voice, slurred and angry, echoed along the corridor. There were distinct sounds of a scuffle.

"Take your hands off me!" yelled the old man.

"Come along, sir," said a younger voice. "You need to sober up."

"There's nothing wrong with me, you bastard!"

"You got drunk and started a fight, sir. We can't allow that."

"Those Yanks tried to take my whiskey off me," protested the old man.

"You'd had too much of it already."

Heritage put his face to the grille in time to see the adjoining cell being unlocked by a member of the crew. Two other crew members were holding a wizened old man who was swearing volubly as he tried to get free. Heritage was about to acquire a neighbor.

"You can't touch me," cried Daniel Webb. "I'll report you to the purser!"

"You're the one on report, sir," said the younger man. "In you go."

The prisoner was thrown unceremoniously into the cell and the door was locked behind him. With his wild imprecations still ringing in their ears, the three men walked off. Heritage had not enjoyed solitude but it was preferable to being forced to listen to the curses of an inebriated old man. He waited until Webb's protests began to fade.

"Hello," he called through the grille. "Can you hear me?"

"Who are you?" growled Webb.

"I'm in the next cell, my friend. I'm a victim of false arrest."

"So am I, so am I. They ought to be grateful to me. Wait till the purser hears about this—and that Mr. Dillman. He was the one who *gave* me the bottle."

Heritage was alert. "George Dillman? The ship's detective?"

"That's the bloke."

"Why did he give you a bottle of whisky?"

"I helped them, see?" Webb said belligerently. "I'm their only witness. And this is the way they treat me. Without me, they wouldn't even know he was dead."

"Who?" asked Heritage.

"The bloke what was thrown over the side of the ship. I was there. I saw it."

"Are you saying that someone was *killed*?"

"Yes," said Webb. "Last night. Right in front of my eyes. This man was clubbed to the deck then pushed over the rail. I watched it all. What do you think of that?"

Heritage sat down on his bunk, his mind racing madly.

ELEVEN

Genevieve Masefield had spent almost a half an hour alone with the prisoner, but progress was extremely slow. At no point did she feel she had won the other woman's confidence. Carrie Peterson told her a great deal about the circumstances that had led her to flee from England with her lover but Genevieve sensed she was holding something back. Time was running out. It was now early evening and Genevieve needed to change for dinner. She brought the interview to an end.

"Thank you, Miss Peterson," she said. "What you told me was very revealing."

"It was such a relief to talk to a woman for a change."

"That's why Inspector Redfern sent me."

"I'm grateful." Carrie searched her face. "Have you reached a verdict yet?"

"Verdict?"

"Isn't that what you were supposed to do?" she pressed. "Ask me questions then report back to the inspector? What will you tell him?"

"Exactly what you've said to me."

"But you must have made a decision about us. Do you think we're guilty?"

"It's not for me to say."

"You must have an opinion."

"No, Miss Peterson."

"Supposing you were a member of the jury."

"I'd need to study all the evidence before I even thought about reaching a conclusion," said Genevieve, moving to the door. "All that I've heard so far is your side of the story."

"John will confirm all the details."

"I'm sure that he will."

Carrie crossed over to her. "We're not killers, Miss Masefield," she said with sudden passion. "We were just trying to start a new life. It was our last chance." A note of envy sounded. "It's so different for you. You're beautiful and intelligent and all the things that I'm not. Wherever you go, men will be attracted to you. I had nobody until John came along. You may think it's wrong that he's so much older than me, but the truth is"—she went on, biting her lip—"he's all I've got. Don't you understand? John was the only man who ever took a real interest in me. Do you think I'd jeopardize my one chance of happiness by committing a dreadful crime?"

"Probably not."

"Tell that to the inspector. He doesn't seem to appreciate the point."

"Good-bye, Miss Peterson," said Genevieve, opening the door. "And I *don't* think it's wrong that there's an age gap between you and Mr. Heritage. To be honest, I find it rather touching. There's no reason at all why people of different ages shouldn't fall in love." She saw tears come into the other woman's eyes. "However, that's not the point at issue, is it? I must go now. Excuse me."

Letting herself out, Genevieve locked the door behind her then walked along to the adjoining cabin. Uncertain whether Inspector Redfern was up yet, she gave a tentative knock. He opened the door almost immediately and invited her in.

"How are you, Inspector?" she asked.

"Fine, fine," he replied. "I gather that you've spoken with Carrie Peterson."

"I listened rather than spoke."

"What did you make of her?"

"She's an interesting woman. There's more to her than appears on the surface."

"I think she's devious and calculating."

"That's not the impression I got."

"Oh?"

"Miss Peterson is still bewildered by the turn of events," said Genevieve. "Only true love could have made her change her life so radically. She staked everything on it. Suddenly, it blows up in their faces. She's bound to be confused."

Redfern was cynical. "I hope you're not asking me to feel sorry for her."

"Not at all, Inspector. I just want you to understand her position."

"In my view, her position is alongside John Heritage as his accomplice. He is certainly guilty," the inspector asserted. "No shadow of a doubt about that. Since they were so close, my guess is that she was an accessory to the murder of Winifred Heritage."

"They were close," agreed Genevieve, "yet she claims she knew nothing about the money that was taken from the pharmacy account. He kept that from her."

"Perhaps, Miss Masefield; though I'm not entirely convinced of that. What he couldn't disguise was the fact that he'd bought the poison that helped to kill his wife. Carrie Peterson had access to the record book at the pharmacy. She must have seen his name there."

"I didn't raise that with her."

"I did. Her answer was evasive. However," he said, indicating a chair, "I'd like to know how you got on."

Genevieve sat down.

"With luck, she may have confided things to you that she concealed from Sergeant Mulcaster and me."

"Judge for yourself, Inspector."

Genevieve gave him a succinct account of her meeting with Carrie Peterson, taking care to present the information without making any personal comment. The inspector was pleasantly surprised at the number of new details Genevieve had elicited from the woman. As he listened, he gained fresh insights into the relationship between the two suspects. Nothing he heard caused him to revise his opinion about their guilt but he was glad to have the additional facts at his disposal.

"Thank you, Miss Masefield," he said. "You've done a valuable job. I had grave doubts about the wisdom of letting you interview her, but I can see now that it's been a profitable exercise."

"I'll be happy to talk to her again."

"How would Miss Peterson respond to that?"

"Warmly, I imagine. She was so pleased to have female company."

"Let me think it over."

"Her overriding concern is for Mr. Heritage," said Genevieve, getting up from her chair. "She's upset that you've moved him out of his cabin. Even though they can't make contact, she felt reassured to know that he was relatively close to her."

He thought it over. "I'll probably have him moved back," he decided. "But not to appease his mistress," he stressed. "It will be more for my own convenience. I don't want to spend any more time in that cell with him. It stinks. I only put him in there as a temporary measure when I lost the services of Sergeant Mulcaster."

"Miss Peterson kept asking where the sergeant was."

"What did you tell her?"

"That he was busy elsewhere."

"Good," he said. "I don't want either of them to know what happened. In fact, the fewer people who are aware of the situation, the better. It would only spread panic and that could hinder the investigation."

"Have you any idea what the motive was?"

"I don't, Miss Masefield, but your colleague believes that he does."

"George?"

"An astute man," conceded Redfern. "You don't suppose he'd be interested in a job at Scotland Yard, do you?"

"Not unless it involved sailing across an ocean," she said.

Redfern grimaced. "He's got more appetite for that kind of thing than me," he said grimly. "This voyage has turned into a nightmare. Quite frankly, Miss Masefield, I don't care if I never see another ocean liner again."

Nobody would have guessed that Paul Taggart was under any strain. When he strolled into the first-class lounge early that evening, he looked poised and assured. His smart uniform helped him to make a pleasing impact on all the passengers who were gathering there before dinner. It was not long before he was ambushed. Wearing a ruby-red gown that reached down to her ankles, Mrs. Anstruther confronted him. Her perfume billowed towards him in a wave.

"Why haven't you locked him up?" she demanded.

"Who?"

"That weird man, Mr. Taggart. The one I reported to you."

"Mrs. Anstruther—"

"He was *looking* at me, in the most upsetting way. Lord knows what disgusting thoughts were going through his warped mind!" she said with a shudder. "I shan't feel safe in my bed until he's under lock and key."

"There's no danger, I promise you."

"I think that there is."

"The gentleman has been spoken to," said Taggart.

"He was no gentleman, believe me!"

"Try to forget him, Mrs. Anstruther."

"How can I, when that dreadful creature is at liberty? You should have seen those mad eyes of his, Mr. Taggart. They were twins pools of evil."

"That's not true at all," he said smoothly. "I'm reliably informed that Mr. Morris suffers from a medical condition that makes his eyes protrude like that. He couldn't *help* the way he looked at you—or anyone else, for that matter. Instead of reporting the man for being a nuisance, you ought to take pity on him."

"Oh," she said, disappointed. "Are we talking about the same passenger?"

"Mr. Morris. Mostyn Morris."

"That's the man. One hears so many things about the Welsh, you know."

"Well, I should pay no attention to them, Mrs. Anstruther. They only lead to silly misunderstandings. Since you found his company unsettling, Mr. Morris has given a firm undertaking to sit well away from you."

"I see."

"There's no call for any more anxiety."

"But I still dream about the way he stared at me."

"I can't do anything about that," he said. "And now, if you'll excuse me . . ."

"Wait," she ordered, grabbing his arm. "I have another complaint."

Taggart took a deep breath. "Not about Mr. Morris again, I trust?"

"No, it's about the lady in the single cabin next to me."

"What seems to be the trouble?"

"I hardly like to put it into words, Mr. Taggart." She looked around to make sure they were not overheard. "Illicit behavior is taking place."

"Could you be a little more specific?"

"She's been entertaining a man in there."

"There's no rule against that, Mrs. Anstruther."

"There should be," she argued. "Immorality is the first sign of a nation's decay. Look at Rome. Look at Babylon." She spoke in a whisper. "Look in the cabin next door to me. It's scandalous."

"What is?"

"The way she conducts herself. I was appalled. When I first met her, I thought she was a nice, quiet, respectable Christian lady. Last night, I saw her in her true colors."

"As what?"

"A scarlet woman!"

"I think you may be exaggerating."

"Am I?" rejoined Mrs. Anstruther. "You should have peeped out of my cabin at midnight, as I did. Do you know what I saw? A man was tapping on her door in what seemed to be a private code. The next moment, the door opened and in he went. I am talking about a spinster here, Mr. Taggart, an unmarried woman who was receiving a visitor at that hour."

"There may be an innocent explanation."

"Only one explanation comes to my mind."

"People are entitled to the benefit of the doubt."

"Oh, there was no doubt about this," she assured him. "When I put my ear to the wall of my cabin, I heard suggestive noises. Need I say more?"

"No, Mrs. Anstruther."

"She was actually *giggling*. At her age!"

"That's hardly a crime."

She pointed a finger. "What action do you intend to take?"

"None, at this stage."

"None!"

"I'm a purser," he said patiently, "not an archbishop. It's not for me to issue any moral guidelines. What people do in private is entirely their own affair."

"Even if they're not *married*?"

"Even then."

"But this happened only feet away from where I lay," she told him. "I couldn't sleep a wink all night."

"I thought you said that you dreamt about Mr. Morris's eyes."

"Did I? Well, that was later, when I dozed off out of sheer fatigue."

"If it bothers you that much, Mrs. Anstruther, I'll see if we can move you to another cabin—yet again. Leave it with me and I'll speak to the chief steward."

"Can't you move *her* to another cabin—and him?"

"Presumably he already has a cabin of his own. Who knows?" he asked, unable to resist the temptation to outrage her further. "Perhaps the lady will visit his cabin tonight. They make take it in turns to use each other's beds."

"What a grotesque idea!"

"They're breaking no law."

"They are, in my opinion."

"Passengers are allowed to invite visitors into their cabins."

"Not for *that* reason, Mr. Taggart."

"For any reason they choose," he said, keen to bring the conversation to an end. "The Cunard Line has no jurisdiction over people's private lives."

"It should have. Standards of decency must be set by someone."

"Not by us. It would be an intrusion."

"The captain will hear about this."

"You'd be wasting your time," he said. "I don't wish to upset you, Mrs. Anstruther, but the lady next to you is probably not the only single person aboard who spends the night with someone else. The likelihood is that it happens all over the vessel. Shipboard romances will always occur. We make it our business not to interfere with them. Good-bye. Enjoy your dinner."

He left her goggling with indignation, and strode briskly away.

When he was asked for his help, Dillman was happy to oblige. It showed that Inspector Redfern trusted him. Since he had an appointment with the captain, Redfern was unable to do the task himself so he asked the American to transfer the prisoner back to his cabin from the cell he had occupied all day. Dillman was pleased to be the bearer of good news. In the course of moving John Heritage back to the second-class area of the ship,

Dillman would have the opportunity to talk to him again. After reporting to the master-at-arms, he was given the key to the cell. Dillman also received a shock.

"Mr. Heritage will be grateful to move," said the master-at-arms. "That drunken old fool was getting on his nerves."

" 'Drunken old fool'?"

"A passenger in steerage. He swallowed half a bottle of whisky and thought he was the world heavyweight boxing champion. It took three men to restrain him."

Dillman was alarmed. "What's his name?"

"Daniel Webb."

"Oh dear!"

"You know him, Mr. Dillman?"

"I'm afraid so," the detective said guiltily. "I gave him the whisky."

"He shouldn't be allowed anywhere near strong drink. It's like giving a box of matches to a fire-raiser."

"Is he still locked up?"

"Yes," said the other man. "Asleep at last, snoring up to high heaven."

Dillman went off to the cells and peeped in on Daniel Webb. Curled up on his bunk, the old man was wheezing noisily. The torn coat and the bruises on his face indicated he had been in a fight. Even from a distance, Dillman could smell the whisky on him. He regretted his benevolence. In giving the old man a present, he had turned him into a menace to other passengers.

Dillman moved to the next cell and unlocked the door. Heritage jumped to his feet at once.

"What's going on?" he said.

"Inspector Redfern asked me to move you back to your cabin."

"Thank God for that!"

"I understand you had a noisy neighbor."

"Yes, Mr. Dillman," said Heritage as he stepped outside the cell. "I never understood what a roaring drunk was until I met Mr. Webb."

"He's peaceful enough now."

"You should have heard him earlier. In fact, I'm surprised that you didn't. His voice was loud enough to reach every part of the vessel. Still, at least, he explained one little mystery."

"Mystery?"

"The disappearance of Sergeant Mulcaster."

"I don't know what you mean," said Dillman, face impassive.

"It was the sergeant who was thrown overboard last night, wasn't it?"

There was a long pause. "Let's get you back to your cabin, shall we?"

By the time she arrived, almost all the other guests were there. Frank Openshaw swooped down on her to clasp her hand and shake it. He beamed with delight.

"We thought you'd forgotten us, Miss Masefield."

"I could never do that, Mr. Openshaw."

"Why stand on ceremony? I'm always 'Frank' to my friends. And I know they all laugh behind my back when I come out with my catchphrase," he added with a chuckle, "but people remember it. I get noticed."

Genevieve smiled. "Nobody could dispute that."

Taking her gently by the arm, he introduced her to some of the others in the cabin. Most of them were strangers to her but she had met Stanley Chase before. In spite of carrying too much weight, he looked very striking in his white tie and tails, and wholly at ease in the surroundings. He was in good spirits, explaining to Genevieve that he had just interested a London banker in a Regency secretaire he had in stock. Iris Cooney was also in sparkling form. For a woman with severe arthritis, she was incredibly zestful, holding a small audience spellbound with a description of a trek she had once made in Africa with her late husband.

Standing on the fringe of the group, silent and forlorn, was Pamela Clyne. She wore a nondescript dress made from a dull brownish material. Among the fashionable evening gowns of the other ladies, it rendered her almost invisible. Long gloves of black lace stretched up to her elbows. Her only concession to style was a gold brooch in the form of a leaf, pinned close to her left shoulder.

When she saw Genevieve in her full splendor, she backed away and simpered.

"Good evening, Miss Clyne," said Genevieve.

"Hello."

"Nice to see you again."

"Thank you."

A waiter brought a tray of drinks across to them and Genevieve took a glass of champagne from it. When he held the tray in front of Pamela Clyne, she shook her head.

"I've had one glass," she said apologetically. "That's all I can manage."

The waiter went off to circle the room. Genevieve sipped her drink.

"Mrs. Cooney seems to be enjoying herself," she observed.

"She always does."

"That's a lovely dress she's wearing."

"It's not as lovely as yours," said Pamela, glancing at her companion's blue velvet evening gown. It exposed both of Genevieve's shoulders. "You're so brave, Miss Masefield. I could never wear anything like that."

"Of course you could."

"I'd be too afraid people would stare at me."

"That's what they're supposed to do."

"You can carry it off."

"So could you, if you tried." Genevieve waved an arm to include the whole room. "Look around you, Miss Clyne. You're among friends. There's no need to be a shrinking violet here. Try to show off a little."

"Oh, I couldn't. It's not in my nature."

With a shy smile, she withdrew to the corner of the room. Frank Openshaw brought his wife across to be introduced to Genevieve, then left them alone together.

"My husband was right," Kitty said approvingly.

"About what?"

"About you, of course. Frank said you turn heads."

"That can be a handicap sometimes, Mrs. Openshaw."

"I wouldn't know about that. The only person whose head I ever turned was Frank Openshaw's. Not that I've regretted it for a moment," she said, looking fondly across at him. "He's been a wonderful husband. My only complaint is that he can't stop making money."

Genevieve laughed. "Most wives would think that was a virtue."

"Well, it is, I suppose. It just means that we'll never be able to retire. We have more than enough money to live on but Frank can't resist making that one extra deal."

"I had a feeling he was talking business with Mr. Chase."

"Yes," said Kitty. "He mentioned that. But there'll be others as well. There always are." She smiled tolerantly. "My husband will be getting people to invest in one of his companies until the day he dies."

"I hope that won't be for a long time yet, Mrs. Openshaw."

"So do I, believe me. My investment is in Frank himself. Oh, look," she said, seeing Pamela Clyne by the wall, "that poor lady is all on her own. Somehow, I don't think she enjoys parties. I'd better go and rescue her."

"Please do."

Genevieve sipped her champagne again and gazed around the cabin. Before she could rejoin the group encircling Mrs. Cooney, she was pounced on by Theodore Wright. He came bounding up to her with a broad grin on his face.

"I was waiting for the chance to catch you alone," he said.

"Hello, Theo." She stood back to appraise him. "Is it really you?"

"Don't say it. I look dumb in this outfit."

"Not at all. You look . . ." Genevieve groped for the appropriate word. ". . . different."

"You're just being polite."

"Perhaps it isn't altogether ideal for you."

Genevieve fought hard to control her amusement. It was the first time she had seen Wright in a white tie and tails. He looked almost ludicrous. The trousers were too short, the coat far too large, and the person inside both of them had no idea how to hold himself. A hand in his pocket, he put his weight on one leg so that he stood at a slight angle. His unruly hair had been covered in some kind of brilliantine then slicked fiercely back in the most unbecoming way. Genevieve warmed to him even more. Other people would have been embarrassed to look so out-of-place at a public function but Wright almost reveled in it. His clownish appearance did not worry him at all.

"Maybe I should have worn a red nose and a wig as well," he said.

"I think you've created enough interest as it is."

"Nobody will notice me beside you, Genevieve."

The intensity in his voice worried her slightly. "Where's your coach?" she asked. "I don't see any sign of him."

"Wes is not coming."

"Wasn't he invited?"

"Yes, but he pulled out. He's still sulking in the cabin."

"Why?"

"No reason," he said casually. He used a finger to loosen his collar. "I'm baking in this thing. It's so warm in here." He sipped his drink. "How are you, anyway?"

"I'm fine, thank you."

"Not often I catch you without Isadora clutching at your skirt."

"She is rather possessive."

"Did she tell you our secret?"

"No, Theo."

"Then I'll say nothing more."

"Why not?"

"Isadora would rather tell you herself."

"Can't you even give me a clue?"

"She'd be real upset if I did that, Genevieve."

He gazed admiringly at her again and she remembered what Wes Odell had said to her. According to the coach, Wright was more than interested in her. The look in his eye seemed to confirm that. He moved in closer to her.

"What kind of a day have you had?" he asked.

"A very pleasant one."

"Anything special happen?"

"Not that I can think of, Theo."

"No surprises?" he probed. "No unexpected gifts?"

Genevieve was taken aback. Realizing at once that he had sent the flowers, she did not know quite how to react. Too gushing a response would encourage him, while too formal a reply might wound his feelings. She opted for a controlled enthusiasm.

"The flowers were gorgeous," she said. "Thank you, Theo."

"Did you guess they came from me?"

"Eventually."

" 'Eventually'?" he echoed, pretending to be upset. "How many other guys would think of sending you flowers like that? I got the idea from this woman up on deck. She was wearing this hat that was covered in flowers." He leaned in even closer. "I was hoping you'd guess right away who it was. Knowing it was me, you'd understand why I didn't need a card."

"Well, no. To be honest, I was rather puzzled about that."

"The flowers said it all, didn't they?"

"I suppose so."

"There you are, then."

She felt uncomfortable. "Does Wes know that you sent them?"

"Of course not," he replied. "He'd tear his hair out if he did."

"Then don't you think it was a little unwise? . . . Don't misunderstand me," she went on. "I was thrilled to receive them and they fill my cabin with the most lovely scent, but I don't want to cause a rift between you and your coach."

"Forget him."

"It's difficult to do that."

"Wes is not here now, is he? So—talk to me."

"That's what I am doing, Theo."

"No, you're not, Genevieve. You're holding out on me."

"I don't mean to."

"Then give me a proper answer," he insisted. "What did you think when those flowers were delivered to you?"

"I thought it was a lovely gesture and I'm very grateful to you."

He became serious. "It was more than a gesture."

Genevieve felt uneasy. Instead of being able to relax in congenial company, she had been put on the spot by a direct question from an admirer. She began to wish that it had been Cecilia Robart who sent the bouquet, not Theodore Wright. The flowers were an indication of his commitment. Staring intently into her eyes, he was hoping for a positive response. Genevieve was glad when Frank Openshaw came to her rescue.

"Hello, Theo," he said, clapping the cyclist on the shoulder. "You're the only person in the room who isn't drinking this wonderful champagne. I know you're in training but can't you let yourself go just a little?"

"I'm afraid not."

"Pity. Anyway, come on, lad. Be fair. We can't have you monopolizing the lovely Miss Masefield like this. You have to share her with the rest of us."

"Sure," said Wright, forcing a smile.

Genevieve breathed a quiet sigh of relief.

The purser was heartened by his stroll around the upper decks of the *Caronia*. Everything was under control. The passengers were happy, the crew was pleasant and efficient, the ship was maintaining good speed, and the general atmosphere was buoyant. Apart from the glaring exception of Mrs. Anstruther, everyone seemed to be content. None of them knew about the callous murder that had occurred on the previous night. Sergeant Mulcaster may have caused a splash in the ocean but his death did not even create a minor ripple among the passengers on the *Caronia*. Paul Taggart was reassured. For the first time that day, he actually began to relax.

Arriving back at his office, he found he had a visitor waiting for him.

"Ah," said Inspector Redfern, "I was hoping to catch you."

"Did you see the skipper?"

"Yes."

"How did you get on with him?"

"Not all that well, actually. Captain Warr can be very prickly."

"He's fine when you get to know him, Inspector."

"We didn't meet in the best of circumstances," admitted Redfern. "Having to report the murder of a colleague is not the most enjoyable duty. The captain was sympathetic but he was also critical. He came very close to blaming me for not keeping a closer eye on my sergeant."

"You weren't to know he was in danger," Taggart said reasonably. "Besides, you expect a trained policeman like that to look after himself. It's not your job."

"I think Captain Warr came to appreciate that eventually. And, in fairness, he was very sorry about the injuries I'd sustained."

"Are you feeling better now, Inspector?"

"Much better, thanks. At least, I was until I spoke with Mr. Dillman."

"Dillman?"

"I'd asked him to say nothing about last night to anyone at all, especially to the prisoners. The captain was equally anxious to keep this whole thing quiet. He wants us to catch the killer before anyone else even realizes there was a murder."

"That's my view as well."

"We're too late, Mr. Taggart."

"Why?"

"The cat's already out of the bag. John Heritage knows the truth."

"I can't believe Mr. Dillman told him."

"He fears that he did—indirectly. Do you recall Daniel Webb?"

"Vividly. My office stank for an hour after he'd left."

"Apparently Mr. Dillman bought him a bottle of whisky in order to coax evidence out of him. Webb went off to celebrate," said Redfern. "Drank half the bottle and got into a brawl with the other people in his cabin. Three members of the crew had to manhandle him. When they put him in the cell next to Heritage, he spilled the beans."

"But we warned him to keep his mouth shut."

"The whisky loosened his tongue, I'm afraid."

"Wait a minute," said Taggart. "All that Webb saw was someone being heaved over the side of the vessel. He had no idea who it was and, in the interests of secrecy, we took great care not to tell him Sergeant Mulcaster's name. How could he possibly have passed it on to Mr. Heritage?"

"He didn't. He simply boasted that he was a star witness in a murder case."

"I get it."

"When he described what he saw, Heritage put two and two together."

"We should have bound and gagged the old idiot!"

"You can see why Mr. Dillman blames himself," said Redfern. "If he hadn't given him that bottle of whisky, none of this would have happened. Because he did, we had a fight in steerage, extensive damage to a cabin, and such foul language from Daniel Webb that the air turned blue."

Taggart fumed. "Wait till I get my hands on him!"

"You'll have to wait your turn. Mr. Dillman is first in the queue."

Daniel Webb had drifted off into a deep sleep. Even when he rolled over and fell off his bunk, he did not rouse from his slumbers. Dillman had to shake him unmercifully before he came awake. The old man got one eye half open.

"Where am I?" he groaned.

"Where you should be, Mr. Webb," said Dillman. "Behind bars."

"Eh?"

"You got drunk."

"No, not me, sir. I never get drunk."

"I can still smell the whisky on you."

"Oh, yes. That was good stuff. I enjoyed it."

"Too well, it seems."

Taking him by the scruff of his neck, Dillman hauled Webb upright then sat him on the edge of the bunk. The sudden movement set off a series of aches and pains. Clutching his head in both hands, the old man winced aloud. He then started to massage limbs that were stiff from their time on the hard floor of the cell. Dillman showed no compassion.

"You forgot your promise, didn't you?" he said.

Webb blinked in agony. "My head is splitting."

"What do you expect if you drink all that whisky?"

"They tried to take the bottle off me—those Yankee bastards in my cabin."

"According to them, you swung it like a club. Mr. Miller had to have six stitches put into a head wound that you gave him. I've just come from him and his story is very different from yours, Mr. Webb."

"Then he's lying!"

"He and his friends were sober. You were drunk. I know who I believe."

"Trust you to side with those rotten Yanks!"

Dillman knelt down close to him. "We warned you, didn't we?" he said into the old man's face. "The purser and I emphasized that you were not to breathe a word of what you saw to anybody."

"And I didn't—I swear it!"

"Then how did Mr. Heritage come to hear about it?"

"Who?"

"John Heritage. The man in the next cell to you."

"Is that his name? He didn't tell me."

"You did all the talking, Mr. Webb, that's why. You opened your big mouth and told him everything you saw on the main deck last night."

Webb was confused. "Did I?"

"You know you did. Because of that, I'm going to recommend that we keep you locked up in here for the rest of the voyage."

"Don't do that!"

"You can't be trusted," said Dillman. "If we let you out of here, everyone on the ship will soon know what happened. We can't take that chance."

"I give you my word, Mr. Dillman!" the old man vowed.

"You gave it to us once before."

"This time I'll keep it."

"Until you get the next drink inside you."

"But you told me that I helped you."

"You did, Mr. Webb. I admit that freely. You gave us valuable evidence and we're grateful to you. But," Dillman said firmly, "this latest escapade of yours has exhausted our gratitude."

"Let me out, sir," implored Webb. "I'll behave. Honest to God."

"Your promises are worthless."

"I can't spend the rest of the trip in here."

"Oh yes you can."

"But there's days to go yet."

"You should have thought of that before you guzzled all that whisky."

"I was thirsty."

"Well, you won't get any alcohol in here," warned Dillman, standing up. "You know what I think about you. I daresay the purser will want to have his say as well."

"Hang on, sir. Don't leave me!"

"Good-bye, Mr. Webb."

"But I can help you again!" urged the old man.

"Only if you shut up for the rest of the voyage."

"I'm serious, Mr. Dillman. You were good to me so I owes

you a favor. It's about that bloke who's locked up next door."

"We've moved him."

"I didn't do all the talking," explained Webb, standing up. "He had his twopenny's worth as well. Moaning hard, he was. I could tell he'd never been locked up before. So I let him ramble on."

Dillman was interested. "And?"

"He said all the usual things. How he'd been wrongly accused and how he'd been threatened by the coppers. Funny thing was, he never told me what they arrested him for. But I guessed, of course," said Webb, with a cackle. "You can't fool an old lag like me, sir. I've listened to a thousand hard-luck stories in prison. They've got him for murder, haven't they?"

"What did Mr. Heritage tell you?"

"Am I right?"

"That's immaterial."

"I never makes mistakes about things like this," boasted Webb. "That's why I can help you, see? When you've spent as much time in a prison cell as I have, you learn to weigh people up. You always know when they're lying."

"And is that what Mr. Heritage was doing?" asked Dillman.

"Oh, yes. He told me a dozen times that he was innocent."

"Did you believe him?"

"No, sir," declared the other. "I can tell you now. That man is guilty."

Isadora Singleton was waiting for her outside the door of the dining room. As soon as Genevieve appeared, Isadora dashed across to meet her. Wearing a striking dress of emerald-green velvet, Isadora also had put on more jewelry than ever before. A visit to the hairdressing salon had improved her appearance as well. It was as if she had made a special effort to be at her best. Contriving to look older and more poised, she nevertheless spoke with the same girlish enthusiasm.

"I've been dying to see you, Genevieve," she said.

"Have you?"

"Where have you been?"

"Mr. Openshaw invited me to join some other guests for a drink."

"You should have told me. I could have sneaked in as well."

"You'd have caused quite a stir, if you had done," said Genevieve, running an eye over her. "You look gorgeous, Isadora. So grown-up."

"Do you think so?"

"Every man in the room will be looking at you."

"There's only one that I'm interested in."

Before Isadora could explain what she meant, Cecilia Robart approached with two other people. Genevieve noticed that Mrs. Robart's gold earrings were in place. Her pearl necklace had now been replaced by a beautiful diamond pendant. Beside her were a tall man with an air of distinction about him and a stately woman with a gracious smile.

"Good evening, Miss Masefield," said Mrs. Robart. "Allow me to introduce Sir Harry and Lady Fox-Holroyd."

Genevieve went through the social niceties. Isadora had already met Sir Harry and his wife but she had not spoken to Cecilia Robart before. While they chatted briefly, Sir Harry gazed in approval at Isadora.

"May I say how charming you look this evening, Miss Singleton?" he said.

"Thank you, Sir Harry," she replied.

"You will certainly make your mark in English society."

"Isadora would make her mark anywhere," said Genevieve.

"How true, Miss Masefield! She caught Lord Eddington's eye, I know that. He found Miss Singleton quite enchanting."

"Is it your first visit to England?" asked Mrs. Robart.

"Yes," said Isadora.

"Well, I hope that you have a wonderful time."

"I'm having one already, Mrs. Robart."

"Good show!" said Sir Harry.

He escorted his wife into the dining room, with Cecilia Robart on his other side.

"That was the lady we saw in the lounge one day," Isadora noted.

"That's right," said Genevieve.

"You couldn't remember her name then, but she seemed to know you."

"Don't worry about her, Isadora," said Genevieve, eager to keep away from the subject of Cecilia Robart. "I want to know this secret."

" 'Secret'?"

"Theo Wright wouldn't tell me what it was."

Isadora flushed slightly. "You spoken to Theo?"

"He was in the Openshaws' cabin this evening."

"What did he say?"

"Nothing beyond the fact that you had a secret."

"More than one, Genevieve." She giggled again. "Shall I tell you what they are?"

"Please."

"Promise you won't say anything to Mother and Father."

Genevieve raised a quizzical eyebrow. "Those kinds of secrets, are they? You can trust me, Isadora. I won't say a word."

"My parents would be so *angry* with me."

"Why? What have you done?"

"I'm learning to ride a bicycle."

"Here on the ship?"

"Yes," said Isadora. "Theo is teaching me."

"I can see why your parents might not be too pleased."

"They're such terrible snobs. But I'm not. I think Theo is marvelous, don't you?"

"Yes," Genevieve said guardedly. "He's a remarkable young man. But how can he teach you to ride without your parents' knowing about it?"

"His bicycles are kept in a storeroom. We were in there alone together. Theo let me get used to sitting on the bicycle while he held it for me. Tomorrow he's going to find somewhere to push me along. I'm so excited."

"Didn't you learn to ride as a girl?"

"No, Genevieve. Mother thought it was not ladylike."

"Wait until she sees you hurtling past on a racing machine."

"That's the amazing thing," said Isadora.

"What is?"

"I'm being taught by the best cyclist in America."

"It's what they call a master class."

"Did you know that Theo designs bicycles?"

"No, I didn't."

"That's what he hopes to do when he retires from professional racing," explained Isadora. "He told me all about it. He helped to build those two bicycles in the storeroom. Wes Odell knows how to coach him but it's Theo who's the expert on the machines themselves. He loves them."

"I'm glad you mentioned Mr. Odell," said Genevieve. "Your parents are not the only ones who wouldn't approve. Theo's coach would be even more upset. Take care, Isadora. If he finds out, there could be trouble."

"Theo warned me about that. It's all part of the fun.'

" 'Fun'?"

"Keeping it from everyone else—except you, that is."

"You said you had two secrets."

Isadora nodded, then waited as more guests walked past them. Her eyes sparkled.

"I wouldn't tell this to anybody but you, Genevieve."

"Then I'm flattered."

"It's very early to say this, I know, but I do so want you to be pleased for me."

"I'm pleased with anything that makes you happy, Isadora."

"It's so strange. I've known him such a short time."

"Are we still talking about Theo?"

"Who else?" asked Isadora, face shining. "I think I'm in love."

TWELVE

Under any other circumstances Dillman would have thoroughly enjoyed his dinner that evening. The meal was delicious, the service was exceptional, and the atmosphere convivial. It was more like a banquet for old friends than a gathering of people who had only met each other a few days earlier. In order to keep his head clear, he allowed himself only one half-glass of wine at the table. His dinner companions found no such need to stint themselves. Seated opposite him, Frank Openshaw noticed how abstemious he was.

"Come on, Mr. Dillman," he urged. "Drink up. You've paid for it."

Dillman tapped his glass. "This is plenty for me."

"Get your money's worth—that's what I always say."

"Frank!" chided his wife.

"It's true, Kitty. I give good value myself and I expect it in return. I'm sure that Mr. Chase works on the same basis," said Openshaw, nodding at Stanley Chase, who sat beside Dillman. "Am I right?"

"Yes, indeed," said Chase. "That's why doing business in America is always such a pleasant experience. The sort of people

I deal with never haggle or complain. If they make up their mind they want something, they pay up willingly. I don't have to *sell* my antiques in the way that I do in England. They sell themselves."

"We have some antique porcelain," said Kitty.

"Who was the manufacturer?"

"Oh, I don't know, Mr. Chase. We bought it because I liked the pattern."

"And we paid a tidy sum for it," Openshaw said proudly, "so we knew it was the genuine article. But you're right about America, Mr. Chase. They have the right attitude to brass. They put it first in their calculations."

"I'm not sure that's altogether laudable," opined Dillman.

"Nor am I," said Kitty. "There's other things in life than money."

"But they all have a price tag on them, Mrs. Openshaw," said Chase.

"Not necessarily," argued Dillman. "Look around the room. The thing that strikes you most is that everyone seems so congenial. You sense a communal friendship. That's something you can't put a price on."

"I disagree," said Openshaw.

"Mr. Dillman is talking sense," declared Kitty.

"With respect, my love, he isn't."

"True friendship is better than all the money in the world."

Chase sighed. "If only that were true, Mrs. Openshaw."

"It is where we come from," she replied.

"Only up to a point, Kitty," corrected her husband. "Even in Yorkshire, a bit of brass helps you to buy the right friends. It's the same here. We all get on with each other like house on fire but only because we can afford to sail first-class. It's like paying a subscription to an exclusive club. You're judged by the size of your wallet."

Kitty bridled slightly. "Don't be so crude, Frank."

"I'm only being honest."

"And it does you credit, Mr. Openshaw," Dillman said pleasantly. "There's some truth in what you say but I still contend that not everything is available for purchase. And I know from experience that the friends you make in business are not quite the same as those you befriend for the simple reason that you like them."

"That's a fair point, Mr. Dillman," said Chase. "I keep on the closest terms with my clients but I don't think I'd invite them into my home. My best friends are those who've been around for years."

"It sounds to me," Openshaw said contentiously, "as if Mr. Dillman is not a true American. All his fellow countrymen take the view that the dollar is king."

"*President* maybe," said Dillman with a smile. "We're a republic."

"Now, that's one thing I do criticize."

"So do I," added Kitty, clicking her tongue. "We have such a lovely Royal Family in England. Don't you agree, Mr. Chase?"

"Naturally, Mrs. Openshaw. My profession is determined by royal blood. I sell Queen Anne chairs, Georgian tallboys, Regency tables, Victorian desks, and so on. It's left me with a deep respect for the monarchy."

Kitty smiled fondly. "I adore King Edward."

"He's very popular over here as well," said Dillman. "Americans—on the East Coast particularly—take a keen interest in the activities of your royal family. The big difference, of course, is that our president wields enormous power. King Edward doesn't. He's only a constitutional monarch."

"We still look up to him," said Openshaw loyally, "and he's a damn sight more use than some of those fools we send to the Houses of Parliament."

The conversation bubbled happily throughout the meal. Dillman managed to take part in it while allowing his mind to grapple with the problems confronting him. The murder of Sergeant Mulcaster took priority but he was also very concerned about the possibility that drugs were being smuggled. Having seen the destructive effects of certain narcotics, he had a deep loathing for those who created the addicts. Somewhere on the ship—perhaps even in this room—was a drug peddler. There was an additional worry: Though the presence of a pickpocket in second class was a minor annoyance, it had to be addressed.

When dessert was over, Dillman did not linger for cheese and biscuits. Excusing himself from the table, he headed for the exit. On the way there, he passed the table where Genevieve Masefield was dining with the Singleton family. He gave her a covert signal to indicate he wished to meet her later on in her cabin.

Dillman was not the first person to leave. When he reached the door, he caught sight of Ramsey Leach ahead of him and hurried to catch up with the undertaker.

"Another splendid meal, Mr. Leach," he remarked, falling in beside him.

"Oh yes, Mr. Dillman," said Leach. "Rather too splendid for me."

"In what way?"

"A stomach ulcer. I'm not permitted to indulge."

"Yes, I noticed how little you were eating the other day," Dillman recalled with a grin. "I put it down to the proximity of Frank Openshaw."

Leach smiled. "He did tend to take away my appetite on that occasion."

"Yet you still ate twice as much as Theo Wright."

"Who?"

"Haven't you met our cycling champion?"

"I'm afraid not, Mr. Dillman."

"Theo is a character. You're bound to see him about. In fact, you could watch him in action if you're still awake at midnight."

"Oh, that's well past my bedtime."

"Most people have turned in by then," said Dillman. "That's why Theo is able to ride on the boat deck without knocking anyone over. He's in training for a big race in France. His coach has put him on a rigid diet."

"Poor fellow! It must be agony watching everyone else eating what they wish."

"Being a champion involves sacrifices."

"So it seems."

"Theo will be in the saddle every day of the voyage."

"Then I wish him well," said Leach with a lugubrious smile. "All I know about cyclists is that I've buried too many of them. They were involved in fatal accidents with motor vehicles."

"That won't happen to Theo. During this race in France, apparently, they close the roads for the riders. Sounds like a sensible precaution." They paused outside the lounge. "Are you glad to be going back to England?"

"Very much so, Mr. Dillman."

"I hope that's no reflection on my country."

"Not at all. My stay there was . . . rather special."

"Did you buy any souvenirs?"

"Souvenirs?"

"Things to remind you of your visit," said Dillman. "In the past, I've seen English passengers boarding in New York with everything from replicas of the Statue of Liberty to huge totem poles. What about your professional interest? Did you see anything you were tempted to buy?"

"Nothing at all, Mr. Dillman."

"That's odd. Most people want to take something back with them."

"Then I must be the exception to the rule," Leach said quietly.

"You're content with happy memories, are you?"

"Those are always the best things to carry home with you." He forced a smile. "Do excuse me. I have to go, I'm afraid."

"Good-bye, Mr. Leach."

Dillman watched him walk away, wondering why a man he had seen leaving his cabin at midnight claimed to retire to bed early every night. Leach had left him with another question burning into his brain. Since he was shipping an expensive funeral casket back to England, why had the undertaker claimed he had bought nothing at all during his vacation?

Inspector Redfern had just finished eating his dinner off a tray when the purser arrived. Paul Taggart looked down guiltily at the empty plate.

"I feel that Cunard hospitality has let you down badly, Inspector."

"Not at all, Mr. Taggart. It was a good meal."

"But you shouldn't be eating it in your cabin like this. We have an excellent dining room. It seems a shame that you can't enjoy the facilities of the vessel."

"Somebody has to keep an eye on the prisoners."

"They're hardly likely to escape," said Taggart.

"I know, but the very fact that they're on either side of me makes me feel on duty. It was different when Ronnie—Sergeant Mulcaster—was here. We could take it in turns to stretch our legs and get some fresh air."

"I suppose so. Well, I've just come from Daniel Webb."

"What did he have to say for himself?"

"I didn't give him the chance to say anything, Inspector. I gave him a real roasting for opening his mouth that way. By the time I left him, he looked well and truly contrite."

"So he should."

"Mr. Dillman had a go at him earlier. He shook the old man up as well."

"How many other people did he tell about what he saw on deck last night?"

"None, he claims."

"Do you believe him?"

"Yes, Inspector," said Taggart. "When he left my office, all he could think of doing was to sit alone in his cabin with that bottle of whisky. He didn't talk to anyone until the people he's sharing with came in."

"That's when he started the fight."

"One decrepit old Englishman against three sturdy Americans."

Redfern grinned. "Sounds like the War of Independence."

"I'd admire his courage, if it wasn't for the fact that it came out of a whisky bottle. Anyway," he went on, "we can feel safe that he told nobody but Mr. Heritage about being a key witness."

"Let's keep it that way."

Taggart was decisive. "We will, Inspector."

"What about the stewards?" asked Redfern. "The ones who helped in the search?"

"They were chosen for their discretion. All they were told was that a passenger had gone astray and that they were to check every cabin to make sure it was only occupied by those whose names were listed."

"I thought you said they searched for the guns as well."

"That was later, Inspector," Taggart explained. "While lunch was being served. Mr. Dillman organized that. He tried to kill two birds with one stone."

"In what way?"

"As well as looking for the missing weapons, he and his team kept an eye open for a cache of drugs we believe is being smuggled into England. We had a tip-off that cocaine and heroin were on board."

"In what sort of quantities?"

"We'll know that when we find them," said Taggart. "I suspect there may be substantial amounts. That's why we're so keen to locate them."

"Any luck so far?"

"None, Inspector."

"It's a pity Sergeant Mulcaster isn't here."

"Why?"

"He had a particular hatred for drug peddlers," said Redfern. "He thought they were another species of murderer. The son of a friend of his became an addict. He was only in his twenties. The sergeant said it was horrible to see the state he was in when they found him. He'd died of an overdose."

"It happens all too often, I fear."

"That's why Sergeant Mulcaster swore to hunt down every

drug peddler he could find. He had a nose for them. You could have used his help."

"He was otherwise employed, Inspector."

"Not anymore, alas . . ." Redfern gritted his teeth. "I want his killer, Mr. Taggart."

"We all do, Inspector."

"I want to catch the bastard and take him back to be hanged. To do that, of course, I'll have to rely heavily on Mr. Dillman."

"Don't forget his assistant," said Taggart. "In her own way, Genevieve Masefield is a very formidable lady. She and George Dillman make a good team. They'll get him."

Throughout dinner, Genevieve Masefield was conscious of his attention. She could not see Theodore Wright but she knew he was watching her. At the end of the meal, much to the disappointment of Isadora Singleton, she excused herself from the table on the grounds that she needed an early night. When her young friend objected, Isadora was scolded politely by her parents. Genevieve gave her a reassuring smile before making her way to the door. Wright was lurking in readiness, however.

"Hold on!" he said, intercepting her as she left the room. "What's the rush?"

"I feel rather tired, Theo."

"But I'm the one who has to be in the saddle at midnight."

"I don't know where you get the stamina," she said.

"Watch me on deck and you may find out."

"I'm afraid I'll be fast asleep by then."

"Then let's have a chat in the lounge," he suggested. "You never did get around to answering that question I put to you. About the flowers."

"They were lovely, Theo. I told you that."

He grinned amiably. "See? You're ducking out of it again, aren't you?"

"Maybe this is not the best time to discuss it," said Genevieve.

"I can't think of a better one. Why don't we talk over a drink in the lounge?"

"Because you're not touching a drop of alcohol, that's why," Wes Odell said harshly, interrupting the conversation. "You're in training, Theo."

"I know, I know," he said irritably.

"You need to let your food go down before we start work again."

"That's not for over two hours, Wes."

"You can rest in the cabin."

"I'd rather be with Genevieve in the lounge."

"Perhaps it's better if you do as Mr. Odell advises," said Genevieve. "It's been a long day for me. I really would like an early night."

Odell was blunt. "You heard the lady, Theo."

"Keep out of this," said Wright.

"Let's go, son."

"No, Wes. Stop treating me like a kid, will you?"

"My job is to keep you on the rails."

"I seem to be in the way," Genevieve said apologetically. "Please excuse me."

"Wait!" exclaimed Wright, holding her wrist.

"Let the lady go, Wes," ordered his coach. "This is between me and you."

"It isn't, Wes. It's between me and Genevieve. So leave us alone."

"Not when you're in this state. Now, calm down."

"This is private."

Odell turned on Genevieve. "I blame you for this, Miss Masefield."

"I'd rather not be involved at all," she said, detaching her wrist from Wright's grip. "We're creating a scene here. That won't benefit any of us."

"Do as I said," warned Odell. "Keep away from him."

Wright was outraged. "You said *that* to Genevieve?"

"It was only for your own good, Theo."

"You dared to tell her to keep away from me?"

"Look," said Genevieve, "I'm caught in the middle here and

it's not a pleasant place to be. I'm sorry for any trouble I've unwittingly caused but I do think it's best if I leave. Good night."

She walked purposefully away and was relieved that Wright did not follow her. He was too busy arguing loudly with his coach. Genevieve did not relish the idea of meeting either of them the next day. When she got back to her cabin, she closed the door behind her and sat down to reflect on the evening. An hour slipped by until she heard a knock on the door. Fearing that it might be Wright, she was a little nervous.

"Yes?" she called.

"It's me," said Dillman.

"Thank heaven!"

She let him in and kissed him gratefully on the cheek. He smiled warmly.

"What was that for, Genevieve?"

"Being you," she said. "To be more exact, for *not* being someone else."

"Such as?"

"I'll tell you later, George. It's personal. It can wait until we've got the important things out of the way. Take a seat."

"Thanks," he said, lowering himself onto a chair. She sat opposite him. "How did you get on with Carrie Peterson?"

"I can't really say."

"Why not?"

"Because she's something of an enigma," replied Genevieve. "I believed most of what she told me because it was patently true, but I never felt she trusted me. It made her very defensive. She withdrew into herself."

"That's understandable, I suppose."

"She's obviously under immense strain."

"Tell me what happened."

Genevieve's account was substantially the one she had given to Inspector Redfern but she added more comment this time. Dillman found it absorbing.

"What's your feeling, Genevieve?" he asked. "Accomplice or victim?"

"I don't see her as an accomplice somehow. And yet, I wouldn't say she was a victim, either. According to her, John Heritage would have been quite incapable of committing murder. But then," she added, "Carrie Peterson is so deeply in love with him that she's blind to his faults."

"Killing his wife constitutes rather more than a fault."

"If he *was* responsible."

"Daniel Webb assures me that he was."

"The old man who came forward as a witness?"

"That's the fellow, Genevieve."

"Why did you ask his opinion?"

"I didn't," said Dillman. "He gave it voluntarily."

It was his turn to talk about an interview with a prisoner. After describing what he had learned from Heritage, he explained why Daniel Webb, a seasoned criminal, had finished up in the adjoining cell. Dillman was rueful.

"It was so stupid of me to buy him that whisky," he said.

"It did the trick, George. It gave us our first vital clue."

"I do wish we had a more reliable witness than Webb."

"Only a drunken man would have been foolish to go out on deck in that weather last night," she pointed out. "That's why the killer felt safe enough to knock Sergeant Mulcaster unconscious before pushing him over the side of the ship. He was banking on the fact that nobody was watching."

"Quite."

"What interests me is Daniel Webb's assessment of the prisoner."

"He was adamant that Heritage was guilty," said Dillman. "How much weight we can attach to his opinion, I don't know. He was still drunk when he talked to Heritage and he was desperate to curry favor with me so that I'd get him released. He's a scheming devil, Genevieve. He may just have been telling me what he thought I wanted to hear."

"You say he has a prison record?"

"Quite a long one, it seems. Minor offenses, for the most part, though he did take part in a bungled bank robbery. He claims that taught him a lesson. Deciding to turn over a new leaf, he sailed for New York." Dillman pulled a face. "He was surprised when the immigration authorities didn't feel that he'd be a model American citizen."

"It was brave of him to try, at his age."

"Yes, Genevieve. But it soured him against my countrymen. That's why he swung the whisky bottle at Ben Miller. Webb attacked the Carver brothers as well. They're only crime was being American. I suppose I should be grateful he didn't attack me."

"You were his guardian angel, George. You gave him the whisky."

"Don't remind me."

"What will happen to him?"

"The purser is going to let him cool his heels in that cell overnight. Mr. Taggart will review the situation in the morning. We must do the same."

Genevieve sighed. "There's so much to review."

"Two murder cases on the same ship."

"Fortunately, one of the crimes took place on dry land. Strictly speaking, it's not our responsibility," she said, "but I have to admit, it intrigues me. The problem is that we've only seen the prisoners separately. I'd like to meet them together."

"The inspector wouldn't permit it. Putting all that aside," Dillman resumed, "tell me why I was given such a lovely welcome when I came in here. You said it was a personal matter. That usually means an unwanted suitor."

"Theo Wright."

"Really? How serious is it?"

"Too serious, George."

"Has he made any kind of declaration?"

"He sent me those flowers," she said, indicating the vase. "There was no card. Theo hoped that I'd guess it was him at once. He cornered me twice this evening to ask me, in effect, if I feel the same way about him. It was embarrassing."

"Can I help in any way?"

"No, it's something I must handle for myself. I've had a lot of practice at keeping other suitors at arm's length, but it's more awkward in Theo's case. I like him. And I was insulted when that surly coach of his ordered me to stop bothering him." Genevieve was angry. "He made it sound as if it was *my* fault."

"Ignore him. Odell has no right to talk to you that way."

"I made that very clear to him, George. What he doesn't realize is that there's another complication for Theo." She looked him in the eye. "This is confidential, mind. Odell must never find out."

"Find out what?"

"Theo is teaching Isadora Singleton to ride a bicycle."

"One of his racing machines?"

"Apparently. Her parents would go berserk if they knew about it. They're taking Isadora to England to dangle her like a carrot in front of the eyes of society."

"I know. The girl is a dollar princess."

"That's what the parents may imagine but Isadora has other ideas. Theo Wright is not just giving her secret riding lessons," said Genevieve. "Without knowing it, he's made her fall in love with him."

The bitter argument with his coach had left Theodore Wright feeling hurt and resentful. He had been forced to back down. Wes Odell had reminded him that his success as a professional cyclist was largely due to expert coaching, and that Theo Wright would never—left to himself—have been able to travel first-class on a Cunard liner. There was sufficient truth in the charge to wound the cyclist deeply, but what upset him even more was Odell's claim that Genevieve Masefield was beyond Theo's reach in every way. Theodore Wright refused to accept that he was socially inferior. In his view, his glittering career in the saddle gave him the credentials to consort with anyone, and he sensed

Genevieve appreciated that. Theo was enraged to hear that his coach had actually warned her to stay away from him, and he was anxious to apologize to her. It seemed to explain her guarded behavior toward him. The one shred of consolation he had drawn from it all was that Genevieve had been thrilled to receive his flowers. His romantic gesture had not been rebuffed.

That thought was uppermost in his mind as he rode around the boat deck with an almost manic dedication. The pedals turned with mechanical precision, the wheels whirred, and the tires whistled on the wooden slats. He was determined to prove to his coach that what he did in his private life would not impair his ability as a cyclist. As he shot past Odell for the fiftieth time, the coach was duly astonished by the speed Wright was maintaining. Fury had put more power into Wright's legs. He was pushing himself as hard as he would in a race, albeit restricted by the limited space.

A handful of spectators had come to watch the training run. Scattered around the boat deck, they stood well out of the way so that Wright could ride unimpeded. One of them stayed alone in the shadows, so nobody could see her. Isadora Singleton was enthralled. She had never seen anyone ride a bicycle so fast or with such consummate skill. Wright picked his way past obstacles as if they were not even there. Isadora was also exhilarated by her own daring, having sneaked out of her cabin when her parents had retired to bed. It gave her an extra tingle of excitement. She stared in wonder at Wright every time he went past. In his vest and knee-length shorts, he was an arresting sight. She could see the muscles in his legs and shoulders. The combination of grace and strength was awe-inspiring. Isadora could have watched all night.

When the training session was over, Wright sat up in the saddle and freewheeled up to his coach. The cyclist was sweating profusely from his exertions.

"How was I?" he asked.

"Pretty good."

"Is that all?"

"No," replied Odell, glancing at his stopwatch. "You were terrific and you know it. You were the Theo Wright of old. Now, put this around you," he went on, slipping a towel around the cyclist's shoulders. "You mustn't catch a chill."

"We need to talk, Wes. About things."

"In the morning."

"This is important."

"So is giving you your rubdown," said Odell. "Come on. I've made some more of that ointment for you. That's what you need now. Forget our differences for one night. It will all look very different in the morning."

"Not to me," said Wright.

When he left Genevieve Masefield's cabin, Dillman did not return to his own. Instead he trawled casually through the lounges in every part of the ship. They were still quite full when he got there and he made sure he studied all the faces with care. One of them, he believed, might belong to the killer of Sergeant Mulcaster. Initially, he had ruled out third class and steerage because passengers there were confined to their own congested areas and unlikely to venture anywhere near the cabin occupied by the Scotland Yard detectives. His experience with Daniel Webb had compelled him to revise that judgment. The old man had shown himself capable of surprising violence; those younger and fitter than him could be lethal. Where better to hide on the *Caronia* than in one of the crowded lower decks? Someone with a grudge against Sergeant Mulcaster might well be traveling in the cheapest section of the vessel.

Dillman's problem was that he stood out. In the first- and second-class lounges, a handsome man in evening dress was a common sight. Among steerage passengers, he was all too prominent and more than one sneering voice could be overheard complaining that he was a toff from first class who had come down to stare at them as if they were wild animals in a zoo. Dillman persisted nevertheless, getting a feel of the place and noting the privations they had to endure. His tour of inspection was long and interesting but it yielded no positive results. It was past midnight when he made his way back up through the various levels, pausing on the promenade deck to gaze out at the sea. Illumined by a half-moon, the ocean was an eternity of restless whitecapped waves. Somewhere in that eternity was the man he had first seen boarding the ship with a shotgun under his arm. Sergeant Mulcaster would not require his weapon now.

Dillman stayed long enough to review what little evidence they had, then moved off in the direction of his cabin. As he turned into the long corridor, he heard a door opening at the far end and stepped smartly back around the corner and into a recess. Footsteps came toward him and, without even looking, he felt certain he knew their owner. It was Ramsey Leach. Carrying the same small case as before, he crept furtively along the corridor and turned left, not realizing that Dillman was lurking in a recess only a few yards behind him. After giving Leach time to reach the end of the passageway, the detective came out of his hiding place and gave pursuit. As soon as Leach went around the next corner, Dillman stretched his legs to increase speed. He reached the corner just in time. When he peered around it, he saw Leach disappearing swiftly into a cabin.

So much, Dillman thought, for the undertaker's claim that he went early to bed. The impression he had given of being without any friends on the ship was also false. Someone had let him in as if he was expected. But the real question hung over the contents of the funeral casket stored below. Dillman wished he could take a closer look at it. Meanwhile he strolled quietly along the corridor until he came to the cabin Leach had entered. After memorizing its number, he went off to bed.

In spite of her late night, Isadora Singleton was up early to watch Theo in action once again. Blinking in the morning sunlight, she stood on the boat deck while he kept to his punishing schedule. She could admire his lithe body and his sense of rhythm more easily now that she could see them properly. Isadora made sure she would not be spotted by Wes Odell, but her feelings for Wright were too strong to be denied. She wanted him to know that she was there to support him. Waiting until he approached yet again, she stepped out to give him a wave. Wright grinned in surprise and blew her a cheerful kiss as he surged past.

Isadora was overjoyed. Her face was still flushed with pleasure when she let herself into her cabin.

Hands on her hips, Maria Singleton was waiting for her. She glared at her daughter. "Where on earth have you been, Isadora?" she demanded.

"I went for a walk."

"This early? It's not even seven o'clock yet."

"I couldn't sleep, Mother."

"Then you should have read a book or something."

"I wasn't in the mood."

"We can't have you wandering around the ship alone at this hour. You're allowed far too much license. I'll speak to your father about it."

"Mother!" protested Isadora.

"What will people think about us?" Maria said in exasperation. "We have to create a good impression on people, don't you understand? Lord and Lady Eddington have been kind enough to take an interest in us. We must do nothing to jeopardize that, Isadora. They have to be *cultivated*. They are our door into society."

"I don't need any door."

"That's foolish talk," said Maria, turning on her heel. "Now, act your age."

"You've never let me do that before," her daughter murmured mutinously.

But her mother never heard the remark.

Isadora felt trapped. Desperate to speak to Genevieve Masefield, she was forced to wait for an hour until breakfast was served in her parents' cabin, then spent a further forty-five minutes in their company. Isadora did her best to conceal her impatience. She did not wish to give her mother cause to restrict her movements even more. When the meal was over, Isadora asked politely if she could get down from the table.

"Where are you going?" asked her mother.

"To write some letters."

"To whom?"

"To whom it may concern, my dear," Waldo Singleton said easily. "Isadora is entitled to write to her friends. You don't have to stand over her and guide the pen."

"Thank you, Father," said Isadora.

"Off you go."

She scampered through the connecting door into the adjoining cabin and took out writing materials. Certain that her mother would look in on her, she took up the pen and pretended to compose a letter. A few minutes later, the head of Maria Singleton popped around the door. Satisfied that Isadora was doing what she should be doing, her mother withdrew. After waiting for a short while, Isadora leapt up, put her ear to the connecting door for sounds of movement then let herself quickly out into the passageway. She hurried off to the dining room and prayed that her parents would not become aware of her absence. At such a critical time in her life, she needed her freedom.

Isadora arrived as Genevieve was about to leave the room. Isadora was delighted to have caught her. Intercepting her friend, she took her aside for a hushed conversation.

"I'll have to be quick, Genevieve," she said. "I'm not supposed to be here."

"Why not?"

"Mummy is on patrol."

"Hasn't she let you off the leash a little yet?"

"No—but that hasn't stopped me sneaking out." Isadora giggled. "I watched Theo in training last night and this morning. And what do you think he did?"

"I don't know," said Genevieve.

"He blew me a kiss."

"That *is* an honor. I hope his coach didn't see you, Isadora."

"I made sure that he didn't. There are two things I need to ask you, Genevieve," she said, looking over her shoulder. "I'm sure you think it's silly of me to have such intense feelings about someone I hardly know but I just can't help it."

"It's not at all silly."

"Theo is really not that much older than me. My problem is that I look and sound much younger than I really am. That's Mother's fault. She held me back."

"She obviously hasn't been able to do that now."

"That brings me to my first question." Isadora became serious. "You're my friend, so give me an honest answer. Do you mind?"

"Mind what?"

"The fact that I love Theo?"

"Of course not."

"I know you saw him first, Genevieve. And he dotes on you."

"Believe me," Genevieve said with feeling, "I have no claims on him at all."

"That's wonderful!"

"But I do have worries about you, Isadora. You're already taking a big risk by letting him teach you to ride. Mr. Odell would take a very poor view of that—not to mention your parents."

"It's a risk worth taking."

"I don't want you to be hurt, that's all."

"But Theo likes me."

"That's not the point. There are other people involved here."

"Not when we're alone together in the storeroom."

"Especially then," warned Genevieve. "You have to be so careful what you do."

"But I can tell him that I love him, can't I?"

"I wouldn't advise it."

Isadora's face fell. "Why not? I want him to *know*."

217

"Have no fears on that score. Theo will know."

"How?"

Genevieve smiled. "Young men have a way of spotting these things," she said.

Dillman had paid enough visits to the second-class lounge to know his way about the room but he had never appeared before in his present guise. Dressed as a steward, he hovered near the door, angling himself so that he could look into a large gilt-framed mirror on one of the walls. In order to keep the place under surveillance he was missing lunch, but he felt it was a worthwhile sacrifice. Two people had been relieved of their wallets in the lounge. His task was to prevent a third passenger from being robbed. There was no guarantee the pickpocket would operate that afternoon. It was a chance Dillman was prepared to take. When lunch ended in the dining room, passengers began to drift into the room in small groups. Some ordered coffee, others called for brandy. Dillman did his share of serving the drinks so that he did not look as if he were keeping watch. Whenever he could, however, he moved back to his position beside the door.

He was not dealing with a common pickpocket, who insinuated himself into crowds in public. This man was selective, choosing his victims with care to ensure a good haul in each case. Instead of searching for the man himself, therefore, Dillman tried to single out a potential victim. Someone old and well dressed was the obvious target, the sort of person who would hardly notice if someone brushed past him and who might not even discover the theft until much later. The earlier victims had both fallen into that category. Surveying the room, Dillman could identify at least another half-dozen people who might tempt a pickpocket. There was no rush. If the man *was* waiting to strike, he was biding his time.

It was an hour before Dillman's suspicions were aroused. Not far from him, a short, stubby man with horn-rimmed spectacles was entertaining a group of friends with anecdotes. Though they laughed obligingly, the only person who found the stories hilarious was the person who told them. Every so often he would let out a shrill laugh and gesticulate wildly. Dillman sensed that his mirth was manufactured rather than real. By keeping one eye on the mirror, he could watch the bespectacled man closely. At the far end of the room, two elderly gentlemen rose from their seats and strolled toward the exit. Almost immediately, a third man got up and ambled casually behind them. He was young, dark, and wore a bland smile. Still watching the mirror, Dillman also took a keen interest in the trio approaching him. At the moment when they passed the group near the door, the stubby man let out such a loud cackle that the two elderly gentlemen both stopped and turned their heads in his direction. Simultaneously, the man behind them appeared to bump accidentally into them. There was a flurry of apologies and all three went out of the room. It was over in seconds.

Dillman followed the younger man as he broke away from the others and made his way out on deck. Taking out a cigarette, he was about to light it when a steward appeared at his side with a box of matches. Dillman lit the cigarette for him and the man pulled on it with satisfaction. He beamed at his companion.

"That's what I call service!"

"I wonder if you could do something for me in return, sir?" said Dillman.

"What is it?"

"Would you give me the wallet that you just stole in the lounge?"

The man glared belligerently. "Damn you! That's a foul accusation."

"It also happens to be true," Dillman said easily. "I saw it clearly. My name is George Dillman, sir, and I'm employed as a detective on the *Caronia*. Two wallets have already been stolen but I daresay we'll find them in your cabin. Would you like to take me there now, sir?"

"I don't know what you're talking about."

"I believe you do."

"This is a disgusting allegation. I'll report you to the purser."

"Are you refusing to take me to your cabin?"

"I most certainly am."

"Then I'll have to ask you to accompany me to the master-at-arms so that he can lock you up while I search your cabin." Dillman stepped in close and seized the man's arm. "I'll arrest your accomplice later when he's finished telling those appalling anecdotes."

Genevieve Masefield also missed her lunch because of the call of duty. Having sifted through what Carrie Peterson had told her, she was anxious to speak to the woman again and secured Inspector Redfern's permission to do so. The interview had the bonus of keeping her away from the dining room and another embarrassing confrontation with Theodore Wright and his coach. Work came first. Talking to the prisoner had two possible advantages. She could either make the inspector's task easier by drawing a confession out of Carrie Peterson or she could offer succor to an innocent woman who was being put through an intolerable ordeal. It was uncertain which result she would get and Genevieve feared she might achieve neither.

Carrie Peterson looked more worn and pathetic than ever. She expressed no pleasure when her visitor let herself in. She barely looked up from her chair.

"Hello, Miss Peterson," said Genevieve. "May I speak to you again?"

"If you have to," Carrie replied dully.

"The choice is yours."

The woman gave a shrug of indifference.

Genevieve ignored it and sat down close to her. "How are you feeling now?"

"Trapped."

"Inspector Redfern says that you still maintain your innocence."

"He was in here for an hour this morning. I've told him the

same things over and over again. But he's already made his mind up." She gave Genevieve a sidelong glance. "So have you, Miss Masefield."

"No, I haven't."

"I can see it in your face."

"I'm trying to be as dispassionate as possible."

"In some ways, that's even worse."

"Why?"

"Because it means *you* didn't listen to what I said, either," Carrie replied with a hurt expression. "You were in here for all that time yet you still can't decide. I know where I stand with the inspector. He thinks I'm guilty. He makes no bones about that fact. Sergeant Mulcaster was the same. At least *he* hasn't come in here."

"He won't be taking you to the bathroom again," said Genevieve. "As you requested, I spoke to the inspector about that."

"Thank you."

"And I'm sorry you feel you failed to convince me."

"I just want someone—anyone at all—to start believing me!"

"But I do believe you, Miss Peterson. Most of what you said tallies with the facts of the case, as I understand them. There are just one or two areas of doubt."

Carrie Peterson fell silent. She went off into a private reverie that lasted so long, Genevieve wondered if she ought to withdraw. The prisoner was in a far less cooperative mood than on the previous occasion. Without warning, she suddenly turned her gaze to Genevieve and spoke in a low voice.

"Do you know what he told me?" she said, eyes filled with fear. "Do you know what Sergeant Mulcaster told me? He thought I ought to know what actually happened when a condemned person was hanged. It was gruesome. He told me about someone called James Berry who used to be the public hangman. One time, the sergeant said, Mr. Berry made a miscalculation. Instead of hanging the man, he let the body drop too far and severed the head from the shoulders." She burst into tears. "That's what I had to put up with, Miss Masefield," she sobbed. "John, too. It would be bad enough if we were guilty, but we're not. It was vile of him to go on like that."

"You'll be spared any more of that kind of thing," promised Genevieve.

"Not if the sergeant has any say in the matter."

"Inspector Redfern is in charge."

"Is it true they've moved John back to his cabin?"

"Yes, Miss Peterson."

"Could you? . . . " She hesitated, torn between hope and fear of rejection. "Could you take a message to him for me?"

"I'm afraid not."

"Just a few words on a piece of paper."

"I'm not allowed to do that."

"It would mean so much to John—and to me. *Please*, Miss Masefield."

Genevieve shook her head. "It's impossible."

Carrie took a handkerchief from her sleeve to dab at her eyes. She withdrew into her shell again.

Genevieve tried to get her talking once more. "I mentioned areas of doubt," she said.

"Did you?" Carrie whispered.

"The chief one concerns the poison that Mr. Heritage bought. Remind me. Why do you think he purchased those particular items?"

"John told me that he was contemplating suicide."

"Even though he had you?"

"It seemed impossible for us to be together at that point. Because of his wife."

"You helped to stop him committing suicide," said Genevieve. "You obviously love Mr. Heritage and feel very close to him, but has it ever occurred to you that he might have used that poison for another purpose without even telling you?"

"That's out of the question."

"You weren't there."

"John would never lie to me."

"Can't you see that you may be convicted of something he did alone?"

"Then I'll willingly die beside him," said Carrie, with a rush of anger. "Except that he didn't—and couldn't—kill his wife. Neither did I."

"That leaves us with an unanswered question, then."

"What's that?"

"Mrs. Heritage was poisoned by somebody. That's incontrovertible. If you and her husband were not responsible—then who was?"

"I've been thinking about that myself, Miss Masefield."

"And?"

"There's only one explanation."

"Go on."

"Winifred Heritage was the most wicked human being I've ever met," Carrie said with venom. "She never forgave John and me for finding some happiness together. He certainly had none inside that house. I can imagine how furious she would have been when she discovered we'd escaped her clutches at last. There's your answer," she said with unshakable certainty. "It was her only way of getting back at us. I believe that she poisoned herself and made it look as if it was a case of murder."

THIRTEEN

George Porter Dillman was pleased to be able to give the purser some good news at last. After all the setbacks they had suffered on the *Caronia*, Paul Taggart was delighted to hear of the successful capture of the pickpocket and his accomplice. It was a good omen. Taggart reached across his desk to shake Dillman's hand.

"Congratulations!" he said. "How did you do it?"

"I posed as a steward in the lounge and kept my eyes open."

"And you say there were two of them?"

"Pickpockets often work in tandem," explained Dillman. "One diverts attention while the other goes to work. The couple I arrested on the *Saxonia* were husband and wife. The lady was very attractive and she certainly knew how to distract someone. In this case, of course, we had two men."

Taggart picked up a pen. "What are their names?"

"Hugo Drew and Peter Harrendorf. An Anglo-American partnership."

"Just like you and Genevieve Masefield."

"Except that our job is to safeguard people's pockets," said Dillman, "not to empty them. Drew is a suave young Englishman who looks completely above suspicion and Harrendorf is one of those gregarious characters who gathers people around him."

"Where are they now?" asked Taggart, writing their names into his book.

"Keeping company with Daniel Webb."

"Did they admit their guilt?"

Dillman smiled. "Eventually," he said. "I had to use a little persuasion. Anyway, I marched them off to the master-at-arms and he's keeping them out of harm's way."

"Did you speak to Webb while you were there?"

"Yes, Mr. Taggart. He begged me to let him out."

"No chance of that. He's too dangerous on the loose."

"He told me he'd finally seen the error of his ways."

"I wonder how many times he's said that?" the purser asked cynically.

"Too many."

"I'll peep in on the old reprobate when I visit the cells. I want to take a look at Drew and Harrendorf in case I recognize them. They may have worked undetected on the *Caronia* before. I'll make sure they never set foot on the ship again."

"They'll be relieved to see you, Mr. Taggart," said Dillman. "By now, I suspect, they'll have grown weary of listening to Daniel Webb. We put them into cells on either side of him so they could both enjoy the benefit of his conversation."

Taggart laughed. "You should have put all three in together." He became serious. "Thanks again. This has cheered me up. What we really need to do, of course, is to make progress in solving the other crimes. The murder of Sergeant Mulcaster must obviously take precedence. It's an established fact. The drug smuggling is an alleged crime. We can't be absolutely certain that it's taking place."

"I believe we can."

"Oh?"

"In fact," said Dillman, "we may well find that it's linked to the murder. I have this feeling that the sergeant's heavy-handed treatment of offenders was his downfall. One man he arrested, Sidney Nicholls, ended up in hospital for a fortnight. Inspector Redfern admitted the sergeant had a short temper. Nicholls was not the only prisoner to feel his punches, it seems."

"Offenders have to be restrained at times."

"This went well beyond restraint, Mr. Taggart. According to John Heritage, the sergeant boasted about the way he'd beaten Nicholls up. Arrest is one thing. Gratuitous violence is another."

"Oh, I agree."

"You only have to look at Webb's case. It took three members of the crew to overpower him but that's all they did. When he was swearing at them like that, they must have been tempted to knock him senseless. Instead, they acted responsibly."

"That's what they're trained to do, Mr. Dillman."

"So was Sergeant Mulcaster."

Taggart nodded in consent. "What was Sidney Nicholls's offense?"

"He was involved in drugs and prostitution."

"That might explain it, then."

"What?"

"The reason the sergeant got too violent," said Taggart. "When I talked to Inspector Redfern yesterday, he told me that Sergeant Mulcaster had an obsessive hatred of drug peddlers. He'd seen the effects of addiction on the son of a friend, a young man in his twenties, who died of an overdose. It made him determined to strike back at anyone involved in the trade."

"The best way to do that is to lock up the dealers in prison, not to take the law into your own hands. But it supports my theory," Dillman said thoughtfully. "Nicholls might be the worst case, but there were other drug peddlers who doubtless felt the wrath of Sergeant Mulcaster. Word spreads quickly in the criminal underworld."

"You feel the sergeant was a marked man?"

"Let's just say, his reputation did not endear him to anyone involved in smuggling or selling drugs. That's what makes me certain that the tip-off you received was genuine. We have someone aboard who's trying to take drugs into England. And that same person," Dillman concluded, "may well be the man who killed Sergeant Mulcaster and tossed his body overboard."

"It would simplify matters, Mr. Dillman."

"Exactly. If we catch the smuggler, we arrest the murderer as well."

Taggart sighed. "It's going to be more difficult than catching pickpockets."

"I know," said Dillman, "but we do have one possible lead."

"Do we?"

"I think so, Mr. Taggart. It concerns that funeral casket."

"Oh, yes. It belonged to a Mr. Leach, as I recall."

"Ramsey Leach," explained Dillman. "He's a mortician from England. Yet when I asked him if he had bought anything during his vacation in the States, he denied it. I don't think something as large as a funeral casket could slip his mind."

"Why did he lie to you?"

"I don't know, but it wasn't his only lie. Mr. Leach insisted that he always went to bed early yet I've twice seen him leave his cabin around midnight. In fact, he was behaving so furtively last night that I followed him."

"And?"

"He made his way to another cabin and was let in by someone."

"You think Ramsey Leach may be our man?"

"I'm not sure," Dillman confessed. "I've been biding my time until I can get more evidence. On the face of it, he's a most unlikely person. Quiet, refined, and very reserved. With a gun in his hand, he might be a very different proposition."

"Would he be strong enough to push the sergeant over the rail?"

"He's wiry rather than muscular but he's used to handling dead bodies in his profession. He would have had no problem. Mr. Leach is an odd character. He has an expression of professional solemnity most of the time. When I bumped into him in second class, however," recalled Dillman, "he was almost jaunty. It was not the face he wears at funerals, Mr. Taggart."

"If he is the man we're after, he obviously has an accomplice."

"That was my belief all along."

"What do you think we should do?"

"If you can loan me the master key again, I'd like to take a look in his cabin when he's not around. The stewards would have peeped in there when we did our earlier search but they were really looking for the stolen firearms. I'll conduct a more thorough search."

"When?"

"As soon as possible."

"What about the cabin he went to last night?"

"I'll check that out as well, Mr. Taggart," said Dillman. "I got the number. Nobody has searched in there properly before."

"Why not?"

"Because it's a single cabin occupied by a middle-aged woman. When we did our sweep of the ship, we concentrated on able-bodied men of a certain age. That may turn out to have been a mistake."

"Take the key with my blessing, Mr. Dillman," said the purser, extracting it from a drawer. "We'll have to make sure neither of them returns to their cabin while you're there. They may turn out to be completely innocent and that could leave us both with red faces." He handed the key over then reached for the passenger list. "We must avoid that."

"We will," Dillman assured him. "I'll identify the pair of them to Genevieve and she can keep an eye on each of them in turn."

"What's the number of the cabin Leach visited last night?"

"Thirty-three."

Taggart studied his list. "And the lady's name?"

"Miss Pamela Clyne."

"Yes, here she is," said the purser, pointing. His eyes bulged. "Good Lord!"

"What the trouble?"

"She occupies the cabin next to Mrs. Anstruther!"

Theodore Wright fulfilled his promise. Having agreed to teach Isadora Singleton how to ride a bicycle, he found a place where they would be unobserved. The long passageway ran between cabins occupied by stewards and cooking staff. Since all of them would be working that afternoon, Wright could begin his instruction in peace. The passageway was wide enough for him to stand beside the bicycle, yet narrow enough for the rider to steady herself with a hand on the wall. Isadora was filled with glee. She not only would learn to do something that had always been denied her, she would be brushing up against the remarkable young man with whom she had become infatuated.

"How do we start, Theo?" she asked.

"It helps if you sit in the saddle," he joked.

"Turn around, then." When his back was turned, she hitched up her skirt and mounted the bicycle. "You can look now."

He swung round. "Okay, Izzy."

"Nobody's ever called me that before," she said with a giggle.

"Don't you like it?"

"I love it."

"Then it'll be my special name for you," he said affably. "Okay. This is what we do," he went on, gripping the machine by the saddle and the handlebars. "Put your feet on the pedals and turn them very slowly."

"Is it safe?"

"Try it, Izzy."

She obeyed his instructions and the bicycle inched forward. He held it steady.

"We're moving," she cried. "We're doing it!"

"We'll do it time and again to build up your confidence, getting a little faster each time. Then," he said, "when you feel good and ready, I'll let go."

"Don't do that, Theo. Please."

"I can't keep doing this forever."

"But I like it."

When they got to the end of the passageway, she was quivering with excitement. It was not simply the fact that she had cycled—albeit with assistance—a distance of several yards. She had also felt Wright's shoulder pressing gently against her. They turned the machine around and went back in the opposite direction, picking up more speed this time. On their third run, Isadora felt able to push even harder on the pedals.

"Well done, Izzy," he said. "You've gotten the hang of it."

"I *knew* that I could do it."

"Keep moving and you won't fall off."

"Not when you're holding me, Theo."

"Enjoying it?"

"I could do this all day."

"By the end of the voyage, you'll be riding around the deck with me."

"Oh, I could never go that fast."

"That's nothing, Izzy," he said. "When I race in France, I'll have to go ten times faster than that. It's not as bad as it sounds. If you stay on the pack, the other riders help you along."

"Not the way that you're helping *me* along," she said with a grin.

It was on the seventh journey down the passageway that he decided to let go of the handlebars, supporting her only by the saddle. Isadora was amazed she still kept going. She had a wonderful sense of achievement. It was only momentary. Losing her confidence, she let out a cry of fear. The machine began to wobble badly. Wright was equal to the emergency. Running along beside her, he grabbed the handlebars and slowed the bicycle down, but Isadora was not only interested in learning to ride now. With her beloved right alongside her, she pretended to lose control completely and fell off the saddle toward him. Wright used one arm to catch her and brought the machine to a halt with the other. He gave her a friendly smile.

"I guess that's as far as we can go for now, Izzy," he said. "Are you okay?

"Oh, yes, Theo," she replied. "It's been amazing."

————

The search of Ramsey Leach's cabin revealed nothing unusual. Dillman was swift but thorough. He looked in every corner of the cabin and the bedroom, kneeling down to look under the bunk and using a long arm to explore the top of the wardrobe. Leach's clothing was sober and conventional. All Dillman found by way of proof that the man had lied to him were some souvenir photographs of Niagara Falls. He could not imagine why the mortician had visited such a place. Before he left, Dillman picked up the small case he had seen Leach carrying the previous night. It was locked and felt strangely heavy. The detective used the blade of his penknife to jiggle away until the catches eventually flicked open. Inside the case were some flannel pajamas and a striped dressing gown but it was the object underneath them that interested Dillman. It explained why the case had been so heavy.

Ramsey Leach owned a large revolver.

After a good night's sleep, Inspector Redfern felt markedly better. Though he was still exercised by the murder of his colleague, he did not neglect the prisoners. He allotted two whole hours to Carrie Peterson in the morning, going through the details once again with painstaking care. In the afternoon, he turned his attention to John Heritage. Contrary to what the inspector had predicted, the prisoner did not gloat over Mulcaster's death.

"Do you have any idea who the killer may be?" asked Heritage.

"Not as yet."

"Daniel Webb claims that he was a witness."

"Pay no attention to what he told you," Redfern said irritably. "Mr. Webb is something of a menace. I can see why the immigration authorities turned him down. And forget about Sergeant Mulcaster. You have a murder charge of your own to answer."

"Granted, Inspector. I just wanted you to know that, although I didn't like the man in any way, I'm profoundly sorry to hear what happened to him."

"Thank you, Mr. Heritage."

"I'm also grateful that you rescued me from the foul cell."

"You can always be sent back there," warned Redfern. "So can Miss Peterson."

"Have you spoken to her today?"

"At some length."

"How is she?"

"As well as can be expected."

"You make her sound as if she's ill," Heritage said anxiously. "Is she? What are her symptoms? I've got drugs in my case. If you let me have it, I'll prescribe something for her. I know that she suffers from headaches."

"Miss Peterson is not ill, I assure you."

"That's a relief."

"She's not enjoying the experience of being locked up, that's all."

"Neither am I, Inspector."

"Then you shouldn't have committed a crime."

Heritage paused. "It was wrong of me to steal from the pharmacy account like that," he said at length. "But it was only money that was owed to me. Stephen had been putting his hand in the till for years."

"I'm not so much concerned with the financial irregularities at the pharmacy," said Redfern. "It's the murder of your wife I'm here to discuss."

"For the hundredth time," said Heritage, controlling his impatience, "I did not kill Winifred. So what is there to discuss?"

"The fact that you haven't shown the slightest grief. You admit that you disliked Sergeant Mulcaster yet you managed to find some sympathy for him. Why is it so difficult to express remorse over the death of your wife?"

Heritage heaved a sigh. "Are you married, Inspector?"

"Very happily."

"Any children?"

"Two."

"Does your wife mind you being a policeman?"

"At times," conceded the other. "She knows there are grave risks in this job. I'm not looking forward to telling her what happened to Sergeant Mulcaster, I know that. It will only alarm her. Mostly, however," he went on, "my wife is proud of what I do."

"Rightly so."

"But we're here to talk about your domestic life and not mine."

"Yours is relevant," argued Heritage, "because your experience may help you to understand mine. You have three things I lacked. A happy marriage, children, and a wife who respected your occupation. My marriage was a living hell, Inspector. It would have been cruel to bring children into that house. As for my work, Winifred spent our whole life together blaming me for not being a doctor or a hospital consultant. Being a pharmacist was not impressive enough for her, especially as I was the junior partner. My wife was the worst kind of snob," he said. "She always wanted a bigger house, better clothes, and a higher status in life."

"And she poured scorn on your place of work, you say?"

"Without cease."

"All the more reason to get your revenge by using the resources of the pharmacy."

"No, Inspector."

"That poison was bought for a purpose."

"I explained that. I contemplated suicide."

"But you drew back at the last moment."

"Yes," said Heritage, troubled by the memory. "I wanted to escape and I wanted to hurt my wife, but I saw that wasn't the right or just way to do it. Carrie—Miss Peterson—would have been desolate. She talked me out of it. That's why I held back."

"Yet you kept the poison in your house."

"Yes, I did."

"Why?"

"I don't know. I wish I'd thrown it away."

"I think you do know, Mr. Heritage. You were using it to kill your wife."

"That's simply not true, Inspector!"

"Then how did she come to die? Somebody murdered her."

"Well, it wasn't either of us."

Redfern watched him in silence for a few moments. He was disappointed that he had been unable to break down the man's resistance. Even after intense questioning over a number of days, the pharmacist clung to the same story.

"Do you know what Miss Peterson suggested?" he asked.

"What?"

"It was when she was interviewed the second time by Miss Masefield, the other detective on board. She works with Mr. Dillman. I hoped that a woman might be able to coax fresh information out of Miss Peterson."

Heritage became wary. "And did she?"

"Oh, yes. A number of discrepancies came to light. But it was Miss Peterson's theory that interested us the most. Even though it sounds more like a clever excuse to me. I'm surprised you haven't suggested it yourself, Mr. Heritage."

"Suggested what?"

"That nobody else was involved. In short," said Redfern, "your wife was so eager to incriminate you both, that she used the poison to commit suicide in a way that would point to you and Miss Peterson as her killers."

John Heritage looked stunned at first but he recovered quickly and even smiled.

"That's it, Inspector," he said, as if he'd just been absolved of the charge. "My wife must have found where I hid the poison. Winifred was always searching my things in the hope of finding letters from Miss Peterson. She'd have done anything to spoil our happiness. This explains it, doesn't it? Winifred killed herself in order to get back at us."

Genevieve Masefield had been frankly astonished at the task assigned to her by Dillman. Given the evidence, she was prepared to accept that the English undertaker merited investigation, but she found it impossible to believe Pamela Clyne could be connected with him in any way. The woman had been too shy even to speak to a man of her own accord, let alone invite one into her cabin. It seemed incredible. When Ramsey Leach had been pointed out to her, he was reclining in a chair on the boat deck, reading a book. It was easy to keep him under observation. Dillman walked casually past her some time later and she knew the search was complete. Her attention could now shift to the other suspect.

Pamela Clyne was taking tea in the lounge with Mrs. Cooney and Cecilia Robart. Sitting near the door, Genevieve glanced through a magazine while watching them out of the corner of her eye. Her earlier impression was confirmed. Everything about Pamela Clyne suggested a nervous spinster who found conversation difficult and the presence of strangers worrying. Mrs. Cooney was using vigorous gestures and Mrs. Robart was also animated as she spoke, but their companion sat there meekly in her seat and contributed little beyond nods, smiles, and the occasional affirmative remarks. Taken at face value, Pamela Clyne seemed as likely to be the accomplice of a drug smuggler as the ship's cat. Genevieve did not, however, dismiss the notion. She had known women before who were capable of disguising their true character completely in order to evade detection. And as demure as she appeared, Pamela Clyne *had* found the courage to cross the Atlantic in both directions. Genevieve wondered what her two companions would think if they realized the reticent Miss Clyne was under suspicion.

Dillman walked past the door to glance into the lounge and Genevieve put her magazine down. It was the agreed-upon signal that she had the second suspect under surveillance. Dillman was free to search Pamela Clyne's cabin. As soon as he went off, another familiar figure came hurrying into the room. Genevieve braced herself when she saw that it was Theodore Wright. He waved cheerily and sat down beside her.

"You certainly like playing hide-and-seek, Genevieve," he said.

"I've been busy, Theo."

"Avoiding me, by the look of it."

"Not at all."

"Listen, I came to apologize for what happened yesterday," he said, sitting forward on the edge of his chair. "I'm so sorry. Wes had no call to try to frighten you off like that. I'll never forgive him."

"He was only doing it to protect you," she said.

"I'm a big boy, Genevieve. Old enough to look after myself."

"Let's just forget the whole thing, shall we?"

"But we haven't had our talk yet."

Genevieve was pleasant but firm. "I don't think there's anything more to say, is there?" she asked. "Circumstances are against us, Theo. I'm very fond of you and I was touched by the flowers you sent, but that's it, I'm afraid. You have your world and I have mine. I'd rather see you as a good friend."

"Oh," he said, visibly disappointed. "That means there's someone else."

"Perhaps."

"I thought there must be. Any guy in his right mind would want you."

"I didn't mean to be a distraction, Theo."

"You haven't been, honestly. You were simply the person who brightened up my day. I love cycling but I do like to relax from time to time. Meeting you was the best thing that's happened to me since we've been on the *Caronia*."

"Don't tell Isadora. She prefers to think that she is."

"Yes," he said, rallying. "Izzy is my most devoted fan."

"Is that what you call her? Izzy?"

"I gave her a proper riding lesson today."

"How did it go?"

"Very well, until she fell off. Don't worry. I caught her."

"I should imagine she enjoyed that, Theo."

"She wants to come and see me riding in France."

"So do I, Theo," said Stanley Chase, catching the last sentence. "Do excuse me for butting in, Miss Masefield," he went on. "I just wanted to tell Theo how impressed I've been by the thoroughness of his preparations."

Wright was pleased. "You've seen me, Mr. Chase?"

"Yes, I was on the boat deck at midnight. I wanted to take a closer look at my investment, you see?"

" 'Investment'?" echoed Genevieve.

"That's right, Miss Masefield. I had a quiet word with Theo's coach and he convinced me that Theo is more or less bound to win the Bordeaux-to-Paris race."

"I am!" said Wright, tapping his chest.

"So," continued Chase, "since I liked what I saw, I decided to place a bet on Theo. As it happens, I pass through Paris every May on my way to a cottage I own in the south of France. I can time it so I'm there when Theo comes bursting through the tape." He turned to the rider. "While you're getting your breath back, I'll be collecting my winnings."

"Thanks for your support, Mr. Chase."

"It does have a selfish element in it, I'm afraid, but there was something else as well. What really convinced me to put my money on you was a chat I had with a Monsieur Fontaine."

"I met that guy," said Wright. "He reckoned that Gaston Vannier would beat me by miles. Boy, has he got a surprise coming!"

"That was my feeling," agreed Chase, "so I had a gentlemanly wager with him. He lives near Paris. I won't have far to go to get my money from him. Monsieur Fontaine was acting out of naked patriotism in backing this chap Vannier. I felt it was only right to support Theo in the interests of Anglo-American relations."

"That's terrific, Mr. Chase."

Genevieve was doubly grateful for the arrival of Stanley Chase. He had cut short an uncomfortable conversation, and so diverted the cyclist with his remarks that Wright seemed to have forgotten all about her. It was just as well. Pamela Clyne and her two companions were just getting up to leave. Genevieve had to delay them.

"Forgive me," she said, rising to her feet. "I must speak to someone."

Dillman subjected the second cabin to the same rigorous search. Nothing incriminating was found. Pamela Clyne's personal possessions reflected their owner. Her clothes were dowdy and the outlay on them modest. She had several small souvenirs of her visit to America, all neatly tucked away in a case. The three books in the cabin were all romantic novels by Ouida. Dillman decided that *Held in Bondage* might give a mild thrill to a maiden lady but it was hardly standard reading for someone involved in smuggling drugs. After a final look around the room, he opened the door to slip away but someone was blocking his exit. Arms folded, the imposing figure of Mrs. Anstruther stood there.

"So *you're* the devil who visits her cabin, are you?" she said.

Ramsey Leach finished another chapter before closing the book. After standing up and stretching himself, he elected to take a walk around the boat deck. It was busy this afternoon. Passengers were promenading or playing games or simply relaxing in the bright sunshine. Children were chasing each other. An old lady was exercising her dog. Leach strolled along until someone came out of a door and loomed over him.

"Hello, Mr. Leach," said Frank Openshaw, clasping him by the shoulders. "Grand to see you again, my friend."

"Yes," Leach replied uneasily.

"My wife was talking about you earlier."

"Was she?"

"Kitty suggested that we ask you to join us this evening."

"I already have dinner companions, I'm afraid, Mr. Openshaw."

"This would be for drinks *before* dinner," the other said amiably. "We like to invite a different group of people in each day so that they can meet in more intimate surroundings. Shall we say, seven o'clock?"

"I may be busy at that time."

"Kitty will be so disappointed if you don't come."

"Oh, I see."

"That's settled, then," Openshaw said with a chuckle. "Good-bye."

Frank Openshaw went striding off down the deck, leaving Leach to regret that he had accepted the invitation. Before he could continue his own stroll, he was approached by a steward. The man gave him a polite smile.

"Mr. Leach?" he asked.

"Yes."

"Mr. Ramsey Leach?"

"That's me."

"The purser sends his compliments and wondered if he could see you in his office. I'll show you the way, if you wish."

Leach was alarmed. He tried to hide his discomfort under a bland smile.

"Thank you," he said. "I can manage on my own."

After the pleasure of being alone with the man she loved, Isadora Singleton was condemned to spend an hour with her parents, taking afternoon tea with Lord and Lady Eddington in their cabin. She was on her best behavior, pleasing her mother and drawing smiles of approval from her hosts. Having been a diplomat, Lord Eddington was a seasoned traveler. When he talked about a posting he once had had to Paris, Isadora's curiosity was aroused. She fed him with polite questions he was only too happy to answer.

Maria Singleton was delighted by the way her daughter was ingratiating herself. Isadora was truly a credit to both of them. It was only when they left the cabin that the problem arose. When they came to some steps, her parents let Isadora go up first. Maria's sharp eye saw something that had been invisible before. Along the hem of the girl's dress at the back was a long, black, shiny mark.

"Isadora!" she exclaimed. "What on earth is *that*?"

Theodore Wright took some time to get over his rejection by Genevieve Masefield. Having relied so heavily on a positive response from her, he was downhearted at his failure. He was also afflicted with guilt. When he tried to view the situation from Genevieve's point of view, he saw how inappropriate his attentions had been. He had inadvertently upset her and he deeply regretted that. In a day or two, Wright decided, when he felt calmer, he would apologize for causing her any distress. Meanwhile, he would keep away from her. His meditation took place at the rail on the promenade deck. Staring out across the ocean, he reflected on what he had lost, then cheered himself with the thought of what he had also gained.

Genevieve Masefield liked him. She made no attempt to hide her affection and clearly valued their friendship. Wright hoped they could keep in touch, perhaps even see each other in London. He had made other friends as well. Notable among them was Isadora Singleton, whose joy at learning to ride was infectious. Wright had a subversive streak. It amused him to be able to help her to defy her parents in secret. It gave the two of them a bond. The Openshaws also had sought his company, and Stanley Chase was so impressed by his cycling that he was actually going to place money on him. Wright remembered the kind interest shown in him by George Dillman, as well. Since he had been on the *Caronia*, the cyclist had made a definite impact. Even his argument with a French passenger about the merits of Gaston Vannier had been good-hearted. He was surrounded by new friends.

Bolstered by that thought, he went back to his cabin. Wes Odell was waiting for him with an accusatory glint in his eye. He closed in on the cyclist.

"You've been talking to her again, haven't you?" he said.

"Well, yes."

"After everything we agreed to last night?"

"I agreed to nothing. You were making impossible demands."

"I saw you in the lounge, sitting alone beside her."

"Only for a couple of minutes."

"A second is far too long, Theo. Don't you see that?"

"You talk as if Genevieve is an incurable disease."

"Exactly," retorted Odell. "She's lethal. It's so obvious from where I stand. What do I have to do to convince you of that?"

"You can stop yelling at me, for a start," said Wright, squaring up to him. "We don't have a contract, Wes. It was all done on a handshake," he reminded him. "I can walk out on you anytime I like."

"Do that, and your career is finished."

"Who says so?"

"Everyone in professional cycling. I *made* you, Theo. Remember that."

"Are you sure it isn't the other way around?"

Odell was stung. "What do you mean?"

"Come on, Wes. You're not the most popular guy in the sport. Lots of cyclists wouldn't let you pump up their tires, let alone ask you to coach them. Without you, I'm still a champ." Their eyes locked. "What are you without me?"

"I'll find someone else to coach."

"In the middle of the Atlantic?" Wright asked sarcastically "Who would you pick? Stanley Chase? Frank Openshaw? Or what about that French guy? I bet he knows the road from Bordeaux to Paris."

"Take it easy, Theo."

"Then stop riling me."

"There's no need for us to bicker like this."

"You started it."

"I'm worried about you, son," said Odell, with an appeasing smile.

"Leave me be."

"And you'll keep away from Miss Masefield?"

Wright exploded. "I'll do what I damn well like, Wes!"

He pushed past Odell and went into the bathroom. Turning on the faucet, he filled a glass with cold water and drank it down in one gulp. He needed a few minutes before he felt able to face his coach again. Odell was sitting down when Wright entered. The coach stared quizzically at him. He opted for a calmer approach this time.

"Why was one of the cycles missing from the storeroom this afternoon?"

Ramsey Leach delayed his visit to the purser for as long as he could. Desperate to make contact with Pamela Clyne beforehand, he could not find her anywhere and resorted to slipping a note under her door. When he finally presented himself at the purser's office, he swallowed hard before knocking and going in. Paul Taggart was seated behind his desk. Dillman was standing beside him. Leach was taken aback.

"Come in, Mr. Leach," Taggart said easily. "We just wanted a little chat with you. I believe you've met Mr. Dillman before."

"Yes, yes," said Leach.

"What you didn't know was that Mr. Dillman is employed by Cunard as a detective. That's why he's here with me now." He indicated a chair. "Do sit down, sir."

Leach lowered himself gingerly into the chair as if expecting a thousand volts of electricity to shoot through it. His discomfort was intense. Beads of perspiration had broken out on his forehead and he clutched his hands tightly together.

"Have you any idea why Mr. Taggart invited you here?" asked Dillman.

"Yes," replied Leach.

"Well?"

"Mrs. Anstruther has complained, hasn't she?"

"She's never stopped complaining," Taggart said bitterly, "but that's not the only reason we wanted to speak to you, Mr. Leach."

"According to the manifest," resumed Dillman, "you have a

funeral casket on board. Yet you told me categorically that you had bought nothing in America."

"I lied to you, Mr. Dillman," admitted Leach.

"Why did you do that, sir?"

"Private reasons."

"Were those reasons anything to do with what the funeral casket might contain?"

"I don't understand."

"I think you do, Mr. Leach," said Taggart.

"It's just an ordinary coffin," said Leach. "Well, strictly speaking, that's not true. It's a very superior product, far better than the ones I normally use. That's why I bought it, Mr. Taggart. I want some copies of it made in England."

"What we're interested in is its contents," said Dillman. "Let me be blunt, Mr. Leach. We have it on good authority that someone is trying to smuggle cocaine and heroin on this vessel. What better place to conceal it than in a funeral casket that you denied even existed until you came here?" Leach loosened his collar. "It's only fair to tell you that I twice saw you leave your cabin at midnight, sir. On the second occasion, I took the liberty of following you."

"Oh my God!" gasped Leach.

"It will save a lot of time if you tell us the full truth."

"The captain can authorize an inspection of that funeral casket," warned Taggart. "We'll find those drugs if we have to rip it completely apart."

"But it's empty, I swear it."

"Then why did you tell Mr. Dillman you had no cargo aboard?"

"I can explain that, Mr. Taggart."

"Explain this at the same time, if you will," suggested Dillman, taking the revolver from a drawer in the desk. "I found it in your cabin."

Leach turned a ghastly white and looked as if he were about to faint.

"Well, sir," said Taggart. "What do you have to say?"

Being an essentially truthful person, Isadora Singleton saw no reason to lie. When they returned to their cabin, both parents stood over her and demanded an explanation. They were flabbergasted when they heard it.

"A bicycle!" said Maria in disgust. "That oil came from a bicycle?"

"Yes, Mother."

Singleton was aghast. "Whatever were you doing on a bicycle?"

"Riding it, of course."

"But you don't know how to ride a bicycle."

"Theo is teaching me, Father."

"Who?"

"Theo Wright. He's famous. He's the American champion."

"What on earth are you talking about, Isadora?" asked Maria. "Are you telling us that you've been sneaking off behind our backs to spend time with this individual?"

"It was the only way to do it."

"No, it wasn't," said Singleton. "You should have come to us for permission."

"Would you have given it, Father?"

"I'm not sure."

"No!" said Maria, shooting him a glance. "Your father and I would have turned down the request at once. A girl in your position doesn't need to do anything as common as riding a bicycle. We have standards. We travel by automobile."

"Yes," said Isadora, "but it's driven by somebody else. Riding a bicycle is something I can do on my own. Theo says it will only take a few more lessons. He's going to France to take part in a race from Bordeaux to Paris."

"I don't care if he's riding from Boston to Buenos Aries," said Maria, with well-bred malevolence. "He is not going to consort with our daughter."

"Theo and I are friends, Mother."

"It's not a friendship of which we approve—is it, Waldo?"

"No, dear," said her husband, taking his cue. "And it's very distressing to learn all this has been taking place in secret. We're shocked, Isadora. You've always been such a truthful person."

"This fellow obviously has led her astray," said Maria.

"But he hasn't," Isadora protested.

"We'll be the judge of that."

"You can't stop me seeing Theo."

"Oh, yes we can, young lady."

"That's cruel, Mother!"

"It's what is necessary," decreed Maria. "Teaching you to ride, indeed! What do you think Lord and Lady Eddington would say? They'd drop us like a stone."

"Your mother is right, Isadora," said Singleton. "You must never see him again."

"That must be made clear to him as well. What's the fellow's name?"

"Theo," said Isadora. "Theo Wright."

"Speak to him, Waldo. Speak to him sternly. Let him know how appalled we are at his behavior. I've a good mind to report him to the purser."

"But he's done nothing wrong, Mother," argued Isadora.

"Of course he has."

"Why don't you meet him?"

Maria grimaced. "The very idea is revolting!"

"But you'd see what a wonderful person he is. Please, Mother."

"No!"

"Father?" said Isadora, hoping for support from him.

"I'm sorry," he said, "but your mother and I speak with one voice here. We've spent our whole lives bringing you up so that you can enter society at the highest level. You've been given privileges few young ladies of your age enjoy. We are not going to throw all that away because you befriend some stray cyclist on a Cunard liner."

"Theo is the American champion."

"That may impress you," said Maria, "but it only horrifies us. What sort of person makes a living by riding a bicycle? It's no better than performing in a circus."

"Don't be such a snob, Mother."

"Standards are standards."

"And that's the last word on the subject," added Singleton, exerting his paternal authority. "The matter is closed, Isadora. I will speak to this person in the most forthright terms, and make sure he never bothers you again.

"But Theo *isn't* bothering me," Isadora wailed. "I love him!"

Waldo stared in absolute dismay. Maria Singleton began to gurgle.

It took Ramsey Leach a long time to pluck up the courage to tell the truth. They waited patiently. Taggart felt certain they had just unmasked the drug smuggler. Dillman, however, was beginning to have doubts.

"We're still waiting," said the purser. "Does this weapon belong to you, sir?"

"Yes," Leach confessed.

"How long have you owned it?"

"A matter of weeks, Mr. Taggart."

"Where did you get it?" asked Dillman.

"It was bought it in New York as a souvenir. I know it was wrong of me to bring it on board without declaring it, but I grew attached to it. I was afraid someone would take it away from me and I couldn't bear that."

"You mean, that you felt you might need it?"

"Not to shoot, Mr. Dillman," said Leach, upset at the implication. "You may have found the gun but there was no ammunition in my cabin, was there? I suppose that I've always had a fascination with firearms," he explained. "I've collected muskets that go back to the Crimean War and I even have a Martini-Henry rifle from the battle of Rorke's Drift." He licked his lips anxiously. "This was going to join my collection, you see. And the reason I don't want to part with it is that I didn't buy it myself. It was a gift."

"From whom?" asked Dillman. "Miss Pamela Clyne, by any chance?"

"No."

"But from somebody rather special, I suspect."

"Extremely special, Mr. Dillman."

"Is that person on board this vessel?"

Leach looked hunted. "Yes. She is."

"Will she confirm that she purchased this weapon for you as a gift?"

"I hope it won't come to that," pleaded Leach.

"Why not?" asked Taggart.

"Because I don't want any of this to come out. If she realized I was here, talking about her, she'd be terribly distressed. I must ask you to respect her feelings."

"We're involved in a criminal investigation, sir. Feelings are not relevant."

"I believe they are," said Dillman, putting the gun down on the desk. "I don't think we need detain him any longer, Mr. Taggart. He's not guilty."

"How do you know?"

"Because I searched the two cabins. Apart from the gun, there was nothing to indicate that either might be occupied by the person we're seeking. We've pursued a false trail and we owe Mr. Leach an apology."

Taggart was surprised. "Do we?"

"Yes," said Dillman. "When I asked him if Miss Pamela Clyne bought this revolver for him, Mr. Leach gave an honest answer. She did not. The lady who did purchase it was Mrs. Pamela Leach. She's his wife."

"Is this correct?" asked the purser, turning to the other man.

Leach squirmed on his chair with embarrassment before forcing the words out.

"Yes, Mr. Taggart," he said. "Pamela and I are on our honeymoon."

FOURTEEN

When he was let out of his cell and taken to the office belonging to the master-at-arms, Daniel Webb thought he was being released. Instead, he discovered, he was only being summoned for interview by Inspector Redfern. Webb began his defense as soon as he walked through the door.

"It was their fault, Inspector," he whined. "Those three blokes in the same cabin as me. Yankee thugs, they were. They tried to take my bottle of whisky away from me and I couldn't let them do that. I earned it."

"Be quiet, Mr. Webb."

"Not fair to keep me locked up like this."

"That's nothing to do with me."

"Speak to the master-at-arms, sir. Get me released."

"Shut up!" ordered Redfern, tiring of the old man's obsequious grin. "I brought you here to answer a few questions. Now, sit down and do as you're told." Webb nodded and took the chair opposite him. "Tell me what you saw the other night."

"What night?"

"The night you slept on the main deck."

"Oh, that," Webb said slowly, thinking he might have a bargaining tool. "I don't suppose you have a cigarette about you, do you, Inspector? My memory's so much better when I have a fag in my mouth."

"I smoke a pipe."

"Then lend me some of your tobacco, sir. I've got some fag papers somewhere," he went on, groping in his pockets. They were empty. "Ah, I remember now. They took all my possessions when they banged me away."

"Quite rightly."

"A man is entitled to some comforts."

"You're not getting any tobacco from me."

"But I'm desperate for it."

"Who cares?"

"I do. Listen," said Webb, smirking hopefully, "why don't you ask the master-at-arms to give you a fag for me? I know he smokes. Then we can talk. See what I mean? You scratch my back and I'll scratch yours."

Redfern was riled. "I didn't come here to offer you a deal, Mr. Webb," he said harshly. "At the moment, you're under arrest for being drunk and disorderly. There's also the charge of grievous bodily harm against a Mr. Miller. If you deliberately withhold evidence from a murder inquiry, you'll find that you stay behind bars even longer. Now, let's have no more of this nonsense. Tell me what you saw."

"Can I at least have a cup of tea?"

"No!"

"All right, all right," said Webb, seeing the anger in Redfern's face. "No need to threaten me like that. I've already been through it a couple of times, but I don't mind telling my tale again."

"Thank you!"

"It all began when I went out onto the main deck. . . ."

Webb's account was rambling and interspersed with all manner of digressions. Yet the essential facts remained the same. He had witnessed the murder of Sergeant Mulcaster by someone who seemed to be holding a gun to the back of the detective's head. Redfern made him go through it twice, to be absolutely sure no detail was missing. Having heard all the old man had to say about one murder, he turned his attention to another.

"I'm told that you spoke to Mr. Heritage yesterday," he said.

"Yes, Inspector. He was in the next cell to me."

"That was when they brought you in rolling drunk."

"I wasn't drunk," insisted Webb. "I never gets drunk, only merry."

"Too merry. You caused mayhem down in your cabin."

Webb smirked. "I like a good scrap."

"So it seems."

"They'll have more sense than to pick on me again."

"They won't get a chance while you're locked away," said Redfern. "Forget about the fight. Tell me about Mr. Heritage."

"Novice, isn't he? Never been arrested before."

"No, he hasn't."

"Doesn't know how to play the game."

"Unlike you," Redfern observed coldly. "Do you remember what you said to Mr. Dillman about him?"

"I liked Mr. Dillman. A real gent, he was. Bought me the whisky."

"You told him something about Mr. Heritage."

"Yes," said Webb. "He's guilty."

"What makes you say that?"

Webb tapped his head. "Brains. Experience."

"Did Mr. Heritage say anything that led you to believe he was guilty?"

"It's what he *didn't* say, Inspector. I mean, he wouldn't even tell me what he was in for. Couldn't see him, of course, but I could tell from his voice what he looked like. And I knew that he was lying."

"How?"

"Too sorry for himself."

"Anything else?"

"Hey, look," protested Webb, "I'm not going to rat on a fellow prisoner!"

"You've already done that."

"All I did was to give my opinion."

"Based on a talk you had with him. Now, stop being so obstructive. What else convinced you John Heritage was lying?"

Webb wiped his nose with the back of his hand. "He's in love, Inspector."

"Go on."

"There's a woman in the case. He mentioned her name half a dozen times. That's why he's pleading his innocence. If you had him on his own, I think he'd own up just to clear his conscience. But he has to think of this woman."

"Miss Peterson."

"She on board as well?"

"Yes, Mr. Webb."

"There you are, then. Mr. Heritage got her into whatever it is that he's supposed to have done, and he feels bad about it. That was his mistake, see? Getting a woman involved. It never works. You always end up feeling responsible for them."

Redfern became pensive, stroking his chin as he reflected on what he had heard from the old man.

Webb made one last bid for a favor. "I suppose there's no chance of a tot of rum, is there?" he said.

Genevieve Masefield was dumbfounded. When she received a visit in her cabin from Dillman that evening, the news he gave her made her eyes widen in disbelief.

"Miss Clyne is *married*?" she said.

"Apparently."

"Then why doesn't she share a cabin with her husband?"

"She does at night, Genevieve."

"What happens during the day?"

"She and Mr. Leach carry on as if they're traveling independently."

"It doesn't make sense."

"It does when you know the full story," said Dillman. "Ramsey Leach is a rather shy man and I gather that his wife is even more bashful."

"She's extremely timid, George."

"That was the very word he used. 'Timid.' It took him six years to persuade her to marry him and another two years of waiting while she kept putting off the day. It wasn't that Miss Clyne—or Mrs. Leach, as she is now—didn't love him. He was keen to stress that point. It was simply that she was terrified about what people would say."

"Why?"

"All sorts of reasons," said Dillman. "To begin with, she's the sort of woman who's utterly self-effacing. She prefers to fade into the background and that's tricky when you have to walk down the aisle in a wedding dress. Add to that the fact that she was a confirmed spinster. She'd given up all hope of ever getting married. But the thing that worried her most, according to Mr. Leach, was the fact that she's five years older than he is. That was a huge barrier for her."

"I don't see why. Age difference is not a crime."

"Pamela Clyne felt that it would set tongues wagging."

"Then she should have ignored them."

"She isn't robust enough for that, Genevieve."

"Has Mr. Leach been married before?"

"No, he's almost as tentative about their relationship as she is."

Genevieve arched an eyebrow. "Are you *sure* he spends the night with her?"

"There's no question of that," said Dillman. "Mrs. Anstruther, the lady in the next cabin, complained to the purser that Miss Clyne entertained a man every night and they kept her awake with their antics. The trouble is, Mrs. Anstruther caught me leaving the cabin this afternoon and thought that *I* was the demon lover."

"How did you talk your way out of that?" said Genevieve, laughing.

"With difficulty."

"So why all this secrecy about being on honeymoon?"

"Mr. Leach explained that. On the crossing to New York, they traveled as man and wife and everyone knew they'd just married. Whenever they went into a public room, it was agony for them. People would watch, whisper, and nudge each other. They vowed they'd never go through that again."

"So they occupied separate cabins."

"Until midnight." Dillman's smile was sympathetic. "I feel sorry for them. All they wanted to do was to sail back home without causing any fuss. Mr. Leach was shaken when he was asked to come to the purser's office. He thought Mrs. Anstruther had complained about the noise in the next cabin and that he'd be reprimanded."

Genevieve laughed again. "For sleeping with his own wife?"

"Silly, I know, but the pair of them are so sensitive. . . ."

"What about that coffin you mentioned?"

"I was misled there," Dillman admitted. "Because he denied having bought anything during his stay, I assumed he was trying to throw me off the track. In fact, it was his wife he felt the need to deceive. His hobby is collecting firearms. When his wife got him the revolver I found in his cabin, he bought her an eternity ring. She wears it under her glove along with her wedding ring."

"Yes, I noticed that her hands were always covered."

"One afternoon in New York, while his wife was taking a nap at the hotel, Mr. Leach called on a mortician whose advertisements he'd seen in the paper. He was so impressed with the funeral caskets he saw that he promptly bought one and arranged to have it shipped back home. But he didn't feel able to tell Mrs. Leach," said Dillman, "and I see his point. What wife would be pleased to hear that the most important souvenir her husband acquired on their honeymoon was a new funeral casket?"

"This is very amusing," said Genevieve, "and rather sweet in its own way, but it does mean that the people we want are still at large."

"Yes," Dillman confessed. "I was completely wrong about Ramsey Leach. He wasn't responsible for Sergeant Mulcaster's funeral arrangements, after all. We can't afford another mistake like that. It was very embarrassing."

"So what do we do?"

"Keep looking, Genevieve. I'm certain those drugs are on board."

"Do you still believe they're linked to the murder?"

"Unquestionably."

"Sergeant Mulcaster's reputation caught up with him."

"I'm afraid so," said Dillman. "What puzzles me is how any-one knew that he was on board the *Caronia*."

"They did cause something of a stir when they arrived, George."

"I know. I saw them."

"So did lots of other passengers. The word got around."

"What spread was the rumor that two murderers were in custody, being taken back to face justice. Nobody knew their names or those of the two detectives."

"Somebody must have recognized the sergeant."

"That's what I thought, at first. But it would be a remarkable coincidence if they had. What are the chances of someone who was arrested by Sergeant Mulcaster in the past, traveling on the same liner?"

"Pretty slim."

"It wasn't the man who was recognized, Genevieve, it was his name."

"I see what you mean."

"How it got out," said Dillman, "I don't know. The two of them took great care to keep out of any public rooms. Apart from an occasional walk on deck to stretch their legs, they hard-ly ever left the area of their cabin. Throughout the day, they were too busy questioning Mr. Heritage and Miss Peterson. Do you take my point?" he asked, running a hand through his hair. "Someone not only discovered their names, they also found out that Inspector Redfern and Sergeant Mulcaster were in second class. Who told them?"

Genevieve's mind was racing. Guilt brought a slight flush to her cheeks.

"I hate to say this, George," she admitted. "But I may be to blame."

Theodore Wright and Wes Odell were in a state of armed truce. The coach was furious because the cyclist had refused to explain why he had taken a bicycle from the storeroom that afternoon. For his part, Wright was simmering with anger because he was being treated like an errant child. Knowing what the consequences might be, neither man wanted to engage in pitched battle in case it would lead to a complete rift. They needed each other. As a team, their success had been uninterrupted. If they split up, their individual futures were uncertain. The atmosphere in their cabin was strained so they dressed early for dinner and went up into the lounge, hoping that greater space would ease the tension. They had just reached the point of being able to exchange civil remarks when Waldo Singleton came over to them.

"Mr. Wright?" he asked.

"That's me," said Wright, offering his hand. "You're Mr. Singleton, aren't you?"

Waldo ignored the handshake. "May I have a private word, please?"

"What about?" asked Odell, sensing trouble.

"This is a confidential matter, I'm afraid."

"I'm Theo's coach. If it concerns him, it concerns me."

"Not this time, Wes," said Wright.

"Why not?"

"You stay here while I speak to Mr. Singleton. I won't be long." Wright led the older man to the far corner of the room where they could talk without being overheard.

Odell watched them sullenly, trying to gauge what was being

said by their stance and gestures. He saw Waldo Singleton bring a hand to his mouth as he cleared his throat. Wright looked relaxed and unworried,

"I'm sure you know what this is about," said Singleton.

"Not really, sir."

"I understand you've been teaching our daughter to ride."

"Is that what Izzy told you?"

Waldo frowned. "Her name is Isadora."

"Yes, of course, Mr. Singleton."

"And she told us nothing at first, which is alarming enough in itself because we brought her up to speak the truth. We noticed an oil stain on her dress."

"From the bicycle chain," said Wright. "I did warn her."

"So you don't deny that you were giving her instruction?"

"Hell no! I'm pleased to introduce anyone to the joys of cycling. There's nothing to touch it. I can't think why Izzy—Isadora—didn't learn years ago."

"That was our decision and we stand by it."

"Your daughter missed out on a whole lot of fun, then."

"That's beside the point," Singleton said sharply. "I'm here to tell you that my wife and I take a dim view of what's been going on. You had no right to conspire with Isadora behind our backs. It was deplorable behavior. In view of that fact, Mr. Wright, I must ask you to leave our daughter alone in future."

"But I like her, Mr. Singleton."

"Your relationship with Isadora is herewith terminated."

Wright blinked in annoyance. "What is this?" he said. "First Wes. Now you. As soon as I get close to a woman on this ship, someone pops up to warn me off."

"Have I made my feelings clear?"

"Very clear."

"Good."

"What you didn't realize, though, is that I have feelings as well. And I don't like to be shoved around by anyone. I want to know what Isadora thinks about this," he said, putting his hands on his hips. "From where I stand, Mr. Singleton, she looks old enough to make her own decisions."

"That's a family matter."

"But I'm involved here."

"Not anymore, Mr. Wright."

"Why not?" demanded the cyclist. "All I did was to give her a riding lesson or two. It's not as if I'm try to elope with her."

"Heaven forbid!"

"We've done nothing to be ashamed of, Mr. Singleton. Judge for yourself. Why don't you and you wife come and watch us practicing together?"

"That's a monstrous suggestion!"

"Why?"

"Listen, young man," said Waldo, raising his voice a little. "I tried to put it as politely as I could but you persist in being obstinate. Let me be more blunt. Without saying a word to us, Isadora formed an attachment with someone whom we consider to be highly unsuitable. If it were not for the unique situation of being on this vessel together, your paths would never even have crossed."

"I'm glad they did."

"Well, we most certainly are not."

"What about Izzy?"

Waldo smarted. "Her name is Isadora."

"Does *she* think I'm highly unsuitable?"

"That's immaterial."

"Let me speak to her."

"No, Mr. Wright."

"If she wants me to scram," said Wright, "then I will, but I have to hear it from Izzy's—sorry, from *Isadora's*—own lips. It's only fair."

"You obviously haven't listened to a word I've said."

"Oh, I heard it, sir. What you're telling me is that I'm not good enough for your daughter. Yet I was simply trying to teach her to ride. You talk as if I'm a prospective son-in-law."

"Over my dead body!" exclaimed Singleton.

Wright grinned. "Thanks for the vote of confidence."

"You're such an exasperating young man."

"That's what all the other cyclists say. But then, all they get to see in a race is the back of my jersey." He gave a shrug. "Look," he said amiably, "I don't mean to be brash, and I'm not looking for a fight with you or with Mrs. Singleton. I like your daughter. She's a great girl. What harm is done if she has a bit of enjoyment on this trip?"

"A great deal of harm, Mr. Wright."

"I'm not a leper, you know."

"Socially, that's exactly what you are. We will treat you as such." Turning on his heel, Waldo Singleton walked off with the utmost dignity.

Odell came scurrying anxiously across to see what the argument had been about. "What did he want, Theo?"

"Nothing," Wright said airily. "Nothing at all."

Before he went to dinner that evening, Dillman paid a courtesy call on Inspector Redfern.

The Scotland Yard detective shook his hand warmly. "I understand congratulations are in order," he said. "The purser tells me you arrested a pickpocket and his accomplice in the lounge."

"A routine assignment, Inspector."

"It proves you know your job."

"That doesn't stop me making mistakes," Dillman said penitently. "Did Mr. Taggart tell you about the suspect we interviewed?"

Redfern smiled. "Yes. Mr. Leach, wasn't it?" he said. "Easy to see why you got hold of the wrong end of the stick there. What a weird marriage those two must have!"

"It's one of the reasons I came."

"To discuss Mr. and Mrs. Leach?"

"No," explained Dillman. "To talk about the false impression you can get when you meet only one person in a partnership.

Ramsey Leach struck me as a lonely bachelor with no interest outside his work. Genevieve had a similar reaction to Pamela Clyne. She'd never met anyone so excruciatingly shy. Yet those two got together at midnight and enjoyed themselves so much that they scandalized the lady in the next cabin. In other words," he continued, "it's only when you put two halves of a partnership together that you understand their true character."

"I think I can see what's coming," Redfern said carefully.

"It was Genevieve's idea, really."

"You want to speak to both the suspects together."

"If possible, Inspector. I know you've kept them apart so that they can't rehearse their lines together. But there could be real value in letting them be in the same room. They haven't seen each other for days, remember."

"Heritage and Miss Peterson remind me of that every time I speak to them."

"Their emotions will be running high. They may well give themselves away."

"I'm not so sure about this, Mr. Dillman."

"It's worth trying," argued Dillman. "Naturally, you'd be there as well. But each of them would suddenly be confronted with an unknown quantity. Genevieve has spoken to Miss Peterson but it would be interesting to see what Mr. Heritage makes of her."

"By the same token, you'd be a new face for Carrie Peterson. Well," said Redfern, thinking it over, "it has its advantages, but it could also work against us. Heritage and his mistress would be able to exchange signals. That's why I opted for divide and rule."

"The interview would be rigidly controlled, Inspector. Sit them well apart and make sure you stand between them. Impress upon them that they'll be sent straight back to their cabins if they disobey the rules, and we'll have no trouble. What do you say, Inspector? They'd be extremely grateful."

"I'm not here to do favors for murder suspects."

"It's their gratitude that might make them open up a little."

"Let me think it over."

"Genevieve and I are at your disposal at any time."

"Thanks, Mr. Dillman." He studied his visitor's evening dress. "You make me feel very envious, looking like that. While you dine in style, I'll have a meal on a tray."

"Even at dinner, I'm still very much on duty."

"Of course." He took out his tobacco pouch and began to fill his pipe. "I took your advice about having a word with Daniel Webb. Evidence from fellow prisoners is notoriously unreliable but I wanted to hear what he said."

"And?"

"He thinks Heritage is guilty."

"That's what he told me."

"According to Webb, the important person is Carrie Peterson. He reckons that Heritage is lying to protect her. If he was in this on his own, says Webb, he'd come clean and take his punishment. But because he inveigled his mistress into the crime, he feels obliged to cover for her."

"Interesting theory. What do you make of it, Inspector?"

"There may be a grain of truth in it."

"All the more reason to question them together," urged Dillman. "Webb is right about one thing. Miss Peterson is the key factor. But for her, Mr. Heritage would still be working at the pharmacy and going home to an unhappy marriage."

"Love does strange things to a man," Redfern said drily, slipping his pipe between his lips before putting his pouch away. "Look at Ramsey Leach."

"I'd rather look at John Heritage—side by side with Carrie Peterson."

Redfern used a match to light his pipe then puffed away. He put his head to one side and looked at his visitor with great curiosity. He removed the pipe to exhale smoke.

"Why have you taken such an interest in this case, Mr. Dillman?"

"Because there's something odd about it."

" 'Odd'?"

"Yes," said Dillman. "On the face of it, we have the classic love triangle. A husband who kills a nagging wife in order to be with his mistress. We've both seen that situation a number of times. What is odd here is that Mr. Heritage didn't *need* to kill his wife. He and Miss Peterson had already made their escape to Ireland. I don't think you'd have pursued him quite so vigorously if his only crime had been to filch from the pharmacy account. There wasn't a large amount of money involved."

"Too little to interest Scotland Yard. We'd have made routine inquiries then given up when we realized they'd left the country. Murder is the only reason my boss would authorize the kind of expenses we've run up. But I take your point, Mr. Dillman," he said thoughtfully. "It is an odd case."

Dillman looked at his watch. "I'll have to hand it over to you for the time being. Duty calls. Genevieve and I have our own work to do."

"Find the killer for me. It's vital."

"That's exactly what we hope to do."

"You have another suspect?"

"Yes, Inspector."

"What's his name?"

"It's a woman," announced Dillman. "Mrs. Cecilia Robart."

Since most people tended to forgather in the lounge before dinner, Genevieve Masefield got there early in order to take up a vantage point from which she could keep the room under surveillance. Theodore Wright was sitting with his coach. He gave her a friendly wave but made no attempt to go over to her. Genevieve took that as a good sign. Pamela Clyne was also there, talking in a corner with the indomitable Iris Cooney and looking like part of the furniture. Once again, she wore long gloves to conceal her rings. Mrs. Cooney was old and sagacious. Genevieve wondered if Pamela had confided her secret to her friend. It would explain why the American woman offered her almost continuous cover. Genevieve noticed that Stanley Chase was deep in conversation with Sir Harry Fox-Holroyd. Fresh from their latest bout of hospitality, the Openshaws led in the group who had just been served drinks in their cabin. Mrs. Anstruther stood in the doorway and scanned the room to make sure there was no sign of Mostyn Morris.

Genevieve soon found herself in conversation with Kitty Openshaw.

"You have a beautiful new dress each time I see you, Miss Masefield."

"Actually, Mrs. Openshaw, my wardrobe is full of old friends."

"Well, nobody would ever guess."

"When it comes to beautiful dresses," said Genevieve, admiring the older woman's silk gown, "yours is very special. It was obviously made for you."

"A birthday present from Frank. He spoils me."

"That's what you get for marrying a bricklayer."

Kitty laughed. "I'll tell him that!"

While they chatted away, Genevieve kept watch on the door and she was eventually rewarded with her first sight of Cecilia Robart. Walking between two other women, she looked composed and elegant. Her gold earrings dazzled in the light and she had reverted to the pearl necklace. The long black evening gown displayed her figure to advantage. Genevieve watched her carefully, uncertain whether such a refined woman could possibly be involved in the terrible crimes. She had never seen Mrs. Robart in the company of a man for any length of time, but that meant nothing. Pamela Clyne had proved that. Even the most perceptive eye could be deceived.

When dinner was announced, the guests began to drift out of the lounge. Dillman hovered near the door, talking to one of the stewards. Kitty Openshaw rejoined her husband, and Genevieve was free to move a little closer to Mrs. Robart. Genevieve waited until they were near the exit before she spoke, making sure that Dillman overheard her.

"Good evening, Mrs. Robart," she said, moving up beside her.

"Hello, Miss Masefield."

"I haven't seen much of you today."

"We spent the whole afternoon playing bridge."

"Did you win?"

"Yes," said Mrs. Robart. "I was lucky enough to have Sir Harry as my partner. I'm a duffer at cards but he carried me along splendidly. What about you?"

"Oh, I've had a very restful day."

"That's the attraction of crossing the Atlantic. There's no rush."

When they got to the dining room, they went their separate ways. Genevieve looked around. Conscious that she had seen so little of Isadora, she wanted to sit close to the Singletons but they did not turn up. Instead she took a seat beside Michel Fontaine. The Frenchman was polite and attentive. After introductions had been made, Genevieve surprised him by mentioning the Bordeaux-to-Paris race.

"I understand that you made a wager with Mr. Chase," she said.

"Why, yes." He pulled a face. "I was so sorry about that."

" 'Sorry'?"

"I like the man. It will hurt me to take his money from him."

"Mr. Chase believes it will be the other way round."

"Nobody can beat a French cyclist in France," he said confidently. "I would bet anything on Gaston Vannier. He is a born winner."

"So is Theo Wright."

"Pah! He will not even finish the race."

"He has tremendous stamina."

"Vannier will—how do you say?—*destroy* him."

Genevieve was about to defend the American when there was a tap on her shoulder. A steward had brought her a note. As soon as she sniffed the scented envelope, Genevieve knew it had come from Isadora Singleton. Making sure that nobody else could read its contents, she opened the missive. One word had been written in block capitals:

HELP!

———

When she had been identified for him, Dillman stayed long enough at the door to take a close look at Cecilia Robart. She did not strike him as the sort of person who would leave a pair of expensive earrings in a bathroom by accident. Like Genevieve, he sensed she simply had wanted to find out who the ship's detective was so that she could be on her guard. He moved off swiftly and found his way to the suspect's cabin, knocking first to make sure it was unoccupied, then let himself in. Eager to get to the dining room before too long, his search was swift but not perfunctory. He found nothing out of the ordinary. The cabin was surprisingly tidy, yet Genevieve had spoken of Cecilia Robart as a rather scatterbrained person. Dillman knew enough about fashion to estimate how costly her wardrobe was, and the other items indicated no shortage of money. It was the wastepaper basket that interested him most. Lying in the bottom of it were a magazine and several discarded cigarette butts. He reached down to extract them and laid them out carefully on the table. There were over twelve in all and they had been smoked since the stewardess had cleaned the cabin that morning. Two different brands had been used. Four cigarettes of one brand had a smear of lipstick on them. The remaining eight had been thrown away when they were barely half an inch long.

Cecilia Robart had a friend who was a heavy smoker.

Michel Fontaine was a charming companion. He flirted gently with Genevieve without making her feel in any way threatened or offended. She was sorry she had to leave the table early but the cry for help from Isadora Singleton could not be ignored. Excusing herself from the table, she looked around for Cecilia Robart. Positioned between Sir Harry Fox-Holroyd and Frank Openshaw, looking completely at ease, she seemed to be keeping up simultaneous conversations with the two men. Genevieve walked past them. When she left the room, she saw Theodore Wright chatting to one of the stewards. He broke away when he saw her.

"You see?" he said with a grin. "I've got a fan, after all."

"You've got lots of fans, Theo."

"That guy has actually seen me race. Comes from Baltimore. He saw me win a big race down there last year and has been dying for the chance to speak to me. What about that, eh?" he asked. "I may not impress the passengers on the *Caronia* but I'm a hit with the stewards."

"You impress us all, believe me."

"No, I don't, Genevieve."

"What do you mean?"

"Mr. Singleton thinks I've crawled out from under a stone. I don't reckon that he'll be in the crowd in Paris to cheer me past that winning line. He found out I'd been giving Izzy—Isadora— some riding lessons. Almost bit my ear off."

"That explains it."

"Explains what?"

"Why Isadora isn't here this evening. I have to go, Theo," she said. "Before I do, promise me you'll definitely win that race in Paris."

"It's in the bag, Genevieve."

"Good. That's what I told Monsieur Fontaine. Don't let me down."

She gave him a farewell smile then hurried off to her cabin to collect a book. From there she went to the Singletons' suite. As she approached, a steward was taking some empty plates away on a tray. The family obviously had dined in private and their meal was over. Genevieve felt able to knock. Waldo Singleton opened the door.

"Oh, good evening, Miss Masefield," he said.

"I'm sorry to interrupt you, Mr. Singleton," she said, "but I'd rather hoped to catch you in the dining room. I have something for Isadora."

"Is that you, Genevieve?" asked an excited voice from inside.

Waldo opened the door wide. "Perhaps you'd better come in."

Genevieve went in and saw the table set for three. Although they were dining in their own suite, the Singletons had dressed for the occasion. Waldo was in his white tie and tails and Maria had produced a turquoise-colored gown with a draped bodice and long sleeves. Around her hair was a pink bandeau. She smiled graciously. Isadora sat beside her mother with a look of gratitude in her eyes.

"I brought that book I promised to give you, Isadora."

"Oh, thank you!" said the girl, recognizing the excuse for what it was. "I've been waiting for that. May I talk to Genevieve in the other room, please, Mother?"

Maria hesitated. "What is the book?" she asked.

"It's a novel by Edith Wharton," said Genevieve. "I bought it in New York."

"No harm in that," remarked Singleton, with heavy-handed humor. "It's not as if you're trying to corrupt our daughter with an English author."

"Don't be fatuous, Waldo," said Maria.

"No, dear."

"Off you go, Isadora."

"Thank you!" said Isadora, leaping from her seat.

She took Genevieve through the connecting door to her own cabin then closed it behind her. As soon as they were alone, she burst into tears.

Genevieve held her in her arms and tried to soothe her. "Theo told me what happened," she said.

"It was dreadful. Father went off to put him in his place."

"Well, I don't think he succeeded, Isadora. When I saw Theo a few minutes ago, he was as lively as ever. Nothing can dampen those high spirits of his."

"I do hope not. I felt so guilty for landing him in the situation."

"He knew the risks."

"We both did, Genevieve. Oh, I could kick myself for giving the game away like that!" said Isadora. "I let the hem of my dress touch the bicycle chain and it picked up some oil. Mother saw it at once. They've banned me from talking to Theo." She crossed to the door that opened onto the passageway and

266

turned the handle. "You see?" she said. "It doesn't open. They've locked me in."

"They can't do that for the rest of the voyage."

"Mother says I'm to stay close to them at all times."

"Won't they even let you talk to me?"

"You're the only exception to the rule."

"That's a relief," said Genevieve.

"Will you help us? Theo and me, I mean?"

"In what way?"

"I've written him a letter," said Isadora, opening a drawer to take out an envelope. "I managed to smuggle out that note to you because the stewardess likes me, but I didn't want to risk letting this fall into the wrong hands." She gave Genevieve the letter. "It's an apology to Theo for the trouble I caused him. An apology and a promise."

" 'Promise'?"

"Two days after we land in England, I celebrate my twenty-first birthday. I'll be able to do what I want to do then. Mother and Father will complain, of course, but they can't really stop me from going."

"Where?"

"To France, I hope," Isadora said excitedly. "I've got money of my own. I want to be in Paris when Theo wins that race."

There was a sharp tap on the door. Maria's voice was peremptory.

"Don't be too long in there, Isadora," she said. "You need an early night."

"I'm just leaving, Mrs. Singleton," called Genevieve, slipping the letter into her purse. She handed the book to Isadora. "You'd better take this."

"What's it called?"

"*The House of Mirth*."

Isadora giggled. "It's not about *my* family, then!"

Throughout dinner, Dillman had studied Cecilia Robart, wondering if she really was a legitimate suspect and, if so, who her accomplice was. It could hardly be Sir Harry Fox-Holroyd, yet he was the man with whom she talked most. When dinner was over, Mrs. Robart went off to the lounge with her companions. Dillman got up and drifted into the smoking room. Several people were enjoying a postprandial cigar or cigarette. The majority of them were men but a few women were there as well, using long cigarette-holders, as much for affectation as for any other reason. Dillman scanned the faces, recognizing a number of them.

The man who interested him most was talking animatedly to two friends. Short, smart, and with a dark complexion, he was one of the few men who preferred a cigarette. Most of them, including Frank Openshaw, pulled on Havana cigars, filling the room with a pungent odor. The short individual was clearly a heavy smoker. Finishing one cigarette, he stubbed it into an ashtray and immediately lit another before continuing his conversation. Dillman counted three discarded butts before he slipped out of the room to escape the stink of smoke.

He loitered nearby until the man he had been watching came out. He gave Dillman a nod as he went past. The detective responded with a smile before moving casually into the smoking room again. Strolling across to the ashtray into which the cigarettes had been stubbed out, he waited until nobody was looking before he picked up some of the butts. A glance told him they were the same brand as those found in Cecilia Robart's cabin. Dillman dropped the butts back into the ashtray and went off to the lounge. The man had now joined a group that consisted largely of ladies. He was making them all titter with amusement. Frank Openshaw ambled into the room.

"Good evening, Mr. Dillman," he said, crossing to him. "We must talk more about those yachts of yours sometime. I've always wanted to be skipper of my own craft."

"That's what you are on the *Caronia*, to some extent, Mr. Openshaw," observed Dillman. "You're far more of a presence among the passengers than Captain Warr."

Openshaw chuckled. "I like to get around."

"Then you'll probably recognize that gentleman over there." Dillman pointed. "The one who's diverting all those ladies."

"Oh, him! Yes, he joined us for drinks this evening."

"What's his name?"

"Michel Fontaine," said Openshaw. "He's a mad Frenchman."

Theodore Wright was troubled. The letter Genevieve had delivered to him had been both delightful and worrying. He was pleased to hear that Isadora Singleton planned to support him in France and was touched by the affection that ran through her letter. At the same time, he was alarmed to hear she had been confined to her cabin that evening as a result of something he had done. Isadora blamed herself for unwittingly revealing their secret and she apologized profusely for anything her father might have said to him. Wright was tempted to go to their cabin and confront her parents, but he saw that that might only embarrass his young friend. Instead he rested on his bunk until it was time to get back in the saddle. Even when he was cycling around the boat deck, he was still brooding about Isadora Singleton, desperately searching for a way to alleviate her suffering. He saw a parallel in his own situation. Wes Odell was watching him as closely as the Singletons watched their daughter. It was a shared problem.

Something else troubled Wright. He felt tired. He was putting his usual effort into the training ride but maintaining nothing like his usual speed. The sequence of late nights and early mornings was affecting him. He always took care to have a long nap in the afternoons but it was not the same as continuous sleep. Because they could only use the deck at certain times, they had been forced to adopt a testing schedule. Wright thought enviously of his French rival. Gaston Vannier would be practicing on the very route that would be taken during the Bordeaux-to-Paris race. It was a huge advantage. Stung by the remembrance, Wright put more power into the thrust of his legs and surged forward.

When he finally came to a halt, however, his coach had no

words of praise. Odell jabbed a finger at his stopwatch. "What's wrong with you, Theo?" he demanded.

"Sorry, Wes. I'm tired."

"Your mind is not on your cycling."

"I need more sleep."

"What you need is more practice," said the coach, taking a small tin from his pocket. "Get back in the saddle for another quarter of an hour."

"I've had enough for one night."

"Do as you're told. Open up."

"What?"

"Open your mouth. I want to give you something."

"Why?"

"Because it will wake you up, that's why. Come on."

Wright opened his mouth and Odell took some flakes from the tin to place on his tongue. The rider swallowed them uneasily. He looked worried.

"Off you go," said Odell. "You've got to ride for twenty-four hours in France, remember. We've must get those miles in your legs, Theo. Show me what you can do."

Wright set off again and was soon cycling with a new vigor.

Inspector Redfern decided to follow Dillman's advice and arrange a joint interview with his two prisoners. The session was scheduled for the following morning. On their way to the cabin, Genevieve Masefield met up with Dillman.

"I was thinking over what you told me last night, George."

"And?"

"I don't think Michel Fontaine is implicated," she said. "I sat next to him at dinner last night. He's an inveterate flirt but I didn't get the feeling he was a criminal."

"I'm going on the evidence of those cigarette butts."

"It's a popular French brand. Other people smoke them."

"True."

"It may not even have been a man in Cecilia Robart's cabin. Those cigarettes could have been smoked by a woman."

"I considered that," said Dillman, "but most women use cigarette-holders. The ends of the butts would have been squeezed to fit into them. I'm not saying that Monsieur Fontaine is our man, but we need to keep an eye on him."

They reached the cabin and were let in. Redfern explained the way he wanted to conduct the interview before going out. He returned first with John Heritage, who was surprised to see Genevieve there. Dillman introduced her. Redfern went off to fetch the other suspect. When she was brought in, Carrie Peterson did not even notice the others at first. Her eyes were fixed on her lover. She tried to run to him but Redfern held her back.

"I warned you, Miss Peterson," he said. "Any impulsive behavior and you go straight back to your cabin. That goes for you as well, Mr. Heritage."

"Of course," said Heritage. "We're just pleased to see each other again."

Carrie was trembling. "How are you, John?"

"I'm fine, Carrie. And you?"

"Much better."

Her words were contradicted by her appearance. She looked strained and wan. During the days aboard the ship, she seemed to have aged visibly. But there was still a hint of defiance in her gaze, and her spirits were clearly lifted by the sight of her lover. After introducing Dillman to her, Redfern made her sit on one side of him while Heritage was on the other. The inspector explained what was going to happen and reiterated his warning that the suspects would be returned to their cabins if they misbehaved in any way. Grateful to be in the same room again, both promised to cooperate. Dillman and Genevieve sat directly in front of them so they could watch their reactions.

"Let's start with the discrepancies, shall we?" said Redfern, consulting his notebook. "There are several details that don't seem to match up. Perhaps you can explain why."

He listed some of the new facts Dillman and Genevieve had elicited from the suspects and asked them to explain why there were slight differences between their individual accounts. Heritage answered with a degree of confidence, giving plausible answers that were also signals to Carrie Peterson to corroborate his testimony. She was more guarded in her replies, agreeing with most of what he said but correcting him on some points. Genevieve had the impression the woman was being slightly more honest. Dillman, too, came round to the view that Heritage was hiding more than his mistress. He was also trying to shield her from their questions by drawing attention to himself. When the Cunard detectives were invited to participate, both of them turned toward Carrie Peterson.

"You believe Mr. Heritage is innocent, don't you?" asked Dillman.

"I know he is," replied Carrie. "We both are."

"How do you know, Miss Peterson?"

"Because it's not in John's nature. He's the most gentle person alive."

"Inspector Redfern and I have both met extremely gentle people who have committed murders," said Dillman. "When someone is put under severe pressure, there's no telling how they will behave."

"John did not kill his wife."

"Then why did he buy that poison from the pharmacy?"

"I've already told you that," interrupted Heritage.

"We'd rather hear it from Miss Peterson." Dillman turned to her. "Well?"

Carrie was distressed. "John bought it because he was considering suicide."

"Is that what he told you?"

"Yes, Mr. Dillman."

"And did you believe him?"

"Of course."

"How did it make you feel?" said Genevieve, taking over. "What did you say when you learned that he was so desperate he was thinking about taking his own life?"

"I was upset."

"Is that all?"

"No," said Carrie. "I was deeply hurt. I couldn't believe John would dream of doing that and leaving me high and dry."

"But I didn't do it, Carrie!" insisted Heritage. "Because of you, I drew back."

"Keep quiet, Mr. Heritage," said Redfern.

"But I want the situation to be understood."

"I think we understand it all too well," said Dillman. "You were faced with an intractable problem. You couldn't bear to live with the woman you hated and you weren't allowed to be with the one you loved. Any man would feel hopeless and desperate in those circumstances. There must have seemed only one way out—to kill yourself."

"No," cried Carrie. "There was another way! I convinced him of that."

"We had the idea that he convinced *you*, Miss Peterson."

She tried to look across at Heritage but Redfern blocked her view. She bit her lip. "It was a joint decision," she said.

"Like everything else we did," added Heritage.

"In that case," said Redfern, "the murder was also a joint decision."

"There was no murder, Inspector."

"Then who poisoned your wife?"

"Winifred must have poisoned herself."

"That's right," said Carrie, taking her cue. "Mrs. Heritage told me that she'd rather die than lose John. And she was capable of dispensing poison of her own. I lost count of the number of vile letters she sent, accusing me of trying to take her husband away from here. They were *dripping* with poison."

Heritage was disturbed. "You never told me about those, Carrie."

"I wanted to spare you any extra pain."

"Winifred actually *wrote* to you?"

"I tore the letters up and burned them."

"Why didn't you show them to Mr. Heritage?" asked Genevieve.

"Because he had enough to endure at home," said Carrie. "John must have told you some of the things his wife did and said. She was vicious. When she turned her fire on me, I was shocked at first. Then I reminded myself I had something she would never have, and that was John's love. So I ignored the letters."

"You should have brought them to me, Carrie," said Heritage, in pain.

"Why?" asked Dillman. "What would you have done?"

"Confronted my wife, of course."

"Would that have achieved anything?"

Heritage was about to answer but changed his mind. He shook his head sadly.

"In other words," said Dillman, "Miss Peterson did the wise thing."

He waited while the two suspects tried in vain to look at each other. A small wedge had been driven between them. Dillman exploited the situation.

"Is Mr. Heritage normally a truthful man?" he asked.

"Very truthful," replied Carrie.

"Have you ever known him to tell a lie?"

"Never."

"But you'd know if he did?"

She faltered slightly. "I think so, Mr. Dillman."

"Have you ever told Mr. Heritage a lie?"

"Of course not."

"Carrie is as honest as the day is long," affirmed Heritage.

"One or both of you is lying to us now," Dillman said calmly.

"Yes," agreed Genevieve. "I'm beginning to think that not everything was a joint decision, was it? How could it be? Until you ran away, you seem to have spent very little time alone together. You worked side by side at the pharmacy, but Mr. Duckham's presence must have been very inhibiting. As soon as the shop closed, Mr. Heritage had to go straight home or he would have faced his wife's ire."

Dillman took charge again. "What Miss Masefield is rightly

pointing out is that neither of you really knew the other person all that well. Yes, I know"—he said, raising a hand to quell the protest that was about to come from both of them—"you were in love and that gives you deep insights into a person's character. Miss Peterson tells us that Mr. Heritage was a truthful man, yet he deceived his wife and his partner. He also deceived Miss Peterson when he omitted to mention that he had rifled the pharmacy account to fund their escape. As for you," he continued, turning to Carrie, "you just heard Mr. Heritage say that you were as honest as the day is long, yet you concealed from him the important fact that his wife had sent you poison-pen letters. Small lies on both sides, I grant you, but enough small lies can become a very big one."

"A denial of your guilt," said Redfern.

Heritage leaped to his feet. "I've had enough of this!" he yelled. "Take me back to my cabin. It's cruel to torment us like this. I'm saying nothing more until we go to court, and Carrie will do the same."

"Will you, Miss Peterson?" asked Genevieve.

"Don't listen to them," Heritage warned. "They're trying to trick us."

"Sit down," said Redfern.

"They've got no real evidence."

The inspector forced him down into the chair. "Sit down and stay there!"

Carrie Peterson glanced around as if noticing something for the first time.

"Where's Sergeant Mulcaster?" she asked quietly.

"Never mind about him," said Redfern.

"But I want to know. He enjoys trying to frighten me. Where is he?"

Heritage blurted out the truth. "He's dead, Carrie. The sergeant was murdered and thrown overboard. You won't have to put up with him again."

Her manner changed in a flash. Heritage had shown some compassion when he discovered the news, but she had none.

A smile of joy lit up her face then she began to snigger. Carrie Peterson seemed unable to control herself. Throwing back her head, she laughed wildly until she was on the verge of hysteria. Genevieve moved across to hold her by the shoulders, trying to calm her down, but the cachinnation went on. It was the vengeful laughter of someone whose enemy has been vanquished. Redfern was taken aback but Heritage was utterly appalled. He had never seen her behave like this.

Dillman waited until Carrie finally managed to regain her composure.

"You killed her, didn't you?" he said. "*You* poisoned Mrs. Heritage."

"Yes!" she exulted. "I killed her on my own. And I enjoyed it!"

Wes Odell knew he was facing the biggest crisis of his career. Theodore Wright had threatened to sever all ties between them. As the cyclist started to pack his bag, the coach implored him to reconsider his decision.

"I'm sorry, Theo," he said. "I only did it for your benefit."

"Keep away from me, Wes."

"Let's talk this over. It's the only way to sort out our differences."

"No," said Wright, tossing clothes into his bag. "The time for talking is over. I've listened to you for far too long."

"But look where I got you."

"It was my legs on those pedals."

"But who was coaching you, guiding you, building you up?"

"I thought that you were, until last night."

Odell touched his shoulder. "Theo!"

"Keep away from me," warned Wright, shrugging him off. "You'll never touch me again, Wes. You're through. Get it? We're finished."

"Well, *you* certainly are," sneered Odell.

"Don't be so sure."

"Where will you be without me in your corner?"

"Standing a much better chance of winning my races, I expect."

"Listen to me, son—"

"No, you listen to me," shouted Wright, rounding on him. "Ever since we got on this ship, you've been on my back. 'Eat this.' 'Don't drink that.' 'Run here.' 'Cycle there.' 'Stand up.' 'Sit down.' 'Keep away from her.' Who the hell do you think you are, Wes?" Wright demanded. "Two really nice things have happened to me since we boarded the *Caronia*. Do you know what they are? I met Genevieve Masefield and I gave some riding lessons to Izzy Singleton. You tried to put the evil eye on both of them."

"I had to, Theo. Don't you understand?"

"No."

"I had to protect you from any distractions."

"You were just jealous," said Wright. "Because *you* can't make new friends, you try to stop me from doing it. You can't bear to share me, Wes, can you? You weren't trying to protect me. You were protecting yourself."

"It's not like that."

"I'm the only person on the ship who'll even talk to you."

"We don't need anyone else!"

"*I* do. I need people I can relax with once in a while."

"Rest has been built into your training schedule."

"How can I rest with you standing over me like a mother hen?" Wright went back to his packing. "I'll speak to the chief steward and get a cabin of my own. And I'll work out my own training program from now on."

"Then you're done for."

"We'll see."

"You're a good cyclist, Theo, and you could have been a great one with me to help you. On your own, you'll never be a champ. Pull out of that race against Vannier while you can. That French guy was right," he taunted. "Vannier will crucify you."

Wright confronted him. "At least I'll have ridden an honest race."

Odell was about to fling a spiteful retort at him, but the glint in Wright's eye deterred him. The coach contented himself with a contemptuous curl of his lip before leaving the cabin and slamming the door behind him. Wright finished his packing. He was about to close the lid of his suitcase when he remembered something. Crossing to the little cupboard that had been used by Odell, he took out a tin of ointment and tossed it into the case. With a feeling of great relief, he let himself out of the cabin and stalked off.

When he turned a corner, he saw Genevieve Masefield coming toward him.

"You're not leaving already, are you, Theo?" she said, noting the luggage. "I know that you're a miracle worker in the cycling world, but even Theo Wright can't walk on waves, surely."

"I'm moving to another cabin, Genevieve."

"Why?"

"I finally saw the light. Wes and I have split up."

"For good?"

"Yes."

"Over what?"

"Over you, among other things," he said. "I'll never forgive him for the way he tried to scare you off. Then there was Izzy. Imagine the rage he'd have got into if he'd known I was teaching her to ride. But the main reason is this," he explained, opening his case to take out the ointment. "He's been rubbing this into my legs."

"What is it, Theo?"

"That's what I want to find out. It felt good at first and it loosened the muscles up. After last night, though, I got to thinking."

"Last night?"

"I was tired. My times were way below the targets I set myself. So Wes slips these flakes on my tongue and suddenly I get a rush of power. It was only after we'd done that I realized it must have been a drug of some sort."

Genevieve's curiosity was sparked. "A drug? What kind?"

"I don't know," he said, "but I promise you this. I've never used drugs to win races before. It's cheating, Genevieve. I've never needed to do that. There are some cyclists who use strychnine tablets to give themselves a boost and there's all kinds of other things they can take. But not me."

"Didn't Wes tell you what he was giving you?"

"No. It's one of the reasons we fell out. He said we were only experimenting in case we could use this ointment in the race. It would give us an advantage, he said, and that would enable me to beat Vannier. But I tell you this, Genevieve," he said earnestly, "I'd rather lose to the guy than cheat."

"I'm sure. Where are you taking that ointment?"

"To the ship's doctor. I'm hoping he can tell me what's in it."

"We've got someone better than the doctor aboard, Theo."

"Have we?"

"Yes," she said. "A trained pharmacist."

John Heritage was in tears when they went into his cabin. Slumped in his chair, he looked desolate as he contemplated the end of his relationship with Carrie Peterson. Confident of his own innocence, he had never dared to question hers. The fact that she had committed murder by using the poison bought by him had left Heritage in despair. He was left with nothing. Inspector Redfern and Dillman had to wait a few minutes while he pulled himself together.

"We've come to ask you a favor," said Redfern.

Heritage looked up. "I'm not in the mood for company, I'm afraid."

"We appreciate how you feel, Mr. Heritage," said Dillman, "and we wouldn't trouble you unless it was very important." He held up the tin of ointment. "This was given to me by Miss Masefield. We believe it may contain a drug and we'd like to know what it is. It could turn out to be a vital clue in our search for someone who is smuggling narcotics on this vessel."

"Why should I help you, Mr. Dillman?"

"No reason, sir."

"Then I'd be glad if you'd leave me alone."

"Of course. I just thought that, as a pharmacist, you'd take an interest. Nobody understands the perils of addiction as much as someone in your profession. There are opium dens in London as there are in New York," said Dillman, "and other strong drugs are being used to destroy lives all over the world." He moved to the door. "I'm sorry to disturb you, Mr. Heritage. We'll have to ask the doctor instead."

"Wait!" said Heritage. He snapped his fingers. "Give it here."

"There's not much left in the tin, I'm afraid," said Dillman, handing it over.

"Will you need anything from your bag to analyze it?" asked Redfern.

"I don't know," said Heritage.

He used a finger to scoop out most of the ointment, then he sniffed it with care. Spreading it onto the palm of his other hand, he examined it more carefully before licking it with the tip of his tongue.

"Well?" asked Dillman.

"Where did you get this?"

"From a professional cyclist called Theo Wright. His coach was using it on him to massage his legs. He also gave Theo a strange substance last night to boost his energy. When he realized he was being given drugs, Theo drew the line."

"I don't blame him."

"Why not, Mr. Heritage?" said Dillman.

"What's in the ointment?" asked Redfern.

"Basically, it's a compound of cocoa butter spiced with something else."

"Go on," said Dillman.

"Cocaine."

Smoking a cigarette, Cecilia Robart was relaxing in her cabin. When there was a tap on her door, she looked up in surprise. She was expecting no visitors. She opened the door and saw Genevieve Masefield standing there.

"Forgive this intrusion, Mrs. Robart," said Genevieve, "but I wondered if I could have a quiet word with you. It's about your earrings."

"But you found them for me."

"I know, but there's something I forgot to mention. May I come in?"

Mrs. Robart was guarded. "Well," she said, "only for a minute. I have to meet a friend shortly."

Genevieve stepped into the cabin and the door was closed.

"Now, then. What's all this about, Miss Masefield?"

"You and me."

"I beg your pardon?"

"I have this strange feeling you didn't mislay those earrings at all," Genevieve said pointedly. "If they meant so much to you, the last place you'd leave them was in a shared bathroom."

"I told you. I can be very empty-headed at times."

"You seem to be a little more organized now," Genevieve observed, noting the tidiness of the cabin. "Now that you don't have to put on an act, that is."

"What on earth are you implying?"

"I've just talked with Sir Harry Fox-Holroyd. It turns out you're not the duffer at cards you claim to be, Mrs. Robart. He says that you have a brain as sharp as a razor. It was you who carried him through that game of bridge."

The other woman shrugged. "I was lucky, that's all."

"Well, your luck has run out, I'm afraid."

"What do you mean?"

"The purser would like to interview you about some crimes that have taken place."

" 'Crimes'?"

"I think you know what we're talking about, Mrs. Robart."

"I wish I did," said the other woman, "and I'll certainly accompany you to the purser. It will give me the chance to complain about your impudence, Miss Masefield."

She picked up her purse and took out a key. Moving to the door, she opened it as if to leave. Genevieve went after her. At the last moment, Mrs. Robart swung round and pushed Genevieve so hard that she stumbled back. Before Genevieve could get to her feet, she heard the key being turned in the lock to imprison her but she was not disconcerted. Anticipating resistance, she had brought some support with her. There were sounds of a scuffle outside the door then it was unlocked again. Two members of the crew were holding Cecilia Robart in a firm grip.

Genevieve smiled. "Now I realize why you pretended to be upset about the presence of two murder suspects on board. You wanted the names of the Scotland Yard detectives, didn't you?"

Mrs. Robart struggled to escape, but to no avail.

"No need to rush off to warn your accomplice," said Genevieve. "My colleague is on his way to arrest him at this very moment. I have an apology to make, you see. When I told you that I worked alone, I was lying to you." Her smiled broadened. "There are two of us."

It took Dillman some time to find him. When the man was not in his cabin, the detective scoured the public rooms in search of him. Most of the first-class passengers were attending a concert in the lounge. Stanley Chase was not among them. When Dillman eventually tracked him down, he was reclining in a chair with his head in a magazine about antiques. He was smoking a cigarette. The detective strolled across to him, pleased there were so few passengers about. They could converse in private.

"That looks like an absorbing read, Mr. Chase," he said pleasantly.

"Oh, hello, Mr. Dillman," said Chase, looking up. "Yes, I never tire of admiring antiques. There's some French Empire furniture in here that's making my mouth water."

"Do you have a special interest in France?"

"Yes. I have a cottage near Castres. I spend all my free time there."

"Do you smoke a French brand of cigarettes, by any chance?"

"I do, actually," said Chase, taking a last pull on the cigarette before snuffing it out between his fingers and dropping it to the deck. "I like them."

"I understand that you're going to watch the Bordeaux-to-Paris cycle race this year. Is there any reason for that?"

"Of course. I've put a bet on Theo Wright."

"You expect him to win?"

"I need him to win, Mr. Dillman. It's a sizable bet."

"Is that why you're trying to safeguard your investment?"

"What do you mean?"

"You supplied cocaine to Theo's coach, didn't you?"

"Is that what Mr. Odell says?"

"No," replied Dillman, "but it's what Theo himself says, and what a pharmacist confirms. Mr. Odell was using a mixture of cocoa butter and cocaine to massage Theo's legs. It's also probable that he put cocaine flakes on his tongue."

Chase put his magazine aside. "What's your interest in this, Mr. Dillman?"

"A professional one."

"I thought you built yachts."

"I did at one time but I work for Cunard now. As a detective."

"You do surprise me," said Chase, quite unperturbed.

"I believe you've met my partner, Genevieve Masfield."

"Yes, a charming young lady."

"She's presently interviewing *your* partner, Mr. Chase."

"Oh—and who might that be?"

"Mrs. Cecilia Robart."

Dillman saw the first flicker of an eyelid and knew that Chase was worried. The other man reached over to lift up a small case, putting it across his knees and opening it so that he could slip the magazine back into it.

"What have you come to do, Mr. Dillman?" he teased. "Are you going to slap me on the wrist and tell me not to be a naughty boy? Drugs are used in all sports. I wanted to make sure Theo Wright had his share of them, that's all. It's a subject on which I've done a little research, you see."

"Oh?"

"Boxers, runners, cyclists—they're all the same, all striving for the extra edge that will mean the difference between success and failure. In France, for instance, trainers give their athletes Caffeine Houdes, a commercial preparation that you can buy across the counter. The Belgians suck sugar cubes dipped in ether. Some people prefer nitroglycerine; others opt for concoctions that contain digitalis, camphor, or atropine. What Theo really needs for endurance is a mixture of cocaine and heroin."

"No doubt you could provide both from your stock."

"Need we get so upset about something that's common practice in sport?"

"But we're not talking about that, Mr. Chase, are we? What we're discussing is the illegal import of drugs into England and the murder of Sergeant Ronald Mulcaster. I believe that you and Mrs. Robart can help us on both counts."

"I've never even heard of this Sergeant Mulcaster."

"No," said Dillman. "I suppose he didn't have time to introduce himself properly while you were tipping him over the rail on the boat deck."

Chase's mouth hardened.

"We have a witness, you see. He actually saw you club the sergeant to death with a revolver. Shall we go and find the weapon in your cabin, sir?"

"No need," Chase snapped, lifting the lid of his case to pull out the gun and hold it on Dillman. "It's right here. I always keep it near me."

"Like Mrs. Robart and her gold earrings."

Chase rose to his feet. "Shut up!"

"It wasn't the antiques that paid for those earrings or for your cottage in the south of France. The big profits are in drug trafficking. Along with the worst kind of human beings. Sergeant Mulcaster knew that."

"He was no better than us," said Chase. "Everyone in the trade knew about Ronnie Mulcaster. He was an animal, hiding behind his police badge. He crippled one man for life and sent a couple more to hospital. Yet he always got away with it. I was doing everyone a favor by getting rid of him!"

Dillman held out a hand. "Give me the gun, please," he said.

"Stand back!" ordered the other.

"There's no way you can escape."

"At least I can take you with me, Mr. Dillman."

"Just give me the weapon before it goes off."

"Not a chance." Chase backed away from him. "Move an inch and I'll shoot."

Dillman remained calm. He glanced over Chase's shoulder and saw someone walking purposefully toward them. It gave him his chance.

"Watch your back," he said.

"You won't catch me like that, I'm afraid."

"I think that Theo may want a word with you as well."

"Turn around, Mr. Dillman. Walk toward the rail."

"You're the one who should turn around, sir. Don't say I didn't warn you."

Wright was twenty yards away now. He recognized the man he wanted.

"Mr. Chase!" he called. "I need a word with you."

Taken by surprise, Chase glanced over his shoulder. Dillman moved swiftly. Diving forward, he grabbed the wrist that held the gun and twisted it back so the weapon was pointing in the air. The two men grappled and moved crazily across the deck as they struggled to get the upper hand. Wright looked on in amazement. Forcing his man toward the bulwark, Dillman smashed Chase's wrist against the rail so that the gun was dislodged. It dropped to the deck with a clatter. Dillman kicked it away before trying to overpower his adversary. Deprived of his weapon, Chase felt a surge of anger and he fought back hard, punching and gouging for all he was worth, but Dillman was much stronger and fitter. He hurled Chase against the rail to take the wind out of him then hit him with a relay of punches to the body and the head. With blood streaming from his nose, Chase eventually fell to one knee. Dillman reclaimed the gun to hold it on him.

"It's my turn next, Mr. Chase," said Wright, bunching up a fist. "There was cocaine in that ointment. I made Wes tell me where he got it from." He dragged Chase to his feet. "You tried to turn me into a cheat."

"Don't worry, Theo," said Dillman, panting from his fight. "He won't be selling drugs to anyone for a very long time."

Paul Taggart was thrilled by the turn of events. He felt the *Caronia* had been cleansed of its ugly stains. Two drug smugglers were in custody and they were also charged with the murder of Sergeant Mulcaster. The purser was delighted with the way Dillman and Genevieve had solved the crimes. When they visited him in his office, he showered them with congratulations.

"The captain insists you join him at his table this evening," he said.

"We'll be happy to accept his invitation," said Dillman.

"Inspector Redfern will be there as well, He's looking forward to eating a meal in the dining room instead of in his cabin. He has nothing but praise for you two. You helped him to get a confession from Miss Peterson."

"Not really," said Genevieve. "We just created the conditions in which it could happen. She'd been under immense strain, locked away on her own. Yet she denied her guilt time and again. When we put her in the same room as Mr. Heritage, however, she couldn't control her emotions quite so well. She gave herself away."

"Whatever happened," said Taggart, "the inspector is deeply grateful."

"We were happy to lend him some assistance."

"Yes," added Dillman. "Even though I went astray at one point when I thought that Ramsey Leach was our man. He and his wife are still pretending they're not married, I notice. Presumably, they only meet at night."

Taggart grinned. "I tried to smooth the path of true love," he added. "I had Mrs. Anstruther moved from the next cabin. It's been left empty now so they can make as much noise as they like without disturbing anyone. But the real triumph of the day was the arrest of Stanley Chase and Cecilia Robart. They were another couple who seemed to be traveling independently yet spent the nights together. Thanks to you two," he went on, "they're both behind bars. It's a time for celebration."

"Not exactly, Mr. Taggart," said Dillman.

"Why not?"

"We still haven't found the drugs. We've searched every last inch of their cabins and there's no sniff of cocaine or heroin. Yet I'm certain it's aboard somewhere."

"They must have hidden it somewhere else, Mr. Dillman."

"Unless they have another accomplice," suggested Genevieve.

Dillman shook his head. "No, the two of them work as a team and they've obviously been doing so for some time. That means they have a system. Well, you heard what Chase said as we locked him away," he reminded them. "He taunted us. He said that we'd never find the drugs in a month of Sundays."

"Then they'll never get off the vessel," said Taggart.

"Yes, they will."

"How, George?" asked Genevieve.

"I don't know," he admitted, "but I have a theory."

As the *Caronia* sailed on across the Atlantic, the vast majority of those aboard had no knowledge of the drama that had been played out inside it. Passengers and crew alike thought it was a routine voyage. When they were on the last leg of the journey, telegraph messages were sent to Liverpool to alert the police and the press. By the time the vessel eased slowly up against its landing stage, a police escort was waiting to take charge of the prisoners, and a battery of reporters wanted to interview

Inspector Redfern. He appeared before the cameras alone. George Porter Dillman and Genevieve Masefield needed to preserve their anonymity, especially as they would be sailing back to New York on the *Caronia*. While the inspector coped with the press, they slipped quietly ashore.

It was over two weeks before the vessel was due to sail again. Before any of the passengers embarked, Dillman was on board, dressed as a steward in the first-class area. Convinced the cache of drugs was still on the ship, he was alert and watchful. His vigilance was eventually rewarded. When the passengers were allowed to board, some brought friends and well-wishers with them. An attractive young woman in a long coat came aboard with a huge bunch of flowers that she wished to leave in a cabin her friends would occupy. She met Dillman in a passageway.

"What number are you looking for?" he asked.

"Twenty-six," she said.

"It's just along here, madam."

"Thank you. I wanted to surprise some dear friends with the flowers."

"Of course."

Dillman led her to the cabin, knowing it was the one occupied earlier by Stanley Chase. He had searched it carefully himself but found no trace of drugs. Of all the cabins in first class, the young lady had nominated that one. There had to be a reason, and he doubted it was connected with any "dear friends." Dillman showed her into the cabin, fetched a vase, then pretended to leave her alone to arrange the flowers. She watched him disappear around a corner before going to work. After taking off her coat, she filled the vase with water from the faucet and hastily put the flowers into it. Kneeling beside the paneling below one of the bunks, she took out a suction pad, licked it, and pressed it hard against the wood. A sudden push produced a click then she drew the pad toward her. A small door swung back on its hinges and allowed her to put her hand inside. She drew out a series of bags that she then concealed in the large pockets sewn into the bottom of her coat, intending to carry it out casually over her arm when she left the ship.

But the system that had worked before had broken down at last. While she was reaching in for the last bag of cocaine, the door opened and Dillman came in.

"So that's how it was done, is it?" he said with admiration. "Mr. Chase told us what an expert he was at repairing antiques. He obviously used his skills in here as well."

"Who are you?" she demanded.

"I'm the person who arrested him," said Dillman. "And it's my pleasure to arrest you as well. I'll take that coat, if you don't mind. But leave the flowers," he added with a smile. "I'm sure the passengers who occupy this cabin will be most grateful."

When Genevieve Masefield came aboard shortly afterwards, Dillman called on her in her cabin. She was thrilled to hear that the cache of cocaine and heroin had been uncovered and a further arrest had been made. The *Caronia* would not be used for drug trafficking again. She had news of her own.

"Have you seen this, George?" she asked, waving a newspaper at him.

"I haven't had time to read any papers today, Genevieve."

"I don't usually look at the sports pages but I'm glad that I did today." She held out the newspaper to show him a photograph. "Theo Wright won the Bordeaux-to-Paris race in record time."

"Without the aid of any drugs, I daresay."

"He had some help. Look at the crowd behind him. Who do you see?"

Dillman examined the photograph more carefully. It was taken as Wright came through the finishing line at the end of the race. Excited spectators were cheering him on. One of them, standing in the front row and beaming happily, was Isadora Singleton.

"Look how much he earned for winning that race," said Dillman, reading the caption. "You missed your chance, Genevieve.

If you'd married him, you might have ended up the wife of a very rich man. Don't you regret that?"

"Not in the slightest."

"Why not?"

"I'm already spoken for," she said, kissing him on the lips. "Aren't I?"